Praise for *Outlawed*

New York Times Bestseller ★ Reese's Book Club Pick

"*Outlawed* stirs up the Western with a provocative blend of alt-history and feminist consciousness... In North's galloping prose, it's a fantastically cinematic adventure that turns the sexual politics of the Old West inside out." —**Ron Charles**, *The Washington Post* **(Best of the Year)**

"North presents a far different perspective on the [Western] genre, one forged by women [and] Black and nonbinary people looking for the freedom, space, and right to exist in a world that largely doesn't want them... Captivating and hard to put down." —*USA Today* **(Best New Books)**

"Fans of Margaret Atwood's *The Handmaid's Tale* are in for a stellar ride where gender roles, sexuality, agency, and self-discovery come together, making North's story as experimental and novel as it is classic." —*The Boston Globe*

"The heroes of the traditional Western were always sure about what made them the way they were; what made a man a man. For Ada and the other 'outlaws' of this spirited novel, the frontiers of gender and sexuality beckon to be explored." —**Maureen Corrigan, NPR**

"A thoroughly gripping, genre-subverting and [genre]-defining marvel of a novel." —**Refinery29 (Most Anticipated Books of the Year)**

"Think *Foxfire* by way of Mattie from *True Grit*, yet North's swashbuckling saga is wholly her own." —*Oprah Daily* **(Best LGBTQ Books of the Year)**

"The characters' struggles for gender nonconformity and LGBTQ rights are tenderly and beautifully conveyed. This feminist Western parable is impossible to put down." —*Publishers Weekly* **(starred review)**

"It's an absolute romp and contains basically everything I want in a book: witchy nuns, heists, a marriage of convenience, and a midwife trying to build a bomb out of horse dung." —*Vox*

"North's *Outlawed* sets a high bar . . . It upends the tropes of the traditionally macho and heteronormative genre while also being a ripsnortin' good read, too." —*The Week* **(Most Anticipated Books of the Year)**

"A Western unlike any other, *Outlawed* features queer cowgirls, gender nonconforming robbers, and a band of feminists that fight against the grain for autonomy, agency, and the power to define their own worth." —*Ms.*

"Earns its place in the growing canon of fiction that subverts the Western . . . A genre- (and gender-) bending take on the classic Western." —*Kirkus Reviews*

"A lovely slow draw in the world of the Old West, a story about the people who don't belong, portraying a realistic, close-minded world that only accepts women willing to fit into a specific mold . . . It's exciting to read a Western tale that features such a range of women and queer characters." —*Booklist*

"This book has me, and you should have this book." —*Glamour* **(Best of the Month)**

"Start *Outlawed* and just try to put it down." —*Sidney Herald*

"A gender-bending, genre-hopping yarn that's part frontier novel, part *Handmaid's Tale* . . . North easily subverts expectations as her characters struggle to find their identities in a patriarchal world." —*BookPage*

"Anna North has written a captivating Western unlike any other, with unique rhythms, dusty lands, and characters like new friends brought in on high winds. A grand, unforgettable tale." —**Esmé Weijun Wang, author of** *The Collected Schizophrenias*

"I'm dazzled by this feminist Western about a world in which women's worth and right to live are determined by the vagaries of fertility. Set in an alternate past, one all too similar to our today, *Outlawed* is terrifying, wise, tender, and thrilling. A masterpiece." —**R. O. Kwon, bestselling author of *The Incendiaries* and *Exhibit***

"*Outlawed* flips the script on the beloved Western genre and gives us the iconic heroine-on-the-run we deserve. Anna North is a riveting storyteller . . . Reader, you are in for a real treat." —**Jenny Zhang, author of *Sour Heart***

"A moving and invigorating complication of the Western, highlighting chosen family, love, and survival among outcasts in another American timeline. As she mines the genre for vital new stories, North beautifully shines a light on our real past and conveys a warning for the future." —**Lydia Kiesling, author of *The Golden State* and *Mobility***

"Fans of Margaret Atwood and Cormac McCarthy finally get the Western they deserve in *Outlawed*, but Anna North doesn't just reimagine a damsel in distress as her own savior. She plays with the promise and danger of the frontier, introducing us to an America we never knew—and one we know all too well." —**Alexis Coe, *New York Times* bestselling author of *You Never Forget Your First* and *Alice + Freda Forever***

Praise for *The Life and Death of Sophie Stark*

Lambda Literary Award for Bisexual Fiction

"I read *The Life and Death of Sophie Stark* with my heart in my mouth. Not only a dissection of genius and the havoc it can wreak, but also a thunderously good story." —**Emma Donoghue,** *New York Times* **bestselling author of** *Room* **and** *Learned by Heart*

"North's prose is as skillful as her protagonist's shot list. Filled with 'the sad fumbling of human love,' Sophie's story examines the relationship between art and suffering." —**Sarah Ferguson,** *The New York Times Book Review*

"A gem full of complex personalities, tragic yet redeeming circumstances, and striking conversations and judgments . . . *The Life and Death of Sophie Stark* is utterly captivating, surprising, and rewarding. You won't forget about it (or her) for a long time." —**PopMatters.com**

"A completely compelling read that asks whether broken hearts and ruined relationships are prices worth paying in the name of creativity." —*Daily Express* **(UK)**

"North is a natural, butter-smooth storyteller, and *The Life and Death of Sophie Stark* is an elegant, kaleidoscopic look at a challenging artist and at the way our lives are, in some respects, only silhouettes made from the perceptions of those who know us." —**Maggie Shipstead,** *New York Times* **bestselling author of** *Great Circle*

"Anna North has woven a circle of longing and frustration around her commanding central character, the enigmatic Sophie Stark. This novel isn't just a character study, though—it's a story of art, manipulation, and dependence. And, in its unique and satisfying structure, it's a narrative high wire act, deftly executed." —**Rebecca Makkai,** *New York Times* **bestselling author of** *I Have Some Questions for You*

"Quietly powerful, beautifully written, with characters you can see and feel." —*BookRiot*

"A fierce, page-turning exposé of a would-be/could-be bright star. 'Friends,' former flames, and critics paint a portrait of an elusive cult filmmaker and the bridges she burned along the way." —*Marie Claire*

"An elegant, intimate portrait of an exceptionally talented woman and her rise to fame . . . Bold and enthralling, *The Life and Death of Sophie Stark* speaks to the costs of creating art and the sacrifices we must make in pursuit of artistic integrity." —*BuzzFeed*

"A bold and graceful novel, executed with incredible artistry. The excellent writing aside, it's worth a read just to meet Sophie, an unforgettable character who can't quite manage to run away from herself." —Michael Schaub, NPR.org

"*The Life and Death of Sophie Stark* is your summer must-read . . . A compelling narrative structure that will engross you and leave you wanting more, all while being completely satisfying and delicious to read." —*HelloGiggles*

"North's engrossing second novel portrays with painful clarity the life of a flawed but highly talented artist. An essential choice for literary fiction readers." —*Library Journal* (starred review)

"In this boldly conceived, superbly executed novel, Anna North explores the life of the brilliant, relentless Sophie Stark and the lives of those closest to her. The result is a portrait of a woman and her films so vivid and so painful that she leaps out of these pages into the reader's imagination. A wonderful novel about art and passion and how we accommodate the other." —**Margot Livesey, author of *The Road from Belhaven***

"Anna North's first novel, *America Pacifica*, was superb, and *The Life and Death of Sophie Stark*, her second, is even better: skillfully designed and deeply felt, of course, but also wholly and mysteriously alive, in a way that many books simply aren't. It explores the way people can be startled and changed—and frequently damaged and betrayed—by a confrontation with art, and proceeds in a round-robin of voices, each entirely natural, entirely human, yet filled with vibrancy and intimacy." —**Kevin Brockmeier, author of** *The Illumination*

"An incisive exploration of artistic integrity and ambition—and a haunting meditation on what it means to truly know another person." —**Jennifer duBois, author of** *A Partial History of Lost Causes* **and** *The Last Language*

"*The Life and Death of Sophie Stark* succeeds wildly at the almost impossible task of making an artist and her art come alive on the page. Anna North captures with fierce clarity the compulsions and ecstasies of creation, the spooky force it exerts on those drawn into a maker's vision. Whether art is a gift or a curse is unflinchingly explored in this tight, suspenseful, and deeply empathic novel." —**Pamela Erens, author of** *Eleven Hours* **and** *The Virgins*

"The novel builds slowly, and, though its denouement is promised by the book's title, it unfolds with a surprising depth of feeling... An engaging exploration of what it takes to make art and, more importantly, what it takes to love those who make it." —*Kirkus Reviews*

"The pinwheel structure of Anna North's *The Life and Death of Sophie Stark* is a narrative triumph—destabilizing and enthralling—and its titular character is a beautiful, peculiar mystery. This novel should have special appeal to readers with an interest in film and filmmaking, but I'd expect anyone who enjoys a good story to like it." —**Owen King, author of** *The Curator*

"As taut and artistically ambitious as its title character, North's novel upends the trope of the lone, tortured genius, considering instead the deeply human consequences of one person's uncompromising vision." —*Booklist*

"North's nuanced prose and emphasis on characterization result in a thoughtful, moving read that explores the creative process and its effects on relationships." —*Publishers Weekly*

"One of North's greatest skills is her ability to tell a story within a story. From the first chapter—where Sophie's girlfriend Allison is telling a traumatic story about her childhood at a bar that Sophie hears and adapts into a film—readers encounter a multi-faceted work . . . North's novel is an intricate, abstract portrait of an artist as a young woman." —*New York Daily News*

Praise for *America Pacifica*

"A dark, gripping, and wildly creative debut with a futuristic end-of-days setting." —*BookPage*

"Anna North's fluid prose moves this story along with considerable force and velocity. The language in *America Pacifica* seeps into you, word by word, drop by drop, until you are saturated in the details of this vivid and frightening world." —**Charles Yu, author of the National Book Award–winning** *Interior Chinatown*

"Anna North has crafted a dangerous, wise, and deeply affecting vision of the future that is also a dark mirror held to our present. At once thrilling and heartbreaking, *America Pacifica* suggests how we shape ourselves by shaping the world." —**Jedediah Berry, author of** *The Naming Song*

"Richly imagined . . . North, a recent graduate of the Iowa Writers' Workshop, is a stylish writer and a good storyteller who keeps the pages turning . . . An entertaining, stylishly written doomsday novel." —*Kirkus Reviews*

"A dark, page-turning debut . . . North cleverly combines elements from other popular modern stories—a brave young heroine on an against-all-the-odds quest on a strange island with shocking secrets . . . The story—and the wealth of detail in a vividly imagined world—is memorable." —*Publishers Weekly*

"A thrilling and often very gripping read, expanding beyond its basic quest narrative to comment on society and the politics of control . . . North weaves in black humor, frank sex scenes, and bittersweet memories . . . An enjoyable and intriguing read." —*Time Out London*

"A richly rendered post-apocalyptic novel set on a Pacific island . . . In her debut novel, Anna North shows us a disturbing vision of the future that is disturbingly similar to our present." —*The Daily Beast*

BOG QUEEN

BY THE SAME AUTHOR

Outlawed

The Life and Death of Sophie Stark

America Pacifica

BOG QUEEN

A NOVEL

ANNA NORTH

BLOOMSBURY PUBLISHING
NEW YORK · LONDON · OXFORD · NEW DELHI · SYDNEY

BLOOMSBURY PUBLISHING
Bloomsbury Publishing Inc.
1359 Broadway, New York, NY 10018, USA
50 Bedford Square, London, WC1B 3DP, UK
Bloomsbury Publishing Ireland Limited, 29 Earlsfort Terrace,
Dublin 2, D02 AY28, Ireland

BLOOMSBURY, BLOOMSBURY PUBLISHING, and the Diana logo are
trademarks of Bloomsbury Publishing Plc

First published in the United States 2025

Copyright © Anna North, 2025

Epigraph: Seamus Heaney, "The Grauballe Man" from *Opened Ground: Selected Poems 1966–1996*. Copyright © 1999 by Seamus Heaney. Used by permission of Farrar, Straus & Giroux, LLC, http://us.macmillan.com/fsg. All rights reserved.

All rights reserved. No part of this publication may be: i) reproduced or transmitted in any form, electronic or mechanical, including photocopying, recording, or by means of any information storage or retrieval system without prior permission in writing from the publishers; or ii) used or reproduced in any way for the training, development, or operation of artificial intelligence (AI) technologies, including generative AI technologies. The rights holders expressly reserve this publication from the text and data mining exception as per Article 4(3) of the Digital Single Market Directive (EU) 2019/790.

This is a work of fiction. Names, characters, places, and events are either the products of the author's imagination or used in a fictitious manner. Any resemblance to actual persons, living or dead, or actual events is purely coincidental.

ISBN: HB: 978-1-63557-966-6; EBOOK: 978-1-63557-967-3

LIBRARY OF CONGRESS CATALOGING-IN-PUBLICATION DATA IS AVAILABLE

2 4 6 8 10 9 7 5 3 1

Typeset by Westchester Publishing Services
Printed in the United States by Lakeside Book Company

To find out more about our authors and books visit
www.bloomsbury.com and sign up for our newsletters.

Bloomsbury books may be purchased for business or promotional use.
For information on bulk purchases please contact Macmillan Corporate
and Premium Sales Department at specialmarkets@macmillan.com.
For product safety–related questions contact productsafety@bloomsbury.com.

For the moss

*The cured wound
opens inwards to a dark
elderberry place.*

*Who will say "corpse"
to his vivid cast?
Who will say "body"
to his opaque repose?*

—SEAMUS HEANEY,
"THE GRAUBALLE MAN"

Time of ending and beginning

A colony of moss does not speak or think in language. But if such a colony could tell the story of its life, it might say this: Once, we flourished. Our capsules popped and our spores spread far and wide. We drank what we needed from the rain and stored the rest in our spongy depths. We made a rich home for ourselves, of ourselves. This time lasted many thousands of daylights and nighttimes, and it was good.

We knew, however, that our flourishing would end, and so it did. One day large wheels came rumbling across our body; iron claws reached down and yanked us up by our roots. In number we were much reduced; our home became dry and barren. This time also lasted many daylights and it, obviously, was not as good.

But our memory and foresight are long—so long, in fact, they are nearly infinite. We knew our time of struggle would end too, and indeed, one day the large wheels rolled to a stop.

A fine day. Wind out of the west. Above our surface, a great panicked scurrying-about. The people come and press their faces so close to us that we might, if we had hands, reach out and touch them.

We have had ample time to observe human behavior, and we can tell they have found something in our flesh, something they did not expect and do not understand. But, of course, we know whose head they draw so slowly from the mud, brushing our remaining tendrils from the temples. Whose shoulders, whose fine, well-protected hands.

A colony of moss does not experience emotions like fondness or intimacy, but if it did, it might say this: We held her. We kept her safe under the surface, in our bath of earth, for many times her lifespan. That we give her up now may seem to be purely random, an accident of excavation. In fact, the hour of her service is at hand.

April 2018

Agnes comes into the coroner's office streaming with rainwater. Eight months in this country and you would think she would have learned to carry an umbrella, but no, she has not.

How must she look now, six feet tall and dripping on the carpet? She is still trying to understand it, the way she is perceived, the imprint her body makes on the world.

"I'm here," she says.

Agnes is very late. She came in on the train, and her phone said you could walk to the office from the station, but somehow instead of shortening as she continued along the road, the distance between her and her destination seemed to dilate, as though the town was growing, new low brown-brick houses appearing in between the houses, new dark-green unfriendly shrubbery. Agnes remembered a story from her childhood: a fairy circle, a hex on the land to trap the unsuspecting. The brownies giggling in the brush as humans stumbled hopelessly, their paths curving ever backward on themselves, bringing them again and again to the beginning.

"Wonderful to meet you, can we get you anything," they are saying, the people in the office, in a way that makes it clear they are annoyed with her. They introduce themselves: Kieran, the coroner, and the secretary, Melinda. Kieran is not much older than Agnes, maybe thirty, but he has all the solidity of adulthood about him—not just a wedding ring on his finger and a picture of a white-haired toddler on his desk, though he has those things, but also a settled calm, a stillness in his body.

Melinda is in her midforties, but with the weariness of someone older: a childhood illness, Agnes thinks, or she has lost someone. She has lived more than her share of life already. Agnes can always sense that quality, and it makes her feel a sympathy she cannot quite express. She apologizes as Melinda takes her sopping coat and her umbrella and hands her a folder.

"I know we sent you the report already," she says, "but I always like to give a hard copy."

Agnes read the report last night in her bad flat with the yellowy walls; she knows the husband's story.

He and his wife were fighting, he says. They fought all the time, as he has never fought with anyone before or since. He believes she hated him. He knows it is not an excuse.

That night, he says, she came at him, trying to claw his face. She had done it before, he says, he has the scar beneath his eye to prove it. This time he stuck his arms out in front of him to try to keep her back. But she lost her footing and fell down the stone stairs to the basement of that house, their little house that used to stand on the edge of the moss, where the factory is now.

No, he says, it was not self-defense. Or, he doesn't know. He does not ask for a lawyer. He is glad they finally found her, he says. When he buried her in the moss, he thought for sure she would be discovered in a day or two. That was in 1961. Ever since then her death has haunted him. She attacks him in his dreams, scratching and screaming. Now he is free.

It is not Agnes's job to pass judgment on the husband. Her only job is to confirm that the woman lying here in the coroner's office in Ludlow, England, is Isabela Navarro, born in 1940 in Málaga, Spain, and that she was killed by blunt trauma to the skull. The folder contains a photograph of Isabela, taken at her wedding in 1959. She is handsome, with a strong chin and high cheekbones, and looks forceful, her head held high. But her shoulders are narrow and rounded forward, a pronounced kyphosis that would surely have led to back pain in middle age, if she had lived long enough to see it.

"Would you like tea or anything before we—" Kieran begins.

"No, no thanks, no," she says, which is the answer he is hoping for, but also the truth. She wants to get to the exam room.

Her sneakers squelch down the hallway. She must buy boots, but what kind, where? Anyway her Chuck Taylors comfort her, they remind her of home, even when their bright red has gone wine-dark in the wet.

In the elevator she and Kieran stand an awkward distance from one another, the quiet chatters in her ears. When they reach the basement he turns to her.

"I should warn you, the remains look"—he pauses—"unusual."

"Unusual how?" Agnes asks.

Kieran shakes his head as he pushes open the exam room door. "You'll see what I mean."

If she believed in God or the supernatural she would call it sacred: the moment when she sees a body for the first time. She remembers, always, the day it came to her that this would be her life. In graduate school, her father had discouraged her from pursuing forensic work—too stressful, was his rationale, all the red tape, the interaction with law enforcement. But when the medical examiner in Las Minas needed an expert in dentition and her adviser recommended her, she felt a pull, not merely because she knew she was the best in the region, but also because she had never encountered a decedent like this before—lying out in the open air, the story of the death unwritten. Her subjects to that point had been in museum collections or computer databases, the questions of their lives all settled and hardened into history.

She drove out to the desert on a white-hot day in August. The remains were still at the find site, in the center of a parched square surrounded by caution tape. The medical examiner and two police officers stood aside for her as she came across the sand.

She can see it now, that first body. It was almost completely skeletonized, the skull whipped pale and clean by the desert wind, the long bones beginning to fissure in the heat. A polyester jacket hung limp over the ribs and shoulders, in color a sun-bleached dirty blue. Four teeth were missing from the maxilla, and this was why the medical examiner had called Agnes: He wanted to know if they had been lost premortem or knocked out at the time of death.

Eye to eye with the body, as she photographed his skull (the chin and brow ridge marked him out, more likely than not, as male), as she bent low to peer inside his mouth and saw the jagged edges where his incisors had snapped off, probably forced backward by a blunt object like the butt of a gun, what overtook her was a calm and tender feeling, a kind of love. This, she felt as she measured the maxilla and mandible, was a person who had been hurt and then abandoned out in the heat, and now he needed a particular kind of skillful care that only she could offer him. She spent hours there on the hard-packed sand, sweating into her coveralls, because she wanted to be sure to get it right, to understand and record his body's story, to witness him. His feet were very long and narrow; he would have had a hard time finding shoes.

From then on it was different, her work, her life. She felt a sense of purpose that was larger than herself, like a voice calling to her across a distance. She feels it every time she works on a case, feels it even now—perhaps especially now, when she is alone and far from home, with nothing else to guide her.

Kieran is right: This body is unusual.

Like metal, is her first thought, a metal cast of a human being. That perfectly made, that detailed. The eyebrows, eyelashes. The tiny lines on the skin of the lips. Agnes is still accustomed to bones blown dry and crackling in the desert wind. This body is as though transformed into something precious—on the taut smooth skin of the forehead, the cheeks, an aureate dark-bright glow. Full fathom five, she lets herself think, she has never been a reader, but she likes that one, her father used to read it aloud to her. Rich and strange indeed.

She circles, taking her photographs. Joy and calm descending on her as they always do, her heartbeat growing regular.

The body lies in the fetal position, the hands folded beneath the head. The legs too are bent and drawn toward the chest. The left leg is skeletonized and the bones of the foot are mostly missing; she counts phalanges, metatarsals, and two cuneiforms lost to the bog.

And yet from the waist up the skin shows almost no sign of decay or degradation. Agnes can see a round scar on the skin of the left arm, perhaps from chicken pox or a childhood accident. Just under the ribs on the right side is a wound at least ten centimeters long, where something sharp has punctured the flesh. It might have been a branch during the body's years in the bog, or perhaps her husband stabbed her before he pushed her down the stairs; "fighting," after all, can mean many things.

The head is bare and shining, the hair rubbed or worn away. The forehead is high-domed, the chin pronounced. Parietal and occipital bones both appear undamaged, but that means little—an impact doesn't have to break the skull open to be fatal. The neck is thin and delicate; Agnes can see the seventh cervical vertebra pushing up against the skin.

The face suggests a young person, the cheeks unlined, the skin smooth around the eyes. But the bones will tell a better story. Agnes is careful not to read too much into the expression—the pressure of the peat may have deformed the skin and facial muscles into new shapes. All the same, there's a surprising animation to the features, the mouth open, a deep furrow in the brow. It does not look like fear—it looks, perhaps, like rage.

"Okay," she says. "Let's look inside."

Kieran lays the body out on the bed of the X-ray machine. His movements are careful but assured.

And then it appears on the monitor above the X-ray bed: the skull. The coroner whistles low. He must be looking at the brain, which is shrunken but extraordinarily well-preserved. You can see the transverse fissure and even the folds of the cerebrum, delicate gray lines against the white. But what excites Agnes is the bone. It has lost some of its calcium to the acid of the bog, as she expected, and it is hard to distinguish in places from the flesh—the effect is one of layers of gauze or spiderweb laid one on top of the other. But the basic structure is intact—now she can see the evidence of impact, a network of microfractures to the frontal bone.

"He said she fell backward, right?" Agnes asks.

"Yeah," Kieran says. "But it was almost sixty years ago. Maybe he misremembered."

Agnes nods. The blunt-force injury those fractures indicate could have been fatal, but Agnes wants a CT scan to be sure. For now she ticks the rest of the head and neck bones off her inventory, all undamaged: maxilla, mandible, cervical verts one, two, three. She flips to the odontogram.

Here she stops.

"We have the dental records?" she asks.

"The dentist in town burned down in 1967," the coroner says. "We were able to get her records from Spain, but they're from childhood. 1953. So there might be some discrepancies."

Agnes pages through the papers in the folder. She looks again at the image on the screen. Something is wrong.

Isabela Navarro's childhood dental records show early signs of decay to the right cuspid and bicuspid, which is not surprising. Drinking-water fluoridation wasn't widespread in Spain until the 1960s, and dental hygiene at that time wasn't what it is today. By the time Navarro disappeared, when she was in her early twenties, she would have had either fillings or severe cavities, perhaps both. But the image on the X-ray screen shows no sign of decay whatsoever—the teeth lie smooth in the cup of the jaw, like stones. And there's something else, even more unusual: The molars are so deeply worn they are nearly flat on top, the cusps all sanded down to almost nothing. Sometimes you can see this level of abrasion in people in their sixties or seventies, but by that age, you'd expect fillings too, even crowns or bridges. It doesn't make sense. Agnes has seen a jaw like this only once before, and it's not in the records the coroner got from Málaga.

Agnes hands the folder back. She shakes her head. A moment of utter confidence, of pure cool clarity.

"I'm sorry," she says. "This isn't her."

New Moon, Third Cycle

It was bright and fine the day we set out for Camulodunon, and the horses were eager and all the auguries were good. I wore my blue dress made of sturdy northern wool, and the red cloak my mother had brought with her from Aremorio, where she was born. I took with me the neighbors' son Crab, who has a calm and easy manner and is good with horses, as well as my youngest brother, my favorite, Aesu. We left early in the morning and took the forest road, the river road having been partially flooded in the recent rain and, according to Crab, still covered in a thick squelchy muck that could snap a horse's ankle.

This was the first long journey I had undertaken in my official capacity, and I admit I felt powerful and sat high in the saddle as we passed by the potter's house and the forge on our way to the moss. I had been the druid for two seasons at that point, and everyone said I was doing very well. I had reformed the record-keeping so that each family's sheep were clearly marked and accounted for, and the lowland farmers could no longer simply claim the upland animals as their own when they wandered across the creek and into the lowland pasture to graze, as was their wont in summer. I had also adjudicated several disputes, including a serious one between Butu the blacksmith's son and his neighbor Duro, who had cut off two of Butu's fingers in a threshing accident. My decision in this case (two sheep and a goat to be paid to Butu's family along with all the grain threshed on the day of the accident) did not satisfy everyone, but I believe it was widely regarded as fair and wise. In addition to all this, I had organized a festival dedicated to our town gods, after which we had the richest harvest in five years, with enough grain to put away for the winter and plenty more to sell at a handsome profit in the summer markets.

So it was with pride but not surprise that I had received the invitation to appear before the new king in the great city to the south. Even my mother had never been granted an audience at Camulodunon, but the young king had made it known that he was anxious to strengthen his relationship with the northern towns, and ours, though not large, was known for the strong swords and helmets from its forge. We brought with us gifts—a shield, three arm-rings, and a drinking cup—as tribute and to show the king the quality of our wares and the advantages of an alliance with us. Crab had packed them carefully into his horse's saddlebags; on my shoulder as I rode I carried a leather satchel, heavy with our offering to the gods.

Unlike the river road, which is well-trod by farmers on their way to market, the forest road is quiet and peaceful, a pleasant beginning to a long journey. With light hearts we passed by the Small Rock and the Large Rock, and the stand of pine that my mother had consecrated to the old druid when he died, and then we arrived at the moss.

It was my first time performing the offering on my own, and my heart pounded in my chest as I accepted the materials from Crab. His mild countenance, his eyes the blue-gray of the river after rain, eased my mind a little as I strapped the heavy satchel to my back and set off on foot.

The morning was warm and the moss was bright with new growth, a carpet of green stretching from the forest road to the river road in one direction, and in the other from the rise where we performed our festivals to the wild woods where the wolves howled and the deer nestled in the shadows with their fawns. All children in the village learned that the moss was treacherous, that what looked like solid ground was in fact a thin skin over murky water that would take hold of an unsuspecting wanderer by the ankles and pull her down and down into the place from which no one returns alive. But only I, as the future druid, had learned the safe path to the place where the gods exchanged with us: our offerings for their favor.

My mother had walked the moss with me many times during my training, showing me how to use the lines of sedge and horsetail as a guide. But once I took on the role of druid, she explained, I would have to go alone. She did not say so, but I understood this as a test, one from which even my mother could not shield me.

At first my path was easy enough—the ground, though soft, held my weight and did not betray me. But when I came to the center of the moss, the most holy and also the most dangerous part because the pools there were the deepest, I made what I thought was the right move and then felt the surface give way, my left leg plunging knee-deep into the wet darkness. Moving as though under its own power, my leg jerked sharply back to free itself, but the muck beneath responded in kind and held me fast, and there I stood half-trapped in the low place that forms the edge of the world.

I was sweating, insects screamed and circled me to bite, and overhead I saw the black wings of the crows whose job it is to pick clean what the gods do not. I remembered, however, a lesson from my mother: that panic drives a stuck body deeper into the moss, and that only the slowest, surest motion will make the mud release its grip. I took a deep breath. I remembered the dance we had performed at the recent festival, in the cool sunrise, the swallows wheeling overhead and the seven of us below, anointed that morning with milk and saltwater for the celebration, our arms sweeping up and back, up and back.

Smooth, calm as I could, thinking of beauty: In this way I freed my trapped leg from the mire. But now around me was all confusion; I had lost count of my steps and track of the landmarks, and I saw only green to the sunrise side and green to the sunset side, green to the forest side and green to the river side, and far off, on the rise, Crab and Aesu on their horses, powerless to help me.

My mother had always told me that if all else failed, I should call out to the gods and they would come to my aid. But herein lay my weakness, the only flaw in what had been, otherwise, a swift and auspicious ascent to the position of druid: I had never been able to hear the gods speak. My mother had taken me to all the holy places within a day's ride of our village—not just the moss, but also the stand of pines, the bend in the river where the stags drank, and the meadow deep in no-man's-land where the ancients had placed the sunset stones. Each was beautiful in its own way, and each time I felt a lifting of the heart as I set foot on the very spot where my fellow druids had walked since the beginning of time and would walk until its end. And yet I soon realized this feeling was not what my mother meant when she spoke of the sublime and ineffable voices of the gods. Next she had given me mugwort to drink, and a tea made from black flowers, but the former made me vomit and the latter made me shiver, terrified, against the far wall of my mother's house for a full day and night, scratching at the spiders I believed were crawling on my skin.

In the end my mother simply advised me to keep practicing, and said that the gods would reveal themselves to me once I learned to pay the proper quality of attention. I did practice, walking to the edge of the moss in the early morning and standing very still, listening as carefully as I could. It unnerved me to hear only the sounds of the birds and animals, the wind in the reeds—the time of the solstice festival was approaching, and I would need to drink the sacred draught before all my assembled neighbors, and speak to them in the gods' voice. Still, concerned as I was, I had also been consumed by the many other duties of my new position, most of which I found more pleasant and less frustrating. Only now did I wish I had spent more time listening on those mornings, before I turned my back on the moss.

Marooned as I was, I tried to attend to the elements as my mother had shown me, but each seemed more oppressive and threatening than the one before. The air was thick with bugsong. The water sent up a fetid stench. The earth slipped sickeningly beneath my feet, as if at any moment I might plunge back into its sticky mouth. The sun blazed in the sky above me, burning the back of my neck and the part in my hair. Only the moss itself seemed benign, its colors more various up close than they had been from far away, pale and deep, gilded and silvered.

Indeed, as I bent low to the ground I could see that the tiny feathered fronds formed a kind of pattern, a lane of vibrant green bounded on each side by a duller tone, like vegetables left in the pot to stew. With a crooked stick I poked the green in its brightest heart, and it gave way: water underneath. I laughed to myself. I looked up at Crab and Aesu on the rise and gave them a wave of the hand.

Stepping only on the dullest patches, I made my way back to the last landmark I remembered, the pine stump that had been split by lightning in my great-great-grandfather's time. From there the going was easy: Guided by the moss beneath me, I made no more false steps, and soon arrived at the semicircle of bulrushes that marks the offering place, my left leg drying in the sun.

Vasso the assistant smith had prepared the offering, and as usual he had been excessive, wrapping everything in three layers of heavy wool and including four figurines he had carved from hardwood—three women and what appeared to be a goat. He was ambitious and hoped to impress me, the head smith, and perhaps the gods themselves with this display of piety, but my mother had always told me that the gods only want what is valuable. I put the figures back in my satchel for the village children, and I removed from its scabbard the real substance of the offering: a broadsword, stout and well-balanced, its pommel stamped with the symbol of our village. Vasso could be annoying but his workmanship was good; I tested the sword against the bulrushes as my mother had taught me, and the sharp blade cut them swift and clean.

I chanted the sacred words, both in my language and in my mother's native tongue. I presented the sword to the sunrise and sunset directions, as well as to the direction of the wide water in honor of my mother's local gods. Then I made my requests: for safety on the road, a successful visit with the king, and—some believed we should be modest in what we asked of the gods, but I knew nothing was ever gained from half measures—an alliance that would yield prosperity and renown for our village. I measured the exact spot with the span of my hands, and then I laid the sword atop the moss and watched it slip beneath the surface to join its ancestors.

I admit I thought I would feel something this time, some holiness, especially after my earlier trial, but all I found in my mind and heart was the satisfaction of a task completed. Disconcerted, I began to make my way back to the rise, and I had reached the edge where the moss dries away to grass when I realized I had forgotten part of the offering ceremony—the appeal on behalf of the dead.

Our village had not buried someone in the moss since before I was born, a man named Inam who purported to be a mystic, but who was regarded by most of his neighbors as simply insane. He fell or jumped from an oak tree onto the forest road and cracked his skull open in the back and died there, looking up at the branches and the sky. No one knew if his was a holy death—a sacrifice of his body and spirit to the gods according to their direction—or if Inam had merely slipped from the oak in the midst of his ravings, and so he was interred in one of the burial pools that ring the moss, which are reserved for the unsettled dead.

The exact site of Inam's burial was not marked in any way, and so I cast my gaze broadly over the whole of the moss as I made the appeal: peace for Inam's family and for all the families of the moss-buried dead, and justice for them and for anyone with a hand in their deaths, if not today, then in the gods' time. I did not expect a response to this request, which had always seemed vague and abstract to me—what use was justice in the gods' time if I was not around to see it?—and I did not receive one.

I returned to the rise with my dress soaked in sweat, my shoes covered in mud, and midge bites swelling hot and itchy at the corner of each eye. Nonetheless I smiled widely at my brother and my friend, and hailed them in a loud voice, shouting that the offering had been a success and the gods had conferred great favor on our journey.

April 2018

Agnes recognizes the woman from the back. She is seated alone in front of Kieran's desk when Agnes walks in, and the curve of her upper spine is unmistakable, much more severe in a woman of her age. Agnes speaks without thinking.

"You must be Ms. Navarro's daughter."

The woman looks at her. She is still dressed for travel, in black slacks and a black wool sweater, a heavy brass necklace like a sheet of armor over her breastbone. She is in her late fifties, her face lined and her hair streaked with gray, and her presence has a weight and gravity to it, the way she turns in her chair but does not rise.

"My name is Dorotea Navarro," she says. "I came here to bring my aunt home."

Kieran enters the room then, looking harried and holding two cups of tea.

"I see you've met Dr. Linstrom," he says.

"Yes," says Dorotea, and then to Agnes, "Maybe you can explain it to me, because I still don't understand. This man,

Mr. Bergmann, has confessed to killing my aunt and burying her body. You have found a body, just where he says he buried her, but you're saying it is not her body? It is someone else?"

Dorotea is obviously angry, but her clarity of purpose is calming to Agnes, who responds with her own.

"It is my determination," she says, "that the remains discovered on Tuesday are not those of Isabela Navarro."

Dorotea leans forward. She is wearing dark-red lipstick. Her gray eyes are sharp.

"If it is not my aunt," she asks, "then who is it?"

In Agnes's last year of grad school, when she was working two days a week at the medical examiner's office in Las Minas, a man came to the front desk with a jawbone in a plastic bag. He was a detectorist, his hair and skin desert-fried, he had found no gold or silver in ten years but he had found this: a bleached-out time-cracked hunk of human skull.

Right away Agnes could see it was not normal. She had this gift, everyone said it, an instinct for the body and its forms. It extends to the living too; she knows when women are pregnant before they show, sometimes she can guess people's jobs by their gait or the way they hold their shoulders. Her father is always surprised by what she can divine, even some of her professors have been impressed, but to her it is no trick or miracle, only the result of years spent looking at each human body with curiosity and care.

This jawbone did not give her much to go on. Only one tooth remained, and it was damaged, split in half by some postmortem trauma. But even half a tooth was enough for Agnes to spot the distinctive pattern of wear: Flour or meal ground by hand in a stone quern contains tiny flecks of rock that abrade the chewing surfaces of the teeth, producing, over a lifetime of such a diet, a smoothed and flattened appearance. The jawbone at Las Minas had belonged to someone who lived in the area between 500 and 600 C.E., likely a member of an Ancestral Puebloan group who consumed a diet high in cornmeal or other stone-ground corn. The fragment was returned, after carbon dating, to officials of the Hopi tribe. Agnes delivered it herself, she felt light but mournful afterward, she had the feeling of a circle closing. The image of the jaw and stone-burnished tooth had slept in Agnes's mind until it was needed again.

"I'm not sure yet," Agnes says. "But I think she lived a really long time ago."

Dorotea nods. She maintains a firm and searching eye contact that makes Agnes sweat under the arms.

"And where," she asks, "is my aunt?"

"We—" Agnes begins, taking a breath, her expertise now exhausted. "We don't know."

Agnes did not deal with families in Las Minas, her work was out in the desert or down in the basement with the cold light. She saw them coming in and out sometimes, pink-eyed, their faces baggy from lack of sleep, and she felt a tug toward them, a desire to give or impart something. But it was not her place; her responsibility, she told herself, was to the dead.

"The police will continue looking for her, of course," Agnes says, uncertainty making her voice sound tight and unconvincing.

"This is the number for the police liaison," Kieran says, sliding a card across his desk. "He's really your best point of contact going forward."

"What will happen to Mr. Bergmann?" Dorotea asks. "Will there be a trial? Or will he go free now because there is no body?"

Kieran's phone lights up. "I apologize," he says shortly, and leaves the room.

"As my colleague says, I think the police liaison—" Agnes attempts.

"I spent a lot of money to come here," Dorotea interrupts. "A lot of money, and I am not a wealthy person. I got the first flight I could. They told me my aunt was here. They told me I could bring her home."

"I'm very sorry if you were given inaccurate information," Agnes says. She heard the medical examiner speak on the phone this way sometimes, in difficult situations: the passive voice, the conditional "if," like a recording on a bus or in an airport. The conversations usually ended quickly; no one argues with the airport voice. Agnes, however, cannot accomplish this effect—her words in her own head sound feckless and whiny. Dorotea leans forward in her chair, looking at once vehement and self-contained.

"Our mother never got over losing her sister," she says. "She had pictures all over the house. I will show you."

She pulls the images up on her phone: Isabela as a girl of seven or eight, standing next to a bicycle; Isabela as a teenager, giving the camera a challenging stare; Isabela as a child again, this time with another girl who must be her sister, both in white dresses and white socks with seed pearls, the sister softer in the face and body with a little bob haircut, Isabela with something mocking in her gaze; Isabela as a young woman, her head thrown back in laughter. The two of them together, maybe fourteen and sixteen—Isabela, the older girl, looks at something outside the frame of the photo, but her sister, still with that softness in her cheeks and chin, gazes upward at Isabela in frank adoration.

Agnes is not a stranger to grief, not exactly. This is what she knows of her own mother, most of it gleaned from her father in small pieces over the course of many years: She liked to paint. She played the violin. She was nearly six feet tall. (Agnes gets her height from her mother, since she was sixteen she has been able to look down at the top of her father's head.) She had a brilliant mind, if she had gone to college she could have been a mathematician. This Agnes's father told Agnes one October evening—the dark falling, that surprise desert cold—when her seventh-grade math teacher had sent her home with a calculus textbook and a note stating that there were no classes appropriate to her level available at the school.

Her mother's parents had eight children, they were part of a fundamentalist religious sect, they were very poor and believed that women, especially, should be educated in the home. Agnes's mother left when she turned eighteen and enrolled in bookkeeping classes at a community college outside Denver, where she met Agnes's father, who was studying electrical engineering. They were married five years before Agnes was born. Agnes's father badly wanted children; her mother consented to have just one. When Agnes was not quite two years old, her mother died suddenly of a heart condition that would have been identified in childhood had she gotten proper medical care.

Until Agnes was ten she had to attend regular appointments with a cardiologist to determine whether she too would develop the condition. Agnes was not told the purpose of the appointments until much later, but she felt her father's fear. When she was very young she believed the doctors might hurt or even kill her; she continued to experience this as a feeling long after she knew it to be false as an idea. She was a shy child, often a half step behind the others, and she was more comfortable with her father than with other children, a preference he did not discourage. The two of them formed a unit, safe and impregnable, as long as they stayed together, she felt—and did this feeling come from him or from within herself, it was almost impossible to tease the two apart—no one could harm either of them, they were protected from loss.

Now, today, Agnes wonders what it was like for Dorotea to grow up under the photographs of the lost girl with the forthright stare. Was it like Agnes's father's house, that warm dark womb smelling of grilled cheese and solder? And what did Dorotea do when she left that place, when she emerged adult from within the walls of her mother's loss, how did she spend her youth and enter into the thick-skinned steadiness of middle age? Did she feel panicked and unequipped, was she confident, how long did it take her to stop looking up for her mother's reaction to whatever she was doing, did she ever stop looking?

"Um," Agnes says, "are you close? With your mother?"

Dorotea looks confused and annoyed.

"My mother died last year," she says.

"I'm so sorry," Agnes says, her face hot. "I didn't realize. I—"

"Close? What kind of a question is that? Was I close with my mother? She was my mother."

"I just meant, it must have made an impact on you, your mother, losing her sister—"

Dorotea narrows her eyes. "What is your job here? You are a student?"

Agnes stands embarrassed in her red sneakers.

"No. No, I'm an anthropologist. I consult with the county on cases involving bones and teeth."

"You came from America to do this? They don't have anthropologists in this country?"

"No, they do."

"Are you some kind of expert, then? They brought you over just for this case?"

"No. I mean yes, I am an expert in dentition, but I came here a while back. I'm a postdoctoral fellow, I don't know if you know what that means?"

"Of course I know what it means," Dorotea says. "For a moment I thought, 'Ah, perhaps they requested someone really special for this case, a woman who has been missing for fifty-seven years.' But no, you are just a very young person, not a student but very recently a student. Perhaps last year?"

"Last year," Agnes admits.

"And you are the one I am supposed to trust when you say these remains are not Isabela's?"

Agnes's embarrassment and insecurity fall away. She knows what she's seen: on the X-rays, in the old records with their handwritten measurements, and on the cold uncanny body itself. She draws herself up so that her eyes look down into Dorotea's eyes.

"Trust me," she says. "These remains are not Isabela's."

Kieran returns to the room, into a magnetic field that buzzes and then dissipates around him. His hair sticks up in the back as though he has been scratching his scalp.

"Unfortunately Dr. Linstrom and I are needed elsewhere," he tells Dorotea. "The police liaison will keep you informed of any developments. If you need help booking your flight back, I think Melinda can help you with that."

Dorotea looks at him, then back at Agnes.

"Oh," she says, "I am not leaving."

○

Agnes does not know what she expected a bog to be like, but not this. Below the rise is a wide, dark, barren expanse of earth, a wasteland. The soil has been deeply harrowed in horizontal lines, the top layers of peat pulled back and cut away, leaving behind black mud and the twisted branches of dead trees, bleached a lusterless silver in the cold. Agnes has a feeling of vicarious pain, like looking at a burn or laceration in living flesh. The sky above is muffled and birdless.

Parked at the eastern edge of the mud are two tractors, one fitted with an enormous, toothed attachment like the blade of a circular saw. A man stands in front of it looking at his phone. Some yards away, in the center of the mud field, is a larger group: ten or fifteen men and women in windbreakers and rubber boots, one of them setting up a barbecue grill, a pair pitching a purple tent. A blond dog is nosing among them, collecting attention.

"Fuck," Kieran says quietly.

Agnes's sneakers slide in the muck as she and Kieran scramble down the rise. The man by the tractor puts away his phone and waves to the coroner.

"How's Emily?" he asks when they reach him.

"She's great, she's great. A handful, you know. How's—it's Charlie, right?"

"That's right. The same. Yesterday he decided he's not going to bed unless we let him sleep with the flyswatter. So, you know what? We just let him."

"You pick your battles," Kieran says. He is smiling and shaking his head, he is at ease. Agnes can imagine him in a backyard somewhere, children running, him lifting a beer.

Kieran gestures at the people with the tent.

"So Officer Taylor called me. What exactly is going on here? Who's this?"

"They're environmentalists," the tractor man says. "I think. They showed up yesterday, after the . . . you know. After the news was on Facebook and everything. They say they're 'occupying' the area, so if we try to operate the equipment, they're going to lie down in the mud. I said we're not even trying to operate right now, because of your investigation. But Fiona, she said we'd better stick around, in case they try to do something to the machinery."

"Idiots," Kieran says.

"Maybe you could talk to them? I don't know if they're planning on letting you dig or what."

"'Letting' us?" Kieran says lightly, but with an edge. "We work for them now?"

He starts across the mud, and Agnes follows. As they walk she sees the landscape is more complex than it first appeared—in the pocks and furrows left, presumably, by heavy equipment, black water has collected, and in the water are green patches, acid-bright, with a look of depth and complexity to them, as though each is composed of many smaller growths. The patches are clearly living but utterly alien; Agnes recalls a comic book her father bought her as a child, in which the hero set foot on a far-off world, where craters bloomed uncannily with blobs of purple mold. She wants to kneel in the muck and take a closer look, but Kieran has already closed the distance between him and the people with the tent, the dog is gamboling toward him with mud on its feet, and a man breaks off from the group and approaches too, so that when they meet they are four. Kieran bends to scritch the dog behind the ears as he begins to speak.

"This is an active investigation site," he says.

The man does not respond directly. Instead he extends his hand. Agnes puts him in his late twenties, perhaps thirty years old, but he moves with the confidence of an older man, or a woman, someone aware of the presence of their body in the world. His skin is light brown; his eyes are green. From the way he stands she can tell he is left-handed.

"Kieran, right?" he says. "I'm Nicholas Bailey. I believe your sister used to take my mum's movement classes."

"Oh right," Kieran says, looking uncomfortable. "Mrs. Bailey, with the, ah—" He gestures stiffly at his head.

"That's right, the white-lady dreads." Nicholas is smiling. "She cut them off, thank God. How's your sister?"

"She's fine, she's great. She, uh, she used to really like those classes. Look—"

But Nicholas has turned to Agnes. He is slightly shorter than her; he looks up into her face. She blinks her gaze away and then back again.

"You're not from here," he says, smiling.

"No."

Where Agnes is from, she used to sit in the backyard at twilight and watch the scorpions scuttling between the rocks. In summer the dry heat would break the blood vessels in her nose. Her first week in this country, her sneakers grew a coat of green mold all over, she had to run them through the washing machine and their color was never the same.

"Little bit of background, then," says Nicholas. "From pretty much the dawn of time until twenty years ago, where we're standing was common land. The people living nearby would come from time to time and cut a bit of peat to keep their houses warm, but for the most part they left it alone. It was home to five species of native butterfly, seventeen species of bird, and, of course, the moss itself, which has the ability to sequester carbon, making it one of the most potent natural antidotes to climate change. Then the council sold the land to the peat company. They brought in industrial cutters and turners and, well, you can see the result."

He pauses for effect. The sun struggles out from behind a cloud and casts weak light on the black mud.

"We've filed suit against the company for environmental harm, and we're confident that we'll win," he continues. "But in the meantime, we have a moral obligation to reclaim this land for its original owners, the people of Ludlow and—not to be too grandiose, but I think this is justified—all the people on earth, who will benefit when the moss is restored to the living, breathing ecosystem it was always meant to be."

In college there was a man, another student, who used to organize Occupy protests on campus. Agnes did not join the protests, she joined in very little at the university, unusual as she was, younger than all the other students and living at home. But she was drawn to this man, the way he could broadcast the content of his mind, as though it was simple to be public in this way. It came naturally to him, even his body moved in accordance with his ideas. Agnes has not thought of him in years, they stopped running into each other, but she thinks of him now, he and this man Nicholas are not dissimilar. Nicholas stands with his shoulders back and his hands spread wide as if to encompass their surroundings. His posture and voice assume an audience.

"Jesus Christ," Kieran says, turning away for a moment and then turning back. "You're only here because we're here, isn't that right? You're capitalizing on our investigation to get publicity for your"—he casts a hand about vaguely in the direction of the tent—"whatever this is."

"It's part of our job to bring public attention to environmental degradation and the prospect of renewal," Nicholas says. "I'm certainly not going to apologize for that. But I'll also tell you that this is a critical time for the moss. You may not be aware of this—few people in the community are—but the peat company is engaged in a final push to extract any remaining resources from the site before it's sold. They already have an interested buyer—I understand they're planning to put in luxury flats."

Kieran shakes his head as though a fly is buzzing around him.

"Look," he says, "none of this is my business right now. We have a body we need to identify."

Nicholas looks confused.

"You haven't identified the body?" he asks. "I thought it was Roger Bergmann's wife. Isabela something? I read that he confessed."

"He did," Agnes says. "It's complicated."

"Complicated how?"

"These remains—" Agnes pauses, she wants to speak well, briefly but with authority. "They're not consistent with Isabela Navarro's presumed time of death. We believe they may be much older."

"How old?" he asks. A new sharpness in his eyes, he stands a little closer.

"I don't know," Agnes says. "Hundreds of years, maybe more. I sent a sample off for carbon dating, but it's going to take a couple of days. In the meantime we need to grid out and excavate the site as soon as possible."

Really the excavation should have begun already. Agnes wishes she had been present when the peat-cutting crew discovered the body in the first place, when they lifted it from the bog. Every moment that the turned earth is exposed to air, every time a rubber boot tramples over the spot where the left metatarsal might lie—

"There's a risk of damaging the evidence," she says.

"Evidence of what?"

Generally in the case of an unidentified decedent, Agnes's first task would be to comb dental records and disappearances looking for a match. In this case, however, if the body really is hundreds of years old, she will probably never be able to put a name to it. It is a disappointment; she likes to know a person, to understand the arc of a life from birth to death and beyond. But her second task, equally important, remains.

"Evidence of how she died," Agnes says.

Nicholas is looking at her still with that sharp focus.

"Why do you need to know how she died?" he asks.

When people find out what Agnes does—the estate agent who showed her the flat, for example, apologizing for the fact that the oven door did not open all the way—sometimes they are disgusted. "I could never do that," the agent said, and she was probably right. Agnes is aware that most people find human remains upsetting. But she is never sure how to respond to their expressions of distaste when her own experience is so opposite to theirs.

"No," was all she said to the estate agent, and the silence hung between them in the ugly kitchen like smoke.

But *why* must someone do it, the work she does? She thinks for a moment. It gives her pleasure to be asked this question and to sense his full attention as she considers her response.

"In this case, with a historical body, the cause of death could tell us something about the time she lived in," Agnes says finally. "Did she have a disease, was she hurt in an accident, was there a war?"

Nicholas nods, he can tell she is not finished.

"But also, the way someone dies is part of the story of their life," Agnes says. "It's like—you know how some people believe the dead can't rest unless we avenge them, or unless they get a proper burial?"

"Sure, of course."

"It's a little bit like that, I think. Something we owe the dead, to find out as much as we can."

"I understand, I do," Nicholas says. His manner is changing again. Agnes feels his focus widen and dilute. "You have a duty. But we have one too. It's our job to protect this ecosystem and bring it back to health. Any kind of excavation here is, of necessity, going to delay that process. Now, if you'd like to make a request, I can certainly put it to our group for a vote—"

Kieran cuts him off. "We're not going to argue with you anymore," he says, "and we're not putting anything up for a vote.

If you're not going to cooperate with us, we'll need to have you arrested for interfering with an investigation. Do you want to go to jail?"

A few of the others have turned to watch them—a woman with long red hair stands windblown on the mud, the dog now sniffing at her feet. The purple tent is finished, and a pair is pitching a blue one.

"We're certainly prepared for that," Nicholas said. "But as I told Stephen"—he gestures at the tractor—"the police may want to consider the optics of arresting peaceful protesters, especially in light of recent events."

"What events?" Agnes asks.

"Kieran can explain that best, I think," Nicholas says. "Nice to meet you, Agnes. I hope you find what you're looking for."

He walks off then across the mud, and Agnes sees the dog bounding again over to him, all the people stopping their work and looking up to see what he has to say.

New Moon, Third Cycle

If Crab and Aesu were disturbed by my bedraggled appearance as I emerged from the moss, they quickly regained their composure, and we continued on in a merry way, enjoying the songs of the thrushes and also of Crab, who knows many funny tunes making light of local leaders. He was in the middle of a particularly amusing one about the druid of Macotonion, who wears a hairpiece made of badger fur, when we rounded a bend and saw two men on horseback in the middle of the road.

They were dressed for battle, each with a breastplate and heavy mail shirt, and though I did not recognize either one, I knew from the insignia on their helmets—two interlocking rings—that they must be Sego's men. I motioned to my companions to stay back, and though Aesu gave me a look, I rode forward until I could speak to the men without shouting.

"Good morning," I said, keeping my voice friendly. "What brings you to the forest road today?"

"It's good to see you, Druid," said the older of the two men, his thick brown beard flecked with white. "Sego sends his regards."

"Tell him thank you," I said. "We missed him at the harvest feasts."

"He's been very busy," said the man, "or he would have come himself. He wanted us to give you a warning."

I heard Aesu's horse step closer to mine, and sensed Aesu's hand on the hilt of his sword. I straightened my spine, trying to tell him with the confidence of my body not to overreact.

"I always appreciate Sego's counsel," I said.

Sego and I had grown up together; we were born under the same star and were inseparable when we were small. When he came of age he inherited some land from his uncle south of the river and began to style himself as a local lord, even raising a small force to raid the Decantae strongholds in the hill country. I did not object to Sego's quest for power—indeed I thought it would be good for our town, and for me as druid, to have a strong ally to the south. But recently Sego's movements had become more obscure to me; he did not come to the drinking hall or contribute to sacrifices, and I no longer felt I knew what he was planning or what he desired. In fact, this was the closest I had come to speaking with him all season long.

"We've heard that you're going to visit the king at Camulodunon," the bearded man said. "Sego believes it's a mistake."

"Why is that?" I asked.

"The king is married to a Roman woman. He speaks Latin. He is practically a Roman himself."

"Wasn't his father king of the Catuvellauni? Who subdued all the southern tribes under one banner? Hardly a Roman lineage," I said.

"He has visited Rome," the bearded man insisted. "I hear he has in his court a Roman doctor, a man from Carthage. In the south they call the king by a Latin name, I can't even pronounce it."

I rolled my eyes. I had heard most of these rumors and they did not concern me.

"So he has a Latin name. So what? My own mother has several foreign names, and I visit with her regularly."

The men looked at each other.

"With all due respect, Druid," the bearded man said, "your duties in town keep you very busy. I don't think you're seeing the whole picture."

"And the whole picture is?"

"The Romans want to control the entire island. They've installed their puppet at Camulodunon and they want to do the same thing here. That's why the king has invited you. He thinks he can easily control you."

I drew myself up.

"Sego should know very well that he's wrong."

"Of course," the bearded man said. "But sister—can I call you sister?"

I waved my hand.

"The Romans are ruthless. The lord at Clindon, a very strong and capable leader, he went to negotiate with them over some land near the Mouse River. He didn't like their terms, so he tried to walk away. They cut out his kidneys and fed them to a crow. Then the crow died."

The younger man gave the bearded man a look. I also was confused.

"The *crow* died?" I asked.

"It was an evil omen," the bearded man said, looking defensive. "The point is, these are dangerous people." Here he puffed his chest out and spoke in his most officious voice. "Sego wants you to know that if you insist on proceeding with this visit, he cannot guarantee your safety."

When we were children, Sego came to sleep at our house so he could go on a boar hunt with my brothers in the early morning. In the night he woke me, timidly poking at my shoulder, so I could walk with him through the yard to the clearing where my father had dug a hole. Of course it was me he roused and not my brothers; Sego always tried to hide his fears from the other boys. On the way to the latrine he wanted to hold my hand. On the way back I refused—I wasn't about to touch his piss-stained fingers—so he clung to a fold of my dress as we walked to our beds.

I thought of this night every time I heard about Sego throwing his weight around, acting like he had always been a powerful man.

"I would never expect Sego to guarantee my safety," I told the bearded man.

Then I motioned to Crab and Aesu and we drove our horses forward at a trot, forcing Sego's men to part and let us pass.

April 2018

"I saw a job listing today," Agnes's father says. "It's a high school, but—"

"Dad, stop it," Agnes says.

"Well, did you find a job?"

Agnes has done what she was supposed to do: She applied for tenure-track jobs as soon as her postdoc began. She did well in the early rounds—her publication history and her grad school transcript were impressive—but the interviews flummoxed her. She arrived in a conference room, on a Zoom call, dressed in her good turtleneck, and she spoke in what she thought was a normal and measured way about her background and interests, but every time she could see the senior professors sneaking sidelong looks at one another, their eyes sliding away from her as she spoke. In response she invariably became more flustered, saying things she knew she shouldn't, she offered unsolicited advice on a pathologist's arthritis, she talked at length about the beauty of a femur she'd once examined, which had split open in a house fire. In the end she received no offers.

Now it is spring and too late for anything but a miracle—a maternity leave fill-in, a sudden departure, a last-minute research assistantship. If something doesn't come up, Agnes will have to go home, move back into her father's house, and admit her experiment with independence has been a failure. Agnes knows this, and also she tries to avoid thinking about it—she does not check her bank balance, she does not make arrangements to move out of her flat, she plans a trip for the fall to visit a museum collection in Scotland.

"I'm working on it," she tells her father.

"I'm just trying to help," her father says. "I'm worried about you."

"I'm fine, Dad," she says. "I just started something pretty interesting."

Agnes made a rule for herself when she first came to this country: When her father calls they will talk about casework, the domain in which she is confident, and in which she enjoys but does not need his input.

In her eight months here she has had four cases. The first was a set of fragments that she determined to be cow bone, the second a woman badly burned in a car crash, for whom Agnes was able to provide a swift identification. The third took more time: the remains of a man found in a makeshift grave during the digging of a new foundation. So much history in the bone—the shrapnel in the left femur, the teeth that grew up poor and never let him forget it, the wear in the shoulder joints suggesting a long life of heavy lifting. But the clavicle, that's what made her smile: the little rounded nubbin on the bone. Very common but it was the first time she had seen it—the shoulders hitch in the birth canal, the collarbone breaks against the mother's pelvis and then, because a newborn's bones are so soft and malleable, heals almost, but not quite, as if it had not broken at all. It made her handle the bones with an extra gentleness, the thought of an old man on his dying day, still carrying the mark of the baby he'd been. She was able to identify him, a sense of peace and accomplishment; his name had been William.

And now this one: a young woman cut down at her most vital. What force remains in her coiled fists, her flexed elbows. That wild face, as though frozen at the moment of crying out, of shouting her attacker's name. A difficult case, certainly—Agnes has never worked with remains like this before, across the world only a handful of people have. And yet she is elated too, it is a joy to face a problem so complex, a challenge to which she is only just equal.

"So head trauma is still a possibility," she finishes, "or it could be blood loss or organ damage from the abdominal wound. I need to talk to a bioarchaeologist, just for starters."

"Do you want me to do a little Googling?" her father asks. "I'm sure I can find somebody."

"What? No, Dad. I'll find someone through the department."

"Just trying to help," her father says. "I know you don't like that kind of thing."

"I like it fine," Agnes says, though in fact she is not sure what she likes, exactly, when it comes to other people. She does not often consult outside authorities in her work; whenever possible she prefers to rely on her own expertise. That she cannot do so in this case is troubling to her—she feels a sense of interruption, a block in what should be an open channel between her and the body. And yet it cannot be helped; she has a job to do and this job cannot be done alone.

"I saw Colin the other day," her father says into the quiet of her thinking.

A stabbing feeling in her gut whenever he mentions Colin, which he cannot stop himself from doing: Colin's rocks, the bookshelf Colin built, remember when Colin this, Colin that. It is the first time, though, that he has reported having seen him.

"Where?" she asks, the first though not the most relevant question she can think of.

"We had lunch at Sam's. They totally changed the menu. Colin had shrimp tacos. He said they were pretty good."

"You had lunch? Why?"

"I wanted to catch up with him," her father says.

"So, wait, you reached out to him?"

"He lived in this house for six years, Agnes. Whether or not you're together, he'll always be my friend."

Agnes and Colin were fifteen when they met; he had moved from Albuquerque with his mother and half-siblings. Agnes was transfixed by him—his physical beauty, his size, the heavy boots he wore, the real tattoo of a lightning bolt on his forearm. (His best friend in Albuquerque had done it in his garage, Agnes later learned, leading to a skin infection that took months to heal.) She assumed he would be quickly adopted by the popular kids, but it emerged that he, like her, was strange—he was bad at sports, liked bands no one else had heard of, and lived in a scary-looking house on the edge of town (one window repaired with duct tape, the roof gutters peeled off and swinging dangerously in the wind). They took to eating lunch together in the shaded area behind the math classrooms, where Agnes had previously been content to eat alone.

Nothing more happened between them until an end-of-year class trip to the Grand Canyon, which was poorly supervised due to the sudden resignation of one of the science teachers. Colin returned from a morning swimming excursion covered in mosquito bites, and Agnes's father, ever cautious, had packed her a tube of cortisone; also, the girls in her cabin had gone canoeing but she had been permitted to stay behind and work on her chemistry packet.

Of course he could have applied the cream himself, but it was wordlessly agreed that she would do it. She was fascinated by Colin's body, the solidness of it, the furrow in his back where his spine lay. Her mind entered a prelinguistic state, a kind of continuous vibration. When she finished with his shoulders she put the cap back on the tube and then shucked off her own T-shirt, unsnapped her bra, and sat before him on the green cot, watching him watch her. She will never forget it—the intake of his breath, the flush at his throat, the look of abjection, almost like sorrow, on his face before he pulled her against his skin.

They did not have sex right away; neither, it emerged, had done so before. They waited for a summer morning when Colin's mother would be at work and his siblings at camp, and Agnes feigned a bike ride to go to his house. In his top bunk, in the room he shared with his little brother, their first time hurt her, but there was something satisfying in the dullness of the pain, like pressing and pressing on a bruise. She bled a surprising amount; when their bodies parted, it looked like they had both been wounded. In his mother's shower he washed first Agnes and then himself; in a daze she biked back home.

That summer was the sweetest time in Agnes's whole life. His beauty shocked her, the way it refreshed itself daily before her eyes; the way he hooked his thumb in the pocket of his jeans; how deft he was, despite the size of him; the way the water plastered his hair to his temples when they snuck into the community college pool at night, the way it made his mouth shine. A new sense added to the first five, a new dimension to her being.

Agnes's father found out about them two weeks into what would have been her junior year of high school, when she was already attending the college nearly full-time—a condom wrapper fell out of Agnes's pocket in the washing machine. After silently placing her folded laundry on her bed with the condom wrapper stacked on top, he was unable to meet her eye for days. However, he did leave a stack of books for her on the kitchen table. Most were years too late, like one called *Your Changing Body* that focused on menstruation, but on the bottom of the stack was a brochure for a local clinic that made clear she could get a prescription for the Pill without a parent present. Paper-clipped to the brochure was a fifty-dollar bill.

After a week of intense awkwardness, during which Agnes and her father stayed as far apart as they possibly could in the small house, he surprised her by coming to her bedroom door one night and asking to meet her boyfriend. She did not know what to say, so she said yes; Colin came for dinner that Friday.

Agnes thinks often about what would have happened if her father had disliked Colin, or even been indifferent to him. Perhaps their relationship would have ended sooner or less painfully than it did. Or perhaps they would still be together.

But what happened was that Colin was himself: eccentric, polite, his gallantry honed by years of too-early responsibility and his interest in electric circuitry already highly developed and lacking only a mentor to nourish it into full flower. Colin's first dinner at Agnes's house ended at her father's workbench in the garage, and from then on he never really left—at first he went back to his mother's house to sleep, but soon he was permitted to stay in Agnes's room. And when his mother moved back to New Mexico with her younger children—Agnes had transferred to the state university as a junior, just eighteen years old, and Colin had started his associate's degree in electrical engineering—it seemed only natural that Colin would move into Agnes's house officially, which involved bringing over a few boxes of T-shirts and a rock tumbler, little more.

Was this the peak of their time together as a family? Maybe it was later, when she applied to grad school, they were so lucky she got into the university's PhD program so they could all be together, one of her professors from undergrad was eager to work with her, she even got a grant to fund her research. The men bent their lives around hers, Colin did the grocery shopping, her father did the taxes, it was understood that she needed to be protected from the outside world as much as possible to focus on her work, when her computer was stolen from the library her father was the one to file a police report and secure a loaner from the university until it could be replaced. They made it easy for her to excel in graduate school, her research on dental weathering won awards, her professors praised her analytical mind.

She cannot put her finger on it, the moment when she began to have a sense of walls closing in. Was it when she stopped driving? She had never been good at it, and then her license expired, and it was easier for Colin to drive her to campus in the morning and her father to pick her up. Or perhaps it was when, very subtly, the men began speaking for her in ordinary daily interactions: ordering for her at the Tex-Mex restaurant, requesting her medications at the pharmacy. At first it was a relief; the waitress intimidated her, that big glossy smile, the jokes she made about Agnes ordering the same thing every time. But then, increasingly, a kind of curtailment, the boundaries of her self growing smaller, her possible futures shutting down.

She has a dozen, a thousand tiny memories like this, but one large one: She had appendicitis, a throbbing ache in the right lower quadrant of her abdomen. She knew exactly what it was when she tried to lift her knee to her chest and the pain made her vision go white. Her father and Colin took her to the hospital. Both came into the exam room—of course she gave consent, she wanted them there, or thought she did, and yet what did she feel when she floated up from a morphine sleep and heard them discussing the results of the test the doctors had performed to rule out ectopic pregnancy?

"Of course, when the time comes—" her father was saying.

"I've been thinking a lot about it," Colin said. "I could take time off from my job."

"So could I," her father said. "And we have the space, if you think about it. If we convert the living room into a bedroom, and then your room could be—"

"I thought that too. Maybe in a few months. I don't want—"

"No, of course, now isn't a good time. In the spring, though—"

"Yeah. Yeah, in spring."

She kept her eyes shut tight until they finished speaking, and then for a long time afterward. She sensed this was important to experience in full: a feeling of displacement, of unreality, as though even her body was not her own.

That month she was finishing her applications for postdocs. Her adviser had encouraged her to apply to positions around the country, but it was decided—how was it decided?—that her first choice should be a university about fifty miles away, where she could commute and continue building up her specialty in the effects of desert conditions. But when she came home from the hospital, her wounds still wet, her belly button swollen into the shape of a T, she looked for the farthest-flung job listing she could find, and without telling Colin or her father, she sent her CV to the university in Manchester.

When she accepted the offer, she came downstairs laughing, almost lightheaded with it, the fear and freedom. She had not considered any of the consequences; she had considered nothing. Did she want to break up? Colin asked her. She had not thought that far. She said perhaps they could be long-distance, they could talk, they could write emails. He left the house and went driving for hours in his car.

"Look, I'm sorry," she says to her father now, shutting her eyes, trying to slow her breathing. "I hope you guys had a nice lunch. I hope he's doing well."

"He is doing well," her father says. "He's building an air-jet loom from scratch, I'm going to go by and look at it next week. He asked about you."

Does she miss Colin, she asks herself sometimes, does she love him still? His holy quiet anger in those days after she told him she was leaving, he had never been more beautiful. When he moved out of their house before she could, how she could not eat, how her father finally began bringing peanut butter and banana sandwiches up to her room where she lay under the covers, more like a little girl than ever, just when she was supposed to become an adult. And now, the shock of their parting no longer fresh, she does often see something she wishes she could mention to him, a chunk of limestone with a shell in it, a ruined castle up near Carlyle, a dry cleaner with a sign depicting, for some reason, a *Tyrannosaurus rex*. What she feels most, though, is a kind of lostness, she has tossed aside the person who could love her in her strangeness and difficulty, whom she could love, who fit his personality to hers and whom she too grew to fit, and it seems impossible that she will find such a kinship again. Maybe she will never find it and will live in loneliness, taking pictures of rocks for Colin and then, later, deleting them.

She has met some men since she moved here, she got an app on her phone. One of them she even liked, his beard, his heavy jaw, a kind of leonine appearance. It was interesting to have sex with him, with someone she did not know, his body was attractive to her in a totally different way from Colin's, he was hairy and smelled good, a kind of whiskey sweetness, although he did not drink. And yet he made jokes that were not funny, and he laughed when she said things that were not jokes, and he called her "cutie," which gave her a feeling of revulsion deep in the pit of her stomach. He began to sense something was wrong between them, and he asked if they were breaking up, and the thought that they might be close enough to "break up" disturbed her so much that she blocked his number and never texted him again.

"What did you tell him?" she asks her father.

What she wants Colin to think of her, if he thinks of her: That she is well, she is strong, she is doing good work. That she is sorry for the way things ended between them but that it was necessary for them both to flourish and grow into the people they were meant to be. She does not want him to know how much uncertainty she feels, or that, just for example, she has not learned to drive in this country and has spent all her money on cabs.

"I told him you're trying to figure out your next move," her father says. "And that, of course, you're always welcome to come home."

New Moon, Third Cycle

We stopped for the night in a small village just past the Gray Hill that was known to Crab because his sister had married a man from there. His brother-in-law's people welcomed us, and we had a very good stew made with mutton and the small spicy herbs that grow in the area.

This village did not have a druid of its own, so the families were very glad to see me, and so many of them were in need of my services that we were obliged to stay an extra day in order to tend to everyone. Most of their requests were simple—a young couple, for example, needed me to perform the naming ceremony for their first child, a baby girl. The baby wailed as I anointed her hands and feet with ochre, and though privately I disapproved of her parents' choice of a name, Gleva, which is silly and insipid and growing entirely too common in recent years, still I presented the child with enthusiasm to the local god, who draws his powers from the hill, and, as a gesture of goodwill and fellowship between our two communities, to our village's deities as well.

In addition to the naming I also cut and braided a young man's hair for his coming of age, inspected an unproductive wheat field, and witnessed the transfer of a fine axe-head from one man to another in repayment of a debt.

Everyone was very grateful and gave me many fine gifts in thanks, including a dress of good soft wool and a sheaf of dried nettles from a nearby dell, which are said to be a powerful remedy for fever and other ailments. On the second day, Aesu said we should be on our way because the sun was high in the sky already and we had delayed long enough, but there was one more family who wanted my attention and I did not want to deny them.

This case turned out to be much more complicated than the others. A young man and woman had been lovers, and the woman, Enica, had become pregnant. When she began to show, her family visited his family to broker a marriage. But in that time the two had fallen out with each other. They did not want to marry, and the man, Linu, began to deny that he was the father of the child at all; he said that Enica had taken up with his best friend, a hog farmer named Bel, and this man was the one who had made her pregnant and should provide for the baby when it came.

When I met them, all parties to this dispute were angry. The young man was sullen, big and red-faced, refusing to meet anyone's eye. The woman was indignant; small and sharp-featured, her belly incongruous before her, she declared that she had only begun visiting the hog farmer after she had broken with Linu, which had happened after she told him she was pregnant.

"He didn't want me once he knew about the baby," she said. "I would've never looked at another man if he hadn't been so cruel to me."

"Our daughter is fifteen," said Enica's mother, a small woman too, with a heavy dark brow that gave her a look of severity. "She only got her blood last year. She never was with anyone before Linu."

She pointed at the young man, who continued slouching and scowling.

"His family has two flocks of sheep and a dozen healthy goats. They can more than support a child. Whereas we—why, my own youngest is still nursing and we lost our last sheep in the winter!"

"Which gives you every incentive to point the finger at my son and benefit from all our hard work these many years," Linu's mother said. She was fat and handsome with a broad, smooth forehead. "Especially since Bel's family is poor."

Then the woman's mother spat at the man's mother, and the male relatives on both sides, silent until now, began to mutter and jostle as though they were about to fight. To defuse the tension, I asked that all parties disperse and reconvene after the midday meal, giving me time to conduct an investigation.

I soon learned that Enica and her family were ill-liked in the village. They owed various debts to various people, and also Enica's mother had once struck a local elder, a very popular and respected woman, with the handle of a spoon. I too found them unpleasant—they failed to offer me a stool in their home, and kept asking how old I was and whether I had even gotten my blood, and making crude jokes about how their menfolk could find out if I was really a woman yet. Linu's family, by contrast, gave me porridge with meat and sheep's milk with honey, and promised to make offerings to my local gods as a sign of respect.

However, I also began to suspect that Enica, and not Linu, was telling the truth. When I spoke with the young man in private he kept repeating the same words over and over, and failing to meet my gaze, and when I asked him questions he became confused and simply repeated himself again. Enica, meanwhile, though rude, was very specific. Young as she was, she knew the signs of pregnancy and could tell me exactly when she had conceived, when she had told Linu, and when he had thrown her over.

Most crucially, the apothecary, an intelligent woman with an impressive knowledge of the local herbs, told me that Enica had visited her in the winter seeking a tonic to end her pregnancy, at least a month before she was ever seen with Bel. The apothecary was no friend to Enica or her family, who owed her money and had insulted her on several occasions. Yet she was an honest woman, and she did not like to see a young person falsely accused or a family default on its responsibility to a new child. Incidentally she had refused to provide the tonic, telling Enica that Linu's family would surely help her when they saw the child, and so she felt partially responsible for the predicament the young woman now found herself in, even though she did not like her very much.

Although I was personally convinced of the reality of the situation, I knew I would need proof to satisfy the young man's family. Luckily I had recently learned of a new ritual performed by the Belgic priests across the water, who were very knowledgeable in matters of pregnancy and childbirth.

With the sun just past its zenith I again summoned the two families to the clearing at the center of the village. I called for a large bowl of sheep's milk and, from the tanner, two sharp needles of the kind used to sew hide shirts.

"Linu and Enica will each prick a finger," I explained, "and let fall a drop of blood into the milk. If the milk curdles, then we will know Linu is not the father of Enica's child. But if it remains smooth and sweet, then Linu is the rightful father and his family must help provide when the baby is born."

There was a great muttering and fidgeting on both sides of the dispute, and Aesu looked at me with worry in his eyes.

"I've never heard of such a thing," Enica's mother said. "Why should I trust my grandchild's future to some foreign magic?"

"This test was developed by the most skilled priests of the Belgae, a forward-thinking people who have produced many wonderful inventions," I said. "It has been performed thousands of times with great success."

Enica's mother rolled her eyes and made a gesture with her hand, as of a duck quacking. Her family and even some of Linu's family laughed at this.

I had not come to this town and offered my services to people in need just to be disrespected in this way.

"I don't know you," I said to Enica's mother. "I don't know your family. Your finances and your affairs are nothing to me. But if you disobey my authority as druid, after you specifically asked for my help, then I will call down my family's gods on your village, and your wheat will rot and your lambs will be stillborn and a great plague will rip through your houses until you come crawling to me, coughing blood onto my threshold, begging me for mercy."

I had never actually called down a curse on someone, and I was not entirely sure what would happen if I did. Would the gods, respecting the skill with which I had learned all the most fell and fearsome incantations, bend their anger to my will? Or would they respond with stillness and silence, as they did when I sought visions?

Luckily, my mother had taught me that the threat of a curse is often power enough. The townsfolk shifted about uncomfortably, scratching their heads and looking over their shoulders. They might not respect me, but they had heard the stories of Bikk and Kunaris, whose people fell out with the High Druid of the northlands in my grandfather's day; they had no desire to become the subject of such tales. Enica's mother looked at me angrily, but then she waved her hand.

"Do the test, then," she said. "It will only prove my daughter right."

One of the elders came forward with the bowl, and the tanner handed me the needles, and as carefully as I could I pricked the man's thumb and then the woman's and let the dark blood drip into the milk.

I excelled at divination, because it did not require me to be able to hear the gods in my mind as my mother could; I had only to learn how to read their signs in the world. I was well-known in my village for my skill with birdsign, which is notoriously difficult because the same falcon or sparrow can have different meanings depending on whether it soars or flutters, sings or cries its distress call. Compared to a complex augury during migration time, this ceremony was quite simple, and I had little doubt that it would prove convincing for all involved.

The townsfolk were hushed, waiting. The milk turned the very lightest pink. Someone coughed. In my mind I began to count to twenty-seven as my mother had taught me: the proper length of time for a bowl divination. When I reached fourteen a man from Enica's family called out, "It's not curdling!"

There was a great commotion, both families shoving to get a closer look at the bowl. Someone even shoved me; Aesu gave the man a look and put his hand to the hilt of his sword.

"Silence!" I called, holding up both my hands as I had seen my mother do. I finished the count before I let them drop.

"The test is complete," I said. "Linu is the father of Enica's child."

The man's family began shouting and complaining.

"It's a trick," said the man's father. "Foreign witchcraft, nothing more."

"I never heard of the Belgae until today," Linu said. "I think she made them up."

Then Enica began crying and yelling.

"All you do is lie and lie," she shouted at Linu. "We shouldn't have to do any of this. We shouldn't have to bring some hoity-toity woman here with her weird milk games. If you just did your duty from the beginning—but no! You're nothing but a weak, pathetic loser."

She tried to scratch the man's face with her fingernails, and one of her sisters pulled her back but her mother pushed her forward again, and then a man from her side began scuffling with a man from Linu's, and I had to shout even louder to be heard over the din, and Aesu and Crab had to unsheathe their swords and hold them aloft before the townsfolk would quiet enough to hear my judgment.

"Linu," I said, "your family will provide half the grain and milk and meat necessary to feed a growing child, along with half the wool and leather necessary to outfit the child in decent clothes. The arrangement shall continue until the child is of age, unless Enica should marry someone else who agrees to provide for the child, in which case your responsibilities are at an end."

Enica spat in the dirt.

"Half? They should pay everything! He's done nothing while I carry his child except lie and drag my name through the mud."

I held up my hand.

"Your family is not destitute. They should share in bringing up the child, just as they would if you were married."

Both families began arguing and bickering, their voices overlapping until I could barely gather my thoughts.

"This is my judgment," I shouted. "I will hear no argument or appeal. You know that my word is law here. You know what will happen if you do not obey."

Then I turned to Crab and asked him to get the horses ready. These fractious townsfolk had grown tiresome to me, and I wanted to leave them to work out the rest of their problems by themselves. As we left the clearing, though, Linu's mother caught my arm.

"We fed you," she said, reproaching me. "We received you in our home."

"And I thank you," I said. "Surely you didn't think it would influence my decision."

The woman scowled, and indeed I had the sensation of all of them scowling at our backs as we departed, even Crab's brother-in-law's family, who had been nothing but kind to us until that point.

As we rode out, I was not particularly troubled by the outcome of our visit; after all, my mother had warned me that a just decision often leaves everyone unsatisfied.

Aesu, however, was in a dark mood, speaking not a word to me or Crab as we rode, but instead glowering from beneath his eyebrows at some point beyond the horizon.

"What's wrong?" I asked him finally, when Crab began to sing a jolly traveling song and he refused to join in.

"You've got to be more careful," he said.

"Careful about what?" I asked.

"You've just made a townful of enemies."

"It was a difficult case," I said. "Someone was bound to be unhappy. Over time, they'll see the wisdom of my decision."

"Will they?" Aesu asked. "The Belgic priests, sister—why on earth did you have to bring them into it?"

"I needed proof," I said, surprised at him. "The Belgic ritual is the latest, most advanced divination."

Aesu shook his head.

"Sister, not everyone is as worldly as you are. The people in that village, a lot of them have never been more than a day's ride from home. When you start talking about divinations from across the water, you just sound crazy."

"You're not giving them enough credit," I said. "Mother made offerings to her family's gods in towns smaller than this one, and no one ever questioned her."

"Because Mother is a politician. She knows how to read people and how to win them over. That's what you've got to learn."

The idea that our mother's success as druid had come through flattery or gladhanding made me angry on her behalf.

"Mother is well-liked wherever she goes," I said. "But her greatest asset as druid was her wisdom."

"All the wisdom in the world is useless if you can't make people hear it," said Aesu.

I did not agree with my brother. I believed that people know justice when they see it, even if they don't like it at first—I felt that if I were to return to the village in two years' time, to find Enica with her little redheaded child, she and her family would thank me, and Linu's family would thank me too, for ensuring the child was brought up fairly and that all her relations did their duty by her.

Still I understood that Aesu was trying to protect me. It was what he had always done, even though he was younger. Once when we were small, we stole and ate a jar of berries that my mother was preserving for the winter. It had been my idea, but when my father lined all the children up to ask who was responsible, Aesu squeezed my hand to keep me quiet, then stepped forward to say that he had eaten all the berries himself. My father beat him with a leather strap until he had welts all down his back and legs. Later I wept with guilt because I had not shared the punishment with him, but Aesu said it would only have hurt worse if he had seen me hurting too.

So I could never be angry with Aesu, nor could I dismiss his counsel the way I might have if the same words came from anyone else.

"I'll think about what you've said," I told him. "Maybe I can learn to be a little more diplomatic."

Aesu nodded, and though he did not speak much for the rest of the afternoon, after a time he took his part in the songs again, and I felt all three of our hearts lift, joyous and full as they should be on our journey to the great city, with the breath of the gods at our backs.

April 2018

Agnes waits for Sunita, the bioarchaeologist recommended by her officemate at the university, in a coffee shop in Manchester. She has never been to this bright café with its chaotic array of posters advertising different sandwiches and drinks, and although she is reasonably sure she ordered a tomato and cheese sandwich, she has instead received something large and complicated on a brioche bun, with sausage, and she is conducting a series of experiments on it, removing and replacing the bread, poking at the sausage patty, taking small bites, as she reviews the carbon-dating report on her laptop.

The technicians have performed the test with the femur sample Agnes sent. They ground the bone down and burned it at high heat and then burned it again and again, until everything that made it bone had fallen away and it was pure and black, and then they put it in a spectrometer and sent Agnes the results. In an unusual step, one of the technicians also called Agnes early yesterday morning, when she was getting ready for class—he had been unable to sleep, he said, he had checked the results several times, he could find no error but he still thought it possible there was something he had missed, would she please let him know if she was able to confirm the age of the remains by other means.

Agnes had agreed; she had taught her class in a haze. She is still staring at the technician's report when Sunita walks in.

The bioarchaeologist is in her early forties, a small woman in a black blazer, large eyes in a round face. She waves to Agnes and points to the counter, then chats easily for a moment with the barista, who pours her a latte in a huge green mug. Sunita's wrist falters as she grips the handle, and Agnes sees the muscles of her arm kick on to compensate.

"You should use a joystick mouse," Agnes says as the woman sits down.

"Sorry?"

Agnes realizes she has said something odd, but it is too late to stop now.

"For your carpal tunnel. You want to avoid repetitive movements that compress the area."

Sunita's left hand flies to her right wrist.

"How do you—"

"You're, ah—I just mean you're favoring your upper arm instead of your wrist. There's a few possibilities, but for women your age, carpal tunnel is really common."

"My age?"

Agnes feels her face heat. Her father was right, she does not like this kind of thing.

"I just meant," she tries, "obviously people can get it in their twenties, but it's more common as you get older, with more wear and tear on the wrist—"

"How old are you?" Sunita asks.

"Twenty-five," Agnes says. "Twenty-six in June."

Sunita looks confused. Agnes can see her doing the math in her head—undergrad, grad school, postdoc.

"I, ah, I graduated from high school early," Agnes explains.

"And they've got you on something like this?" Sunita asks.

Agnes feels a protective instinct. She sits up straighter in her seat and grips her laptop with both hands.

"I'm the anthropologist under contract with the coroner's office. So yes, it's my case."

Sunita looks hard at Agnes. She is trying to suss out something. What substance exists to Agnes, what counterweight to her youth and inexperience? Agnes swallows and holds her gaze.

"Well," says Sunita slowly, "I hear you have quite a find on your hands."

"Maybe," says Agnes. "The technician was worried it might be a mistake."

"Right, we'll definitely work on other dating methods. But the remains are consistent with other bog bodies of the period—you've looked at Anne Stilwell's work? Or Bancroft?"

"Of course," Agnes says, though she has only just begun to familiarize herself with the relevant research, the handful of other bodies in museums across northern Europe, their names epithetical and incantatory. The Huldremose Woman. The Raspberry Girl. Even within this small and strange society, only a very few resemble the body lying in the vault in Ludlow in their perfect preservation, their faces expressive, their skin plump as though with life. And none has quite the alchemical quality that Agnes sees, even now, in her mind's eye, a human being turned to brightness beneath the earth.

"Right, okay," Sunita says. "So we'll do a soil analysis first, and then we'll look for artifacts that can help us out with dating.

The coroner's office, I assume they're giving you whatever you need?"

"They're kind of dealing with a lot right now," Agnes says. She has an email from Kieran on her phone with the subject line "Dorotea," which she has been too nervous to open. "And they're a little under-resourced. They don't have a CT scanner, for instance, which wouldn't usually be a problem, but with this level of soft tissue preservation—"

"Of course, we'll do that," Sunita says. "But really our first priority should be the site. Something this well-preserved, there's a good chance of finding grave goods."

Agnes squirms in her chair. She's been nervous about this— that any new people she brings in will have their own priorities, their own research interests that will conflict with what Agnes needs to do.

"Grave goods, sure," she says. "But first I really want to establish cause of death."

Sunita raises an eyebrow. "Have you worked on a body this old before?"

"Yes," says Agnes, thinking of the jawbone. "Kind of."

"Right, then you'll be aware that we may not be able to reconstruct the chain of events the way you're used to with more recent decedents."

Agnes nods. She understands this rationally, but she does not accept it. She has been given a duty, and she will discharge it. She believes she will find out how this body died.

"Our best bet is the burial site," Sunita continues. "If we can find evidence of execution, for example—"

"Do you think she was executed?" Agnes asks.

"That's one theory about a lot of these bodies," Sunita says. "I thought you read Stilwell."

"I just started," Agnes admits.

"Okay, take Hillerod Man. When they first dug him up—this was in 1940, I think—they found marks around his neck. And then when archaeologists went back and excavated the bog, they found a leather noose."

Agnes remembers the fractures to the body's skull. Did she stand cold on a platform, waiting for a club to come down? Did she howl in fear, did she lift her face in strength and resignation? Did someone catch her when she fell?

"There's been some debate about him, more recently—some questions about whether the neck markings were actually made postmortem. But one thing we know is that bog burials were unusual, even at the time. Most people were buried in normal graves, in the ground. So your decedent, if she ended up in the moss, she was probably there for a reason. Once we excavate the find site, we might be able to figure out what it was."

"That might be a little bit of a problem," Agnes says. "The site is being, um, occupied right now."

"Occupied?"

"An environmentalist group," Agnes explains. "They're suing the peat company for control of the moss. They say it's super important from a climate perspective."

"That's certainly true," Sunita says. "Peat bogs are very effective carbon sinks. I'm actually part of a task force on peatland protection. But surely this group should understand the importance of our work as well. Have you talked to them?"

"Our work"—the phrase discomfits Agnes. The body is neither Sunita's property nor her responsibility. And yet there is no other way to say it: Agnes cannot do this without her.

"A little," Agnes says.

"Well, look, just explain to them what we're doing, the momentousness of this discovery, I'm sure they'll get it. We're on the same side."

○

"I won't lie, it's fascinating," Nicholas says. "A two-thousand-year-old body, right here in the Ludlow Moss. Can I see a picture of her?"

It is not strictly ethical to show him photos from an active investigation, but Agnes needs his help. Is there also a way in which she wants to impress him, to see his reaction when she pulls up the image on her phone, this extraordinary person, this rare transfigured human being whom it is Agnes's privilege to know? Indeed, Nicholas looks at the image with a kind of sweet awe. She sees that she has captivated him, captured the attention of someone who is used to the attention of others.

"This is amazing," he says.

"I know," she says. "What's really cool are the teeth, but you can't see them here."

"What's cool about the teeth?" he asks.

"They, um, they tell us she had a lot of grit in her diet, that she was eating stone-ground grain. That's actually how I knew how old she was, the tooth surface, I've seen something like this before."

"You're the one who figured it out?" he asks her. "That she's ancient?"

"I mean, my colleague did the carbon dating. But yeah, they brought me in to do the ID and I kind of said, 'Wait a second . . .'"

"So are you going to be famous now? 'Dr. Agnes Linstrom Discovers a Bog Body.'"

"I didn't discover her," Agnes says.

Agnes does not want to become famous—she does not even particularly want to be celebrated in her field. But the thought has occurred to her—if she is associated with a major discovery, especially if she can publish quickly, she may find herself with more career opportunities. She may not have to go home. This is not her first thought, when she thinks of the body, but she does not resist it. Her father has always taught her that the path to a good life is to use her gifts fully, and it strikes her as fair and right that if she can serve well in this case, she should be rewarded.

Nicholas looks again at the photograph.

"Who do you think she was?" he asks. "And why was she buried here? These bog burials were ritualistic, weren't they? I read—"

"We don't know yet," Agnes says, her words fast and eager. She has made him understand, she thinks. Of course anyone would understand when confronted with the importance of her situation. "When we excavate, we'll be looking for anything that might tell us about her, weapons obviously, anything to indicate violence, but also things like fibers, pottery, any items she might have been buried with, honestly I'm not even the biggest expert on some of this stuff, my colleague Sunita, she can explain more about how we handle a historic grave site, especially one like this, that's been so exceptionally preserved for so long—"

Nicholas interrupts her, his face apologetic.

"The thing is," he says, "we've already started the process of rewilding the moss."

"Rewilding?" Agnes asks.

"Come on," he says. "I'll show you."

They descend the rise and walk south along one of the furrows to a spot just yards from the find site, where the redheaded woman and another man kneel by a rusty metal pipe emerging from the mud. The woman inserts a rock into it. Agnes's excitement shades into anxiety.

"A peat bog depends on water," Nicholas explains, speaking again as though to a larger audience. "It rains, the sphagnum sucks it all up and holds on to it, pools form, then come the bugs, the voles, the birds. The sphagnum creates a whole ecosystem. You take away the water, though, and the sphagnum dries out, and then everything else dries out along with it. That's what the peat company did when they built this drainage system in the nineties. They took away the water, and it killed the bog."

The woman stands and brushes crumbles of mud from the knees of her jeans.

"Luckily they never updated the drainage system," she says. "It's just these old pipes. All we have to do is plug them up, and the bog will flood again next time we get a good rain."

Agnes glances involuntarily at the sky. A few fluffy white clouds idle at the horizon.

"But if you flood it," Agnes says, "we won't be able to dig."

The woman shrugs, her face is not unkind but she clearly does not care about what Agnes is saying. "Maybe you can do your research somewhere else," she offers.

"No, look, that's not how it works," Agnes says. "This body was buried *here*."

"Have you ever considered that maybe this body should have stayed buried?" the redheaded woman asks. Her face remains utterly pleasant. "No offense, but her people must have put her here for a reason. Do you think they wanted her to be poked and prodded by people who didn't know her or care about her?"

"I do care about her," Agnes says, although this is not the language she would have chosen. She would not say "about"; she would say "for."

"We know you do," Nicholas says. "But think about this: Don't you think the best way to honor her memory would be to look after the place where she was buried? Like Leah says, her people put her here for a reason. Obviously the moss was important to them. Don't you think they'd want to see it restored?"

"So restore it," Agnes says. "It seems like a good idea, honestly. Just wait until after we're done excavating."

Nicholas gives her a skeptical look. "I was looking up other archaeological digs in Britain," he says. "I saw this Neolithic site in Orkney, really cool stuff. They've been excavating for ten years."

"I'm not going to be here for ten years," Agnes says. She is aware, very keenly, of the clock ticking down.

"Listen, if you want to draw up a proposal, setting clear limits of time and space on the excavation, we can present it to our community," Nicholas says. "But I think you should take a longer view of things. Yes, you found a body here. But is the body really what's important? Or is it the conversation the body opens up about the earth, the past, the future—is that what really matters?"

He annoys her now, this speechifying. She remembers the man she knew, the Occupy protester. "Like a used-car salesman," Colin once said.

"The body is what's important," she tells Nicholas, and she stalks away across the rise, her hands balled up into fists.

To reach her car she has to pass again by the yellow tractor, where the man, Stephen, has been replaced by two women. One of them is very short, wearing a bright-blue dress and impractical stack-heeled boots. She is interviewing the second woman, who is older, perhaps sixty, with an easy confidence in her body that draws Agnes near almost without her realizing it. Agnes means to walk past them, she is still angry, she is in no mood for conversation. But the first woman—she holds a microphone, has very long sleek hair—calls out to her.

"Excuse me, are you Agnes Linstrom?"

It would be too uncomfortable simply to ignore her, even though Agnes wants to. Agnes was never called upon to speak to the press in Las Minas; when the department received a request in one of her cases, the medical examiner handled it himself.

"Sorry," Agnes says, maintaining a physical distance. "I'm working right now."

"Come on, Grace," the other woman says. "Don't bother her. I'm sure Kieran can give you what you need."

"I'd love your perspective, though," Grace says to Agnes. "Especially coming from the outside into this complicated situation."

"I don't know if it's complicated," Agnes says.

"That's what I've been saying." The older woman extends a hand, rough and short, the thumbnail split down the middle. "I'm Fiona. I'm one of the bad guys."

By process of elimination, Agnes infers that she must be talking about the peat company. "I'm not really interested in taking sides here," she says.

"No, nor should you," Fiona says. Her face is angular and humorous; she is missing the first bicuspid on the left side, giving her smile a jaunty appearance. "I told Kieran, she must be tearing her hair out, getting dragged into all this. Last thing you need."

"You know Kieran?" Agnes asks.

"I know pretty much everybody," Fiona says. "And I agree, it's quite simple. You've made a major discovery here. You need space to work. Everything else comes second."

Agnes must look skeptical, because Fiona laughs.

"Look, I'm not a science person, but even I understand what a big deal this is. It could put this town on the map in a real way. That's good for me, it's good for you, it's good for everybody here—even if they don't necessarily see it that way."

Agnes does not care about putting this or any town on the map. But there's a directness to Fiona's speech, her gaze, that she appreciates.

"It's a big deal," she agrees.

"I'll leave you to it, then," Fiona says, stepping a comfortable distance away from Agnes, lifting her hand in goodbye. "But if there's anything I can do to help, let me know."

Time of people talking

A colony of moss has no need or desire to mark the passage of time. But if such a colony did choose to comment on its days, it might say this: We enjoy the respite. No wheels roll over us, no blades cut, no scoops tear into our body. In the quiet, slowly, we begin to increase.

A colony of moss has no interest in or even awareness of human activity. But if it did, it might say this: They walk and walk. We feel their feet and hear their voices above us. Their brief lives allow them only a narrow field of vision, and they have only the barest understanding of the consequences of their actions. We, however, who have seen across the retreat of the glaciers, the warming of the air, and sunrise, sunset, equinox, and solstice so numerous as to be almost without number, see how they play their parts in a larger design, and are satisfied. We are even—dare we say it?—excited.

Waxing Crescent, Third Cycle

My mother had told me stories of the great cities over the water, the armory at Avallon and the magnificent gardens of Domnonia. But no mere story could prepare me for the sight of the fortification at Camulodunon. We approached the city through the forest to the northeast, half-dark even at midday, a place of unfamiliar magic. My mother had given me a tincture for protection, made of meadowsweet from our valley and other herbs that carried the power of our local gods, and I administered a dose each to Aesu and Crab before taking some myself as soon as we entered the wood. Yet still I felt fear when I saw it, looming in the dimness: a wall of earth twice as tall as any man, too steep to climb and studded, for good measure, with sharpened rocks and spear-points to slice open the hands and knees of anyone who tried to summit it. Surely, I told Aesu, there must be a gate in the wall, and we were turning our horses west to look for it when we heard a shout at our backs: "Dismount!"

I had heard nothing of their approach, and yet the men were all around us, at least a dozen strong, armed with spears and clubs, their heads and bodies so thoroughly encased in heavy armor that they might have been iron statues placed in our path by some terrible sorcery—except that the one whose helmet bore a red plume, who seemed to be their leader, turned his thickly bearded face to Aesu and said again, "Dismount."

"I am the Druid of Bereda, on the Greenstone River in the north country," I replied. "We have come on the king's invitation to visit this city."

"I don't care if you're the emperor," the leader said. "Nobody rides into Camulodunon."

Aesu shook his head at me. Even in the green-gray shadow I could read his lips saying, "We should go."

I shook my head back.

"Do I have your word that if we dismount, you will take us to the king unharmed, like the invited guests we are?" I asked the leader.

His laugh rang in the forest.

"Little Druid," he said finally, "Brocchus here killed his own mother with a chisel. Lucianus slaughtered an entire town in southern Gaul just because he felt like it. Me personally—well, I drowned my best friend and took his wife, and then two weeks later I drowned her too. So if you'd like our word, we'll happily give it to you, but I'm not sure how much it's worth."

I looked at Aesu. "We should go," he mouthed again.

I looked at Crab. He glanced frantically between me and Aesu, an unfamiliar panic on his face. I knew I was responsible for these men, my dear friend and my brother, as much as I was for myself.

But, indeed, I was responsible for all the people of Bereda. It was their interests I represented on my journey to this city with its fanged walls and murderous guards, and their interests that compelled me now to dismount my horse, look the leader in the eye with all the courage I could gather, and say, "We will rely, then, not on your word, but on your fear of what the king will do to you if you harm his honored guests."

The leader snorted. He motioned to the man at his right—hungry-faced, gray-bearded—who unhooked a length of rope from his belt and roughly bound my hands behind my back. Then he pressed the point of a spear between my shoulder blades and commanded me to walk forward. I could not see if the other guards did the same to my companions or worse; I could only think of Sego's men and their warning, and wonder if perhaps my judgment was not as strong as I had always thought.

The men marched me through the wood along the edge of the wall, and after a time I saw that our path began to curve; the wall was not straight but rounded, and I was beginning to think that we would march in a full circle when the woods began to open, and I saw ahead of us an enormous ditch, as deep as a river but dry at the bottom, stretching alongside the wall. We followed the ditch for another long while, long enough that I passed through fear to curiosity and then to boredom, and then finally we came upon a break in the wall guarded by four huge men.

The leader with the beard called to them, and they disappeared for a moment and then returned with a wooden plank, which they lowered over the ditch for us all to march across.

As soon as we passed inside the wall my uncertainty fell away. I held my head high again; I felt a soaring in my heart, for the majesty I saw was such that I was sure I had been right in leading us to this place, even if we had faced difficulty along the way. Stretched out before us were farmsteads, richer and more modern than the ones at home, with golden wheat piled high for the milling and oxen pulling iron plows that glittered in the sun. Beyond these, the land sloped upward in a gentle hill, on which were clustered houses so close together that one could step from threshold to threshold with barely a stretch of the leg. The men led us into a narrow lane that wove among these dwellings, some of which, I realized, also served as smithies, tanneries, and other workshops and places of trade—at one point we walked by a butcher tipping a bucket full of hog's blood directly into the lane. The mingled sounds of men shouting, children laughing, spoons against plates, coins jangling, and looms singing made my heart beat faster in my chest. I lifted my face and took a deep draught of air to breathe the city in, and after I recovered from the scent of a nearby goose shed, I could detect on the breeze the spices of unfamiliar foods and the smoke of unfamiliar offerings. My mother, I thought, must have felt this way when she stepped off the barge and took the air of Albion into her lungs for the first time. I still could not see Crab or Aesu, but I hoped that they too felt the import of the moment, the power that comes with walking for the first time in the presence of new gods.

Near the top of the hill we came upon another ditch, deeper than the first, and another wall, higher than the first, and again a brace of huge men let us through, and before I could see what was on the other side I was thrust to the dirt with such force that my eyes went black, and my ears filled with the sound of bees.

April 2018

"Sorry," Agnes says, "I must have the wrong office." Instead of Sunita, she sees a girl sitting at the desk, with a book and a laptop open in front of her. The girl wears a baggy purple sweatshirt with sleeves that come down all the way to her knuckles, and her hair pours down her back in many long braids. She is thirteen, maybe fourteen, the look of a child still, she has not finished growing. She fidgets, picking up a phone and putting it down again, her left foot bouncing. Her shoulders are hunched and pulled up to her earlobes, some tension screwing the muscles tight, but the face she turns to Agnes is bright and open.

"Are you the anthropologist?" the girl asks. "My mum went to get coffee. We were up kind of late."

"I'm Agnes," says Agnes, looking behind her down the empty hallway.

"I'm Ruby," says the girl. A stiff wave of the hand, jokey and self-conscious. Agnes recognizes the vocabulary of movement, the gestures of that age. But she does not know how to talk to teenagers; in junior high she made her attempts, she remembers a trip to the mall, a crop top, a shiny brownish lip gloss. The other girls were not unkind, Erin split a food-court cookie with her, Nicole told her the makeup brought out her eyes. But also they did not invite her out again, and she did not ask, easier to spend her weekends beating her father at computer games, and her weeks greeting her classmates with an expression of generalized politeness, avoiding focusing her eyes on any particular person, so that she moved through school in a kind of fog, within which it was easy to ignore and be ignored. And then later there was Colin, and she had no need of other friendships. Why accept anything less than the incandescence of his attention? Why struggle?

This girl, however, is easy in her speech and manner.

"You don't read Latin, do you?" she asks Agnes.

"Sure don't," Agnes says. "Sorry."

"It's okay," the girl says. "Hardly anybody does."

Agnes glances into the hallway again; still no sign of Sunita. When she turns back, the girl is still looking at her.

"What, ah, what are you working on?" Agnes asks, aware that she should be trying to make conversation.

"It's Livy," Ruby says. "Most of it is pretty easy, but this part is complicated. It's where Romulus kills Remus."

Agnes only barely remembers these names from a ninth-grade world history class during which she mostly looked out the window. She senses, though, that Ruby expects them to be familiar to her, part of the corpus of knowledge common to adults.

"What's complicated about it?" Agnes hedges.

"Well, first Livy says there's a battle over auguries. Remus sees six vultures, so he says, 'That makes me king of Rome.' But then

Romulus sees twelve vultures, and he's like, 'No, I'm the king of Rome.' Then their guys fight it out and Remus dies."

"Is there a wolf in this story?" Agnes asks, trying to pull together the shreds of her recollection.

Ruby waves her hand. "That's way earlier. Anyway, the confusing part is then Livy says the more common story—the *vulgatior fama*—is that Remus actually jumps over the walls of Rome to make fun of Romulus, and Romulus gets angry and kills him."

"Seems like they need higher walls."

"Not the point," Ruby says. "The question I'm supposed to answer is, which one is Livy saying is the real story? Birds or walls?"

Agnes looks over Ruby's shoulder at the book, intimidating chunks of unfamiliar language interspersed with snatches of English. Agnes took Spanish in high school; she liked the sound and feel of it, the *erre* on the tongue. Her textbooks, though, were much simpler, with big type and faded photographs of clear-skinned teenagers hanging out at fountains.

"You're doing this in school?" Agnes asks.

The girl shrugs. "My mums got them to let me work ahead."

Agnes remembers the meeting she and her father had with her high school guidance counselor, his list of her teachers' concerns about her—she clearly understands the material, but she doesn't participate in class, she doesn't engage with peers, perhaps she could join a club or sports team, something to bring her out of herself a little. Instead her father enrolled her in science and math at the community college. She remembers the joy of it, the first time she had been truly excited by school: the revelation that was the second derivative, a concept in math that so clearly and uniquely explained something in the world. In chemistry the litany of the metals, stannous plumbic cupric ferrous. How she would race home from the bus stop to show her father, and later Colin, her mind seeming almost to overflow.

"It must be birds," Ruby says. "If the more common story was true, he'd just give us that. I think he's telling us the birds story because that's the real one."

Sunita returns with three drinks in a cardboard tray. She moves with a kind of clipped determination, Agnes has the thought that she is pushing through something. She sets a drink down in front of her daughter: icy, topped with whipped cream.

"This is your *one* this week," she says. "Agnes, I see you've met Ruby. Ruby, this is the scientist I was telling you about, from the States."

"I know, Mum," Ruby says, rolling her eyes. "And I *know* about the coffee, you *told* me."

"Then consider this your reminder," Sunita says, loving but annoyed. "Did you do your maths homework?"

She rolls her eyes again. "I'm doing my Latin."

"I'm very glad you're doing your Latin, but your maths, if I'm not mistaken, was due yesterday."

Ruby theatrically turns the paper over. "Fine," she spits.

"Don't speak to me that way," Sunita says. "Agnes and I are going down the hall to do some work. When we get back I expect the maths to be done."

Agnes follows Sunita down the hallway in the fluorescent light, fascinated and a little frightened by her open exercise of authority. Her father rarely made rules for her, he did not force her to do work she did not want to do, which is probably why her grades in English and history were so dismal.

"Sorry about that," she says to Agnes at the door of the scanner room. "She's been having some problems at school. We're working on it."

The scanner room is painted gunmetal gray, with that dry-cold bite that Agnes has come to associate with all rooms in which once-living tissue is laid bare for examination. She is habituated to it, even prefers it, accustomed as she once was to the desert heat; now when she feels goosebumps her mind seems to become more alert and agile. For this reason her father and Colin installed a high-powered air conditioner in her bedroom when she was finishing her dissertation; she would emerge for meals with blue nail beds and a buzz of barely interrupted focus, her skin shocked by the relative warmth of the rest of the house.

"Ready when you are," Sunita says.

Agnes nods. When she opens the container, Sunita draws a single breath. Her features sharpen, her whole body seems to organize itself. There is a new purpose to her carriage and movement.

Together, wordless, they lift the body out. So light, so small in their arms. On the scanner bed they unzip the bag.

What strikes Agnes this time is the power of the body, its depth of color and detail against the flat light, the antiseptic chemical smell of the lab. How clear that this material is human, has being, force, and moment, even now, especially now, that it has been under the world and back out and retains its form and essence still.

"Jesus," says Sunita quietly.

"What?" Agnes asks.

She wants to know, she finds, what does another person see in this time-carved form, this shape of polished vital matter?

Sunita breathes out. Her eyes are wet with tears.

"She's so beautiful."

Agnes feels a rush of fellow feeling. She wants to put a hand on Sunita's shoulder, but she senses it would be inappropriate.

"She is," Agnes says instead.

Sunita places her own gloved hand, not on the body, but next to the head, as though adjusting a pillow.

"Little one," she asks, "what happened to you?"

They move aside from the scanner bed, unspeaking. Sunita presses a series of buttons and the body slowly disappears inside the tube. The scanner begins to hum.

"Where are we with the find site?" Sunita asks, her voice businesslike again.

"Kind of nowhere," Agnes says. "The protesters aren't budging. They're actually trying to flood the moss right now. We're just lucky it hasn't rained in a couple days."

"They can't do that," Sunita says. "You have to talk to them. Did you talk to them?"

"I talked to them," Agnes says. "I think the next step is to get the police involved, unfortunately. I can talk to Kieran—"

Sunita's face clouds. "I'd rather not do that if we can avoid it. With what happened last year, I just—"

"What *did* happen last year?" Agnes asks.

"There was an anti-Brexit protest outside the council office," Sunita says. "Maybe twenty, twenty-five people, mostly students. No reason there should have been a police presence there. But, you know, the commissioner wanted to look tough, he had his campaign to think about, so he sent a dozen officers out there. Of course, somebody threw something, there was a fight, and one of the officers punched a boy in the chest and he had a heart attack and he died. He was seventeen years old. His sister was in Ruby's class."

"That's horrible," Agnes says.

Her father never got the newspaper when she was young; he was always so eager to protect her from distractions, as though any foreign material could damage the crystalline structure of her mind. Even still she feels at a remove from the events of the world. And yet she knows what it is to stop a heart, to send a body from life into death.

"I might have one other idea," Agnes says now.

The scanner beeps. Sunita presses a few buttons and it hums again.

"What is it?" Sunita asks.

"Well, there's a person from the peat company. It seems like she wants to help us. I don't know what she can do exactly, but there's a lawsuit—"

"Look, peat extraction is absolutely one of the most environmentally damaging industries on the planet," Sunita begins.

Before she can finish, though, the images begin to come up on the monitor. They are clear compared to the ghostliness of the X-rays, Agnes can see the details of the soft tissue, the pale-gray filigree of the brain. She feels a calm energy moving through her own body, her breath regular, her hands still. They begin with the head, where Agnes counts three small hairline fractures of the frontal bone at an angle that suggests contact with a flat surface: a fall or push to the ground. Such a fall could have been fatal, certainly, especially if it caused bleeding on the brain—which, even with remains as well-preserved as these, would be difficult to identify so many years after death. Agnes waits for the reconstruction to render on the screen. She peers close.

"What are you looking for?" Sunita asks.

And there they are. At the margins of the breaks, the bright white of callusing, the bone beginning to heal itself. The process appears well on its way. Agnes would estimate this skull has done weeks or even months of work to put itself back together. Another month and it would have been good as new.

"Hello," Sunita says, waving an impatient hand at Agnes, who now realizes she has said none of this aloud.

"Sorry," she says. "I was just looking at the skull fractures."

"And?"

Agnes has the feeling of a door closing, all the possible paths beyond it falling dark, falling away.

"And I don't think that's how she died."

Waxing Crescent, Third Cycle   ☽

I came to on a kind of low table, fitted with one very soft cushion the length of my entire body and another, even softer, wedged under my head. A man was kneeling next to me, blowing something that smelled like sweat or piss directly into my face.

"Salt of ammonia" were his first words to me.

"What?" I asked.

"You asked the name of the medicine. It's salt of ammonia. Very useful in cases of fainting."

"I didn't faint," I said, the immediate past coming back to me now along with a throbbing headache. "I was thrown to the ground. Where is my brother? Where is my friend?"

As soon as I said it I heard Aesu's voice. "Leave her be," he said, pushing the man aside.

"Now do you agree we should go home?" he hissed. "They nearly killed you. They knocked out Crab's tooth."

Crab, I saw, reclined on a cushioned table like mine, looking swollen and furious.

"What is the meaning of this?" I asked. "We were invited personally by the king, and we have been kidnapped, beaten, and left nearly for dead. How does the king explain himself?"

The man shook his head. In appearance, he was unlike anyone I had seen before, with delicate features, brown skin, and large eyes the color of honey.

"The guards at the wall are under the command of Mattonius, the king's cousin. They don't always see eye to eye."

"And who's in charge here," I asked, "the king or his cousin?"

"The king has already disciplined Mattonius," the man said. His speech was strange to me; it reminded me of the few times I'd met traders from the far northwest, the way they spoke our language with their own music in it.

"The entire company of guards on the northern flank have been lashed," he went on, "and Mattonius's allowance for provisions for the month has been cut in half. He and his men will dine on gristle and gruel."

"And will the king personally apologize to us?" I asked.

"The king does not apologize," the man said. "The king is the king."

Aesu stood up. I was proud of him, his height and strength, my little brother, whom I had held in my arms when he was not yet one day old. How he rose so quickly to defend our honor.

"Then we're leaving," he said. "My sister has important work to do in the north. She has no time for someone who insults us."

The man held up his hand, on which glimmered a gold ring inlaid with green stones.

"I'm sure the king will make you rich gifts in recompense for your suffering. Once you've recovered your strength, he will receive you himself."

My brother knelt by my side again.

"We should never have come," he said. "It's true what they say. This king is weak. He can't control his own guards. His friendship is worthless to us."

But when I sat up and looked around me, what I saw was strange and wonderful. Instead of a hearth, the room was lit by a small pottery vessel that produced flame from its spout. From the ceiling hung herbs of every variety: sweet cicely and hogweed and many I could not begin to identify, with flat broad leaves or clusters of pale flowers. All along the walls were shelves busy with jars and bottles, which I presumed to contain tinctures and powders; my mother had a few such in her house for divination and treating everyday ailments, but I had never seen so many in one place before, nor could I fathom the power of someone who had such an array of substances at his fingertips.

"Are you the druid here?" I asked.

He laughed. "I'm a doctor," he said. "And you need something for your head if you're going to be in any state to meet with the king."

He turned from me and began to rummage among the bottles on one side of the room. I took this as my cue to do the same on the other side, removing stoppers and smelling the contents, some acrid, others sweet, others with scents I could not easily name, but only grasp at descriptions for: like grass burned with twigs and leaves, like rainwater over stones. I was holding a black jar whose stopper was especially sticky when the doctor turned around.

"Put that back," he insisted, nearly shouting.

"I was just looking," I said. "I wouldn't steal from you."

"If you stole that one you'd regret it," he said. "Three drops are enough to kill a grown man."

He measured, instead, a pale powder out of an earth-colored jar and mixed it in a bowl of water.

"Drink this," he said, "for your head."

"She's not going to take anything you give her," my brother said, but I did not believe this man had any reason to harm me, or to lie to me about the milky preparation in the bowl. Also I was curious about this new potion, its taste and effects, whether I could replicate it at home. I lifted it to my lips and drank. The mixture was bitter, like wormwood, but almost immediately I felt the pressure in my head begin to lift and my balance return.

"There's so much we can learn here," I whispered to Aesu. "Let's meet with the king and see what he has to say. Then we can leave if you still want to."

"Are you ready?" the doctor asked, hearing us talking.

I rose to my feet, and even though I could tell my brother still disagreed with my decision, he offered me his arm to steady me as I followed the doctor out of the house in which we had lain. Crab followed behind, cursing softly with his injured mouth.

We entered an open space planted all around with lush trees, their branches heavy with a kind of dark fruit I had never seen before. On either side as we walked were houses, larger and finer than those we'd seen below in the town, with foundations of stone and frames of fine-hewn, highly polished oak that shone in the sunlight. I tried to peer inside each one as we walked past: I saw a man counting a pile of coins the size of a bale of hay, a woman applying red paint to another woman's cheeks, and children in fine clothes sitting in a neat ring, singing in a language I had never heard.

Before I could come even close to satisfying my curiosity, the man ushered us into the largest house of all, this one protected by two huge guards carrying battle-axes and wearing helmets inlaid with gold.

Inside the air was thick with a spicy perfume, and near the doorway a man was playing a tune on an instrument with four strings, a music that gave me an uncanny shiver, like a white crow or a rainstorm when the sun is shining. Yet the many men and women gathered in the house seemed to ignore the music entirely. They sat or lay on tables piled high with cushions, some of them drinking from intricately worked cups, others eating the dark fruit from the trees outside. Their clothing was finespun with patterns that even our best seamstress back home never could have managed; the women had painted faces and wore their hair in complicated plaits pinned behind their heads; the men had their hair and beards trimmed short, as though to resemble boys.

The only familiar feature of the house was the hearth in which a fire blazed. Just in front of it, inside its innermost circle of heat and light, a man and a woman sat upright in high-backed chairs. The woman sat on the right; she was thin, long in the face and body, with dark hair and eyes an unusual deep brown like the heartwood of an oak. The man was shorter than her, muscular, with a coiled strength in his body that reminded me of Sego, the summer when I saw that we were no longer children and he was becoming a man. His eyes were very blue and he watched us intently and searchingly, his gaze moving from one to the other.

I had thought of nothing else for weeks but the great city of Camulodunon, but I realized I had not prepared myself for this moment: I had no idea what to say to the king. Should I be deferential, take a knee or even press my forehead to the floor, and shower the king with compliments about his greatness? Or should I be confrontational, taking the king to task for the way his guards had treated us, perhaps mentioning the fine gifts we had brought him that had been confiscated along with our other belongings, and whose whereabouts I still did not know? I decided on both—I would take a respectful tone but hold the king to account. After all, as a druid I too was deserving of deference. I bowed my head only very briefly before speaking, but in that moment I heard the king shout, "Aesu!" His voice was deep and loud, seeming larger and older than his body. "I've heard so much about you! Come, eat and drink with us!"

As though from beneath the floor came big men with tables and padded benches for us to sit on, and women with shining hair carrying trays of fruit and meat. Aesu hesitated, anger and suspicion still heavy on his brow, but then he gave a slow nod and sat opposite the king. I sat next to him, facing the queen.

"Tell me if this is right," the king said to my brother, leaning close, less than an arm's length between them. "I heard that in the battle of the Small Willow River, you took a man's head off with a shovel."

"That man was my cousin," Aesu said. "I took no pleasure in it. I do what I have to do to defend our land."

"Of course," the king said, more sober now. "I don't know if you know, but my younger brother joined with the Trinovantes to attack this very city. I had to kill him with my own hands."

Aesu nodded. He took one of the dark fruits from the table and put it in his mouth. He said nothing but I could tell he was warming to the king. He was always moved by the discharge of duty, especially at great cost.

"Tell me," the king said, "what do you make of the Brigantes in the north? Are you concerned?"

I was not concerned about the movements of the Brigantes since they were several days' ride from any of our grazing lands. My brother, however, seemed to have many opinions, speaking in a low voice to the king, more animated than I had seen him in weeks. Crab too became involved, leaning across me on the bench to correct Aesu on matters of local gossip. Then the queen, hitherto still and silent, motioned to me to sit on the little cushion by her side.

"Did you know the king is not his father's eldest son?" she asked me, turning away from her husband, who remained absorbed in his conversation with my brother.

"I don't know anything about his family," I said.

"He isn't even the second eldest. And there was a sister too, a very wise and formidable woman. She would have ruled well."

The queen's voice was edged, like the doctor's, with the language of a foreign land. I had not until that day considered the sound of my own tongue—the harshness and spareness of it like our fields in wintertime. In the queen's voice I imagined I could hear fruit trees and sunshine. I could hear gold.

"Do you know why he became the king, even though by all rights the crown should have gone to someone else?" she asked me.

"It sounds like he's ruthless," I said.

The queen waved her hand.

"The Trinovantes? He loves to tell that story. The truth is Bracius was not even his brother by blood. No, he became the king because he understands people. He knows what they want and how to bring them over to his side."

She pointed to Aesu, now appearing to explain something by drawing with his finger on the table next to the tray of food. I saw how I had failed to speak to this side of my brother, had neglected to consult him in matters of policy and instead simply gone my own way.

At the same time, I heard the words not only as explanation, but as warning.

"Does he know what I want?" I asked.

She looked at me with neither benevolence nor malice, perhaps with resignation. Her eyes were set very deep in her face, lined with a black paint, with small creases just beginning to make themselves visible at the corners.

"He'll figure it out," she said.

She motioned with her hand, a wide swooping gesture, and the musicians at the edges of the room began to play a livelier tune. A woman approached, short and laughing-eyed, and pulled Crab up to dance. Another, more demure, offered her hand to Aesu, and after a moment he took it. Only then did the king look me in the eye and beckon me to him.

April 2018

"Thanks for coming out here," Fiona says. "I used to have an office in town, but the rent was so expensive."

The bagging plant sits next to a stable, at the southeast corner of the moss. If Agnes listens closely she can hear the horses whinnying. The plant itself stands empty and silent. Fiona walks her past the assembly line, a U-shaped metal track longer than Agnes's whole flat, above which squats, at one end, a kind of metal cage like a freight elevator. The ceiling is several stories high and the walls are made of corrugated iron; the floor is cement. Everything is still. One man punches numbers into a control panel; Fiona waves to him as they pass.

"We had to furlough almost everybody," Fiona says. "Some of them quit and got other jobs and, honestly, I don't blame them. Eddie Morris, he got a job up in Manchester, working construction. I told him, 'When all this is over we'll hire you back at twice the pay.'"

She leads Agnes into a smaller room off the factory floor, with bags of peat stacked up in the corners. The room has a pleasant smell, humid and sweet, that makes Agnes think of a greenhouse.

"I wish I could offer you tea, but we're pretty bare-bones here," Fiona says. "Water?"

"I'm fine," Agnes says. "Listen, I, um, I don't really want to get in the middle of things here, but—"

Fiona holds up a hand.

"Please," she says. "I understand. This isn't your fight. You just need to do your job."

Against her will Agnes feels her shoulder blades relax down her back.

"I don't know what to do," Agnes says. "I can't work if they won't leave."

They sit in metal chairs on either side of a dented metal desk. The desk is piled with binders and papers; in the center blooms a purple orchid in an earthenware pot.

"I wish I could do more," Fiona says. "What I can offer right now is advice."

Fiona pulls two granola bars out of a desk drawer, opens one, and pushes the other across the desk to Agnes.

"My dad was a miner," she says. "I'm no stranger to protesting. And ninety percent of protesting is PR, right? That's not a judgment, it's just the truth. You're trying to get noticed, you're trying to change people's minds."

Agnes thinks there is something more, she thinks sometimes to protest is to record, to enter into history.

"So what Nicholas and his crew need is good press, and what they really *don't* want is bad press. You can use that."

Agnes chews the granola bar. It has chocolate chips. Sometimes when her father picked her up from school, he would bring a two-pack of cookies from the vending machine at his office, and they would sit right there on the curb and share.

"How?" she asks.

"If I knew, I'd probably do it myself," Fiona says, smiling. "But then, it's not so effective coming from me. Like I said before, I'm the bad guy."

Agnes smiles, fears she should not communicate sympathy with this woman, and continues smiling anyway. Fiona rummages again in her desk and pulls out a business card.

"Remember Grace, the reporter?" she asks, handing Agnes the card. "She's lovely, and I'm sure she'd love to hear from you anytime."

"Thanks," Agnes says, rising. She holds the granola bar wrapper in her fist. She wonders if there is a way to stay here, in this warm room, with the smell of earth and the soft, speckled face of the flower.

"I can take that," Fiona says. She throws the wrapper in what must be a wastebasket concealed beneath the desk. She stands too, and extends her hand.

"Let's keep talking," she says. "You don't have to be on our side, or any side. But you're smart, and I can tell you think critically. That's not so common these days. I hope we can be friends."

○

Agnes feels calm and strong, like maybe she has figured out something, and she walks into the coroner's office with her shoulders high and what she thinks is a confident expression on her face.

"Thanks for coming," Melinda says. "I know this isn't really your business right now."

Kieran is drinking an energy drink out of a can. His large, square, handsome face is stony with annoyance.

"She's in the records room," he says.

Melinda picks up a white box of donuts from her desk.

"Here, bring these," she says. "She's probably hungry; she's been in there a while."

The records room is mostly full of filing cabinets, but in one corner is a kind of nook containing a faded pink loveseat and a coffee table with a tissue box on it. A painting hangs on the wall, an abstract image of horizontal stripes in blue and gray and cream. Dorotea looks alert and rested. She wears a black wool sweater and a green silk scarf, gold earrings in her ears. She is not sitting on the couch when Agnes enters, but standing at one of the cabinets, paging through a folder.

"Oh I'm sorry, that's confidential," Agnes says, unsure if it actually is.

Dorotea hands the file to her.

"It's very interesting," she says. "This office was so active at one time."

"I think it's still pretty active," Agnes says, absently placing the folder on top of the cabinet to be refiled later.

Dorotea makes a scoffing sound in her throat. "In the case of our aunt we have seen no activity at all."

Agnes sets the donuts on the table.

"The coroner has been working very hard," she says.

Dorotea raises an eyebrow. "Really? Has he started to dig since I arrived?"

"No, but there have been some unforeseen delays," Agnes says.

"Yes, Mr. Davies explained to me. A protest. He said you have been speaking to these people. That's why I wanted to speak with you."

"There's not much to say," Agnes says. "I'm in, ah, ongoing conversations with the protesters. I don't have anything to share yet, but when I do—"

Dorotea waves her hand impatiently.

"What have you been saying to them?" she asks.

Agnes straightens her spine.

"I told them our investigation has unique scientific importance," Agnes says, "and that remains like these are extremely rare, and that if we don't excavate soon, crucial evidence could be irrevocably lost."

Agnes feels that she sounds very serious and convincing, but Dorotea shakes her head.

"No no no no no," she says. "You think everyone cares about your ancient body, but no one cares about your ancient body. Listen to me. You tell them there is a grieving family here, and they are preventing us from laying our aunt to rest."

"I think they're aware of that," Agnes says.

Dorotea shakes her head again. "Our mother bought a plot next to her for Isabela. She didn't even do that for our father. All we want is to bury our aunt with her sister. You go and you tell them that."

Agnes watches Dorotea speak, the gathered force of this person. She thinks too of the business card now zipped into the pencil case she uses as a wallet.

"No," she says. "Come with me. You can tell them."

Waxing Crescent, Third Cycle ☽

"I'm so sorry to delay our conversation," the king said. "I sensed your companions were ill at ease."

"My brother was uncertain about coming here," I said. "It didn't help that your guards nearly killed us."

The king laughed ruefully.

"Yes, that's a problem that needs to be dealt with. I hope he feels reassured after our talk."

Aesu was dancing close to the woman in the firelight. She was whispering in his ear. At her throat she wore a necklace of unusual stones, glinting, the color of blood.

"I think he does, for now," I said. "But I don't know if I do. When you invited us, I was eager to come and see for myself: the great king at Camulodunon. Now that I'm here, though, I realize I want to know why exactly you asked us in the first place."

The king took a long breath.

"It's no secret that my time on the throne has been contentious," he said. "A lot of people thought I should've kicked the Romans out. A lot of people still do. What do you think?"

I looked around me at the platters of unfamiliar fruit, the women now stirring a dark liquid in a broad golden bowl.

"I don't know the Romans," I said. "But this world contains wonders far beyond our shores, and it is our duty as much as our privilege to learn about them."

The king smiled.

"I thought you might say something like that. The thing is, not everyone agrees with us. You know that as well as I do. In the north particularly—your friend Sego, for example, has been recruiting a force to challenge my men at the Oak Fort."

This surprised me. I knew Sego did not like the Romans, but I had not realized he felt strongly enough to bring fighting men together—or, indeed, that he had the influence to do so, outside of our immediate region. He had grown more powerful than I'd imagined.

"This is where I need your help," the king went on. "You have influence in Bereda and for miles around. The people look up to you. I invited you here to ask you if you'll be my ally in the north, and make your support known among your friends and family and the people you serve."

"My support for you and my opposition to Sego?" I asked.

I thought of Sego's men on the forest road. I was angry at him, and I had been looking forward to having it out with him on my return, but I had no desire to become his enemy.

"It doesn't need to come to that," the king said. "If you're successful, maybe he won't even be able to raise a force at all."

"But if he does," I said, "you'd ask me to rally fighters against him? My oldest friend, whose mother fed me from her hearth when I was little more than a baby?"

"I understand it's difficult," the king said. "But consider your constituents. You've seen the strength of my men, and those are just the city guards. Don't you want your people on my side when the time comes for battle?"

"Is that a threat?" I asked.

"I don't want to threaten you," the king said. He lifted his hand and a woman came forward, honey-skinned and very beautiful, holding forth a goblet of the dark brew. I hesitated, then took a sip. The taste seemed to tingle on my tongue, like mead but deeper and richer, with a perfume of fruit and summer herbs.

"What is this?" I asked.

The king only smiled.

"Please, enjoy yourself tonight," he said. "Rest. You've come such a long way. Tomorrow, my men will send for you. There's something I want you to see."

April 2018

Dorotea is more at home on the moss than Agnes expected. She walks carefully in her fine little leather shoes—her feet, Agnes notices, are tiny—but her face has a faraway look. She casts her eyes over the twisted branches, the crumbled, chewed-up earth.

"So," she says to Agnes. "Somewhere here."

Despite her youth, Agnes has a living will; she wrote it years ago, when she first began working with the dead. It does not stipulate a particular burial spot—Agnes thought about whether she would want her body to lie among trees or near water, and decided she did not care. Her instructions, which she keeps printed out in a folder labeled IMPORTANT PAPERS, state that her body should be donated to the teaching hospital at the university back home for use as a cadaver and then, if possible, buried in such a way that it can decompose naturally and fertilize the ground. Wherever this happens, Agnes does not think of it as a resting place. Her body will not rest, it will be active, as busy as it was in life, and just as much hers.

And yet Agnes knows too that people care where their loved ones lie, they do not want them in a place of dishonor, the side of a highway, a trash dump, a place where mere objects are discarded and through which others travel thoughtlessly on the way to somewhere else. Is the moss now such a place, ruined and plowed under, a wasteland where someone sought to hide his crime? Whatever it is, Dorotea has a spot in mind for her aunt's body and it is not here, lost to her, somewhere under the peat.

"We'll find her," Agnes says.

Agnes intends this as reassurance, but Dorotea seems to take it as something else, she nods, her expression turns inward.

"Yes, we will."

As they approach the encampment, Agnes realizes the protesters are dismantling their tents. She does not see Nicholas, so she approaches the redheaded woman, who is pulling up tent stakes with a loose-limbed ease.

"Are you guys leaving?" Agnes asks. It is possible that the suit has been decided and no one has told her.

"No, of course not," says the woman, smiling. "We're just moving the tents up to the rise over there to get ready for the rewilding."

Agnes casts an eye across the mud. The furrows are dry now, but she can picture them filling with water to overflowing.

"Is Nicholas here?" Agnes asks. "I need to talk to him."

"You're Dr. Linstrom, right?" the woman says instead of answering. "I'm Leah."

It should be no surprise that this woman recognizes her, but Agnes still finds it unnerving. "Hi," she says.

"Nick is actually in court right now," Leah says. "But I'm happy to talk to you."

Agnes hesitates. "This is Dorotea Navarro," she says. "She's Isabela's niece."

The introduction does not change Leah's demeanor—she is hale and comfortable, at home.

"Pleased to meet you," she says, and, more somberly but no less assuredly, "I'm sorry for your loss."

"Thank you," Dorotea says. "I came here because I want to bring my aunt's body home."

"I understand," Leah says. "The last few weeks must have been so hard for you and your family. If you'd like, I'd love to walk the land with you, so you can pay your respects, maybe say goodbye—"

"No," Dorotea says. "This place is where my aunt was killed. I do not want to spend time here. What I want is my aunt."

Leah inhales. "Look," she says, "I know what it's like to lose someone. My husband died of a drug overdose."

They must both look surprised at the word "husband," because she gives a practiced laugh. "It's a lot of fun being a twenty-four-year-old widow. Everybody really knows exactly what to say to you."

"I'm sorry," Dorotea says.

"Thanks," says Leah. "Yeah, it was awful. What helped was working on something I believe in."

"This protest," Dorotea says.

"I don't really think of it as a protest. I mean, it is that. But also—like, before I came here, I was working out west, near Hoylake. There's a toad there, it doesn't look like much, kind of like a rock honestly. And it's really finicky about where it will breed, like the size and shape of the puddle has to be just exactly right. Anyway, we spent a whole winter and spring occupying this one strip of land maybe the size of, like, a living room, and it was my job to make sure all the trash was picked up and the area was clear so the puddles could form. And it worked. When we started there was one toad on that strip of land, but she must have found a mate from somewhere else because by the time we finished we counted twenty toads. I held one of them, they're about the size of your palm. I could feel its heartbeat. That's how I think about this work, I guess. It's just saving what we can."

Agnes understands as well as anyone what is happening to the world. She has read the IPCC report, she knows the scale of what is possible: the species lost, forests gone to wasteland, empty skies, flowers blooming their last into a sweltering April. Disease-bearing mosquitoes sweeping north and south from the equator, cities falling into water, babies and old people suffocating in the heat. And yet it has all been too large for her mind to hold, her attention cannot find a place to rest, it slides back into what she knows well, a broken tooth, the delicate precious goblet of a skull.

A toad, though. A single living being is easy to understand, and she pictures it quite clearly now: the work she stands athwart in order to do her own. "The bad guys," she remembers Fiona saying.

Dorotea, however, appears unshaken in her purpose.

"I do not have something I believe in," she says. "I work in a bank. I helped my sister with her children when they were younger. My life is very ordinary."

"My life is ordinary too," Leah says. "That's what I'm trying to tell you—"

Dorotea holds up her hand. "I need to find my aunt's body so I can bury her with my mother. And I think we can work together on this."

Leah is confused, but smiling. "How do you mean?"

"An archaeological dig, I understand it might not seem very valuable to you. Or to most people. But a grieving family, and especially after all these years, I would think you would be more sympathetic. Certainly I think the public will."

The smile slips.

"Agnes knows of a journalist, a young woman. What is her name, Rose?"

"Grace," Agnes says quietly.

"I'd like to tell Grace that, despite your concerns, you were kind to us and stood aside so that we could find our aunt. I think that would be good press for you and your group."

She keeps her voice light, but looks Leah hard in the eye. "I know you don't care about things like this. You care about the earth. I respect that. But everyone can use good press, especially when they have legal troubles."

Leah meets her gaze. There is a hardness in her too.

"I'll take your request back to our community," she says. "We'll be in touch when we've had time to discuss."

Then she turns to Agnes. "I saw you talking to Fiona the other day," she says, gesturing to the west where the bright metal machines hulk over the moss.

She smiles, this time it is not kind.

"She's nice, isn't she? Always knows the right thing to say."

Time of biding time

A colony of moss does not express preferences for certain people, living or dead. But if such a colony of moss did decide to reveal its favorites, let us just say this: You might be surprised.

Such a colony might elaborate: We are not above some pettiness. We like a soft footfall. We like a person who does not stand between us and the sun. We like people with a lot of nitrogen in their blood. We are not always proud of our preferences, but we have them.

We try to remind ourselves, however, that no matter what might please or irritate us in the moment (for example: chanting), each person has a use to us, one which may not become clear for many lifetimes.

Waxing Crescent, Third Cycle ☽

I slept long and deeply in the great house of the king, on soft cushions pulled close to the fire. When I woke the light was streaming through the windows with the intensity of midmorning. I looked about me and was disturbed to see that I was entirely alone in the wide round room, but before I could get up to search for Crab and Aesu, a woman entered, the same who had served me the strange draught the night before. She set before me a tray piled high with plums and pears and bread as white as milk and lofty as goose down, and told me that the king had ridden out with Crab and Aesu to inspect the troops, and that he would return to meet with me in the evening.

"He invites you to eat and bathe, and to tour our gardens," she said. "You may take home with you any seeds or cuttings you wish. The king would be happy to see our flowers blossoming in the north."

I was annoyed with both the king and my brother for leaving me behind. Though it was true I had not studied battle tactics and weaponry as Aesu had, I should still have been invited to any formal inspection of troops in deference to my station as druid. In reaction to this slight I refused to comply with the king's instructions—I accepted the bath, in a beautiful bronze tub inlaid with patterns of fruit and flowers, but I did not allow the women to plait my hair in their complicated styles, and I refused the robe they offered me, though it was woven of soft cloth the color of sunlight.

When I had dressed myself again in my own good dress and cloak, I set off not for the gardens as the king had instructed but instead down the hill in the direction of the town. When I reached the wall defending the king's compound, the guards stood in the path to block my way, but I straightened my back and spoke from deep within my belly:

"I am the druid of Bereda, a guest of the king, and I command you to let me pass."

One of them raised an eyebrow at my words, another laughed, but after conferring in whispers for a moment they stood aside and let me through.

The city below was even more exciting than I remembered. Near the top of the hill the houses were tall and fine, with shuttered windows and bronze fittings on the doors, but as my path led me downward, the people's dwellings became more motley, some with doors and windows of hide, some open to the weather, some painted in bright shades and some with unusual large boards hanging from their roofs bearing markings I could not understand. Here along the crowded lanes and alleyways the noise was riotous, and I could hear my own language but also other tongues, some soft and guttural like my mother's, others bright and sharp as a blade. For a long time I wandered only listening, trying to match these new sounds to what I saw around me, the fish for sale, the children fighting, the woman in a red cloak with bright paint smeared over her sleepy face.

Finally, near the bottom of the hill, an alley opened onto a wider street lined with merchants and their wares; I had never seen so many in one place. In our village we traded with one another simply, milk for wheat, a goat for ducklings, the sinking of a roof post for the weaving of a shroud. A merchant from the south came once or twice a year in the summertime, but typically his stock was already depleted from the journey and consisted of a few caps and cook pots little better than what we could produce ourselves. Here I saw carts piled high with crockery in yellow and blue and violet, hung with blood-brown sausages, bowing under the weight of great slick fish with ice-green scales and jellied eyes pointing skyward. One of the tradesmen displayed on his cart an astonishing quantity and variety of cheeses, nothing like the soft white curd we ate at home but hard and pressed into wheels and wedges, straw-colored, bright orange, even veined with blue. By this time it was midday and I was hungry, so I asked for a slice of the blue concoction, offering as payment some of the herbs I carried with me, which, unique to our region and mixed specially by my mother, were sure to be of high value in the south.

The cheese merchant, however, only looked at me with a bewildered expression.

"It's two sestertii," he said.

"Ses—" I began, rummaging in my satchel. "I may have a few bronze potins, but I assure you the herbs are worth much more. I can show you how to mix a tea for fever, or prepare a bowl for divination—"

"Go away, girl," the man said. "If you're hungry you can go to the scrap heap like the other beggars."

I was slightly embarrassed by this encounter, but undeterred in my exploring, and soon I came upon a cart bearing nothing but a wooden board with blue and white stones set out upon it in an irregular formation that reminded me of dancers at a festival. A few men gathered round the cart, and one in particular seemed minutely focused on the stones, finally moving one of the blue ones as I approached. Then the man behind the cart, small and nondescript with a gray pointed beard, moved a white stone a few spaces and took the blue stone from the board. A loud groan erupted from the onlookers and the one who had moved the blue dropped some coins on the table and slunk away.

I had never played anything quite like this at home, but I had always been good at games. As a child I routinely beat older children and even adults at Soldiers and Sentries and Three Riddles; privately, my mother told me it was because I had an imaginative mind. The only game I ever lost at was dice, about which my brothers used to tease me, asking why the gods couldn't tell me the numbers in advance.

Now I found myself drawn to the stones game, and as I watched the next match and the next, I began to understand the rules: Each piece could move one space at a time, either forward or to the side, unless it encountered an enemy piece at which point it could not only capture the enemy but also move an extra space. The game ended when the first piece reached the opposite side of the board.

After a time the man with the pointed beard took notice of me and beckoned me forward, asking if I wanted to play.

"I don't have any money," I said, remembering what had happened with the cheese merchant.

"First one's free," the man said, neither smiling nor unsmiling, his face wan and mild. I accepted, and after giving up a piece early in the game recovered to beat the bearded man handily, inspiring crows from the audience. One man, large and square-jawed, clapped me on the back with a meaty hand and shouted, more to his compatriots than to me, "I'll stake you for the next one. I like to see a girl beat old Nannygoat here."

I did not like being referred to merely as a girl, but this did not seem the moment to insist on my title. And as I was gaining mastery of the game I had no desire to stop.

"Whatever you like, Andauer," said the man with the pointed beard, arranging the pieces on the board. "It's nothing to me."

The second game was even easier than the first, as I found I could begin to anticipate my opponent's moves. I thought I could detect the slightest furrow in his impassive brow as my blue stone leapt one of his white and reached the edge of the board. It was gone again when he reached into his satchel and drew out coins for Andauer, his winnings.

But Andauer held up a hand and looked at me for the first time, conspiratorial.

"Double or nothing?" he asked.

At the beginning of the third game I felt a calm comfort in my moves, as easy as following the steps of a harvest dance. But after I captured my first white stone, the bearded man took two of mine in quick succession, and I found myself on the defensive, moving to avoid him rather than to advance my position. My palms grew slick as I moved the pieces, and I felt the silence of the gods as keenly as I ever had, the loneliness of their refusal.

When his blue stone reached my side of the board, the bearded man did not rejoice, but merely opened his hand to receive Andauer's money. Instead Andauer raged.

"She tricked me!" he shouted, and then, turning to the bearded man, "Is she in cahoots with you?"

"I never tricked anyone," I protested, and, my pride wounded, "I still won two out of three."

"You lost the one that counted," Andauer snarled, slamming coins down on the cart's surface. "Well, you'll pay me back."

"I told you," I said, "I don't have any money. I have these herbs—"

"I don't want your herbs, girl," Andauer said, grabbing me by the arm and pulling me close to him. I could smell his breath and sweat. I turned in desperation to the bearded man, but he only gazed impassively as Andauer began to drag me away. The other men seemed to converge around me, boxing me in. I could see nothing but their rough cloaks, but I could hear something at a distance, beneath their laughter and clamor: the sound of hoofbeats.

April 2018

Nicholas's voice on the phone surprises Agnes. It sounds different when separated from his physical presence, his context among the people who trust and listen to him. He sounds younger, stripped of something.

"You didn't need to threaten us," he says.

It is early morning, a Saturday. Agnes is sitting cross-legged on her couch, eating Nutella toast and looking at the CT scan images on her laptop. Now that she's all but ruled out head trauma as a cause of death, she concentrates on the abdominal wound, the dark slice through the pale tissue. The penetrating object, whatever it was, appears to have missed the vital organs, but it pressed deep into the flesh; she would have bled badly. Still, Agnes sees signs of healing here, a soft web of scarring, the body stitching itself back together from the inside out. An infection, she thinks, and she sees some of the indicators—the heart is reduced in size, and its shape is unusual, the left ventricle appearing dilated. *Possible markers of sepsis*, she could write in her report, and no one would disagree with her. But the kidneys, spleen, and liver are remarkably well-preserved and show no sign that Agnes can see of septic changes. The sense Agnes has, looking at each scan one after the other, is of a body that was functioning well up until the time of death, not one lingering days or weeks in septic shock. She badly needs to speak to a pathologist, and Sunita has someone she trusts, an old friend who will treat the project with the gravity and discretion it requires. But this person is busy, is always busy, and so here is Agnes, alone with her judgment, which is almost always enough, but in this case is painfully not.

"I didn't threaten you," she says to Nicholas. She thinks of Leah, her strong snub-fingered hands carefully clearing away soda cans and plastic bags from the tall grass by the ocean, and she feels guilt in her throat, a physical clutching.

"I thought we were friends," Nicholas says.

The word surprises her, it gives her an unexpected flush of happiness.

"We can be," she says. "I mean, we are, we are friends."

"Then why did you tell Dorotea to go to the press about us?" he asks.

"I didn't," Agnes stumbles, "I didn't *tell* her—"

"She had the idea on her own? Right when it was most convenient for you?"

"It's not, that's not what this is about. Convenience, I don't—"

She trails off, she considers hanging up the phone. She wants him to understand without her having to explain, is this not what friendship is?

"And you're hanging out with Fiona all of a sudden? Do you understand what her company does, Agnes? I thought you were a scientist."

She puts the phone down on the couch cushion, stands up, and slides the remainder of her toast into the trash. When she returns she is not ready to hang up just yet, she wants to hear him, the way emotion tightens the timbre of his voice.

"Agnes? Agnes? Are you there?" Nicholas is saying.

"I'm here," she says.

"Look, ordinarily I wouldn't be angry. I'm used to opposition in my work, I expect it. I just thought you would understand what we're trying to do."

"I do understand," Agnes says. "I think I do. It's just—look, it seems selfish to you, probably. Maybe it is, I don't know. But I have one thing I know how to do in my life. I don't work for the university, I don't work for the coroner—I mean, I do, but really, I work for the decedent. The body. I have a responsibility to her. And so I get what you're doing, I do, I respect it, but I have to do my job here. It's not a choice. I have to."

They are quiet on the line for a moment. The sun is nudging up above the tops of the buildings across the street, goldening the gray sky.

"I don't think you're selfish," Nicholas says finally. "I'm disappointed, but I don't think that."

"I'm glad," she says.

"We talked about it," he goes on, "me and Leah, all of us. We decided we'll allow access so the coroner's office can dig for Isabela Navarro's body. And during that time, if you want to excavate the immediate area where the other body was found, we won't try to prevent you."

She almost does not believe him.

"Are you serious?" she asks. "We can dig?"

"Yeah." He sounds confused. "I mean, Dorotea was convincing. Wasn't that your goal?"

"I didn't—" she begins.

The word "goal"—it makes her sound savvy and calculating, a mastermind formulating a plan, when really, she has been stumbling clumsily forward, like a child just learning to walk. "My goal is just to do my work," she says finally.

"And now you can," he says. "For a while at least."

"For a while?"

"We can't let an excavation just drag on forever," he says. "Once they find Isabela's body, everything stops."

Agnes does some mental math, the size of the moss, the size of the coroner's team, the complexities of drift and settling over nearly sixty years. It could take months to find Isabela, indeed they might never find her. She realizes she has known this, even as she walked with Dorotea across the mud she knew it, and yet she allowed the other woman to speak for her, to do what she could not. She made an instrument of Dorotea, of her strength and righteous grief. Not such a child, perhaps, after all.

"I understand," is all she says. "Thank you. Thank you so much."

○

The next day, cold and bitter with a wind out of the north, they finally begin to dig. Kieran's team starts at the southeast corner of the moss, closest to where Bergmann and Navarro once lived. Agnes and Sunita, along with two of Sunita's postgrad students, Yasmin and Oliver, set up a small shelter near the dig site, a tarpaulin roof over a few tables and lab benches, a toolbox, a crate of sifters and sieves. Then they make the grid: Sunita hammers the sturdy nails into the earth, Agnes ties the string. When they are finished they have nine squares, each one meter on a side. It satisfies Agnes to see it, finally: The wasteland rolls away on all sides, but here, in the center, a little order. The size of a small house, Agnes thinks. A shrine perhaps, an altar.

When they first strike the earth with their trowels a hush falls, as though something significant is about to be uncovered. What

Agnes finds instead is peat: layer upon layer of it, both more complex and more monotonous than she expected. Beneath the topmost layer of hard-packed black mud is an altogether stranger substance, a loose matrix of interlocking threads or hairs with a powerful, almost musky smell. It is like a hide under the earth, Agnes almost expects it to rear up beneath them, a mouthless, eyeless beast, shivering and quaking to life. Beneath this layer is another more like the first, but when Agnes looks closely she can see the life there, the way the fibers have been pressed against one another over centuries until they fused into something new, it is not unlike what has happened to the body, Agnes thinks, except that while the body has been polished to a high shine, this layer of earth has been compacted into darkness, into blackness, Agnes thinks of the vacuum of space, she thinks of stars collapsing. And beneath the black layer is another layer of hide, and another of blackness, and sometimes they split and interpolate, double back on each other, some stack thin as tree rings and others fat as wedding cake, it is dizzying to sift through them, day after day, a week, with nothing to interrupt their chaotic yet continuous repetition.

Agnes is not used to long hours in the field like this; usually the examination of the find site is supplemental to her work, which happens in the lab. The soil itself begins to take possession of her; she finds it in her clothes, her hair. At night her shower runs black with it, she falls asleep and wakes up to its animal smell, she has the sense of being buried alive.

Sunita too seems troubled. She is on the phone several times a day, she plucks the hair at her temples, and when they pick up lunch she orders only coffee or fries. Once Agnes sees Yasmin embracing Sunita and feels uncertain, should she be trying to help, should she be asking what is wrong? But what does she have to offer this woman anyway? A tenure-track professor, a mother, Sunita has good sturdy sensible boots, she drives to the dig in her own car. Agnes does and says nothing.

On the eighth day of the dig, the sun comes out on the moss and for a little while Agnes thinks she sees the glitter of metal everywhere. She keeps abandoning the careful system by which she meant to move through her portion of the grid a centimeter at a time to chase something flashing at the corner of her vision, which turns out to be nothing—a piece of pine branch, a wet root, at least once, Agnes thinks, a speck of dust in her own eye.

In the afternoon Sunita's wife, Tianna, comes to the moss with Ruby. The whole family looks exhausted and wrung out; Ruby looks even smaller and more hunched than before. Tianna installs her daughter under the shelter with her laptop and a sandwich. She and Sunita speak together briefly; then they embrace and Tianna leaves.

For a time Agnes submits herself to the dizziness and monotony of the dig, the repetition of peat layer on peat layer. Then Ruby wanders over to her corner of the site, the incline of her shoulders indicating curiosity.

"What's that?" Ruby asks, pointing near Agnes's left foot.

"What's what?" Agnes sees nothing.

"There's something sticking up out of the ground," the girl says. "Here, I'll show you."

"No, you can't come in here like that—" Ruby is dressed in a T-shirt and leggings, her shoes uncovered. "Can you just tell me, like, on the clock?"

"On the clock?"

"You know, one o'clock, two o'clock, three o'clock—"

"No, I don't know what that is. It's like, right by your foot. You're going to step—oh."

Agnes looks at the bottom of her sneaker, the worn treads obscured by a plastic cover and a thick layer of mud.

"The other one."

Clinging to the mud on her right foot is a large, soggy oak leaf. Agnes peels it away.

"This?" she asks.

"Sorry," says Ruby. "It looked like something."

There's a vulnerability in the girl's voice that Agnes didn't hear when they first met, a tightness.

"It's okay," Agnes says.

Ruby is still standing there, she is not leaving. They stare at each other. Agnes wants to say something to her, something fun or reassuring, what does an older person say to a younger person, where does one learn this skill?

"Here," Agnes says finally. "Do you want to learn how to dig?"

Ruby shrugs. "Sure."

Agnes leads her over to the shelter where she rummages in a cardboard box until she finds shoe covers, a jumpsuit, and a hairnet. Sunita looks over from her section of the dig while Ruby is dressing. Agnes gives her what she thinks is a desperate look, like, *Come over*, like, *This is your kid*, but Sunita smiles, gives her a thumbs-up, and keeps digging.

Agnes has always been a mediocre teacher. She enjoys some parts of teaching anatomy: talking about bone tissue, for example, the hungry osteoclasts, the teeming marrow, the body's scaffolding so much more alive than it seems at first, than it seemed to Agnes before her first biology professor—a sharp-eyed short woman with a face like a falcon—revealed it to her. The students, however, do not seem to enjoy her. Her teaching evaluations last semester were full of complaints like "Lectures were confusing," and "Did not prepare me for the exam." So she approaches Ruby with a certain amount of anxiety, expecting the girl to become annoyed with her at any moment.

"The important thing is consistency," Agnes tells Ruby as they squat in the dirt. "You want to make sure you're going over every square centimeter with the same care."

At first Ruby is eager. Agnes shows her how to scrape away a thin layer of peat with a trowel, then deposit the result in a bucket for sifting. For a few minutes she watches the girl work. She is quick, almost furious; her hands and arms are gratified to be employed.

But when the bucket is almost full, Ruby lays down the trowel and sits in the dirt; she rolls up one of her sweatshirt sleeves and begins to rub at her arm, then scratch. Agnes is not going to say anything, probably the girl is fine, maybe she has a bug bite. But the moment goes on and on, Ruby will hurt her body, she is going to break the skin.

"Are you okay?" Agnes asks.

Ruby jerks upright.

"Yeah, fine."

"Sorry," Agnes says. "I didn't, um. I know you're fine."

Ruby picks up her trowel, looking aggrieved and embarrassed. They both scrape at the dirt for a moment in silence.

"Whatever," she says. "My mum probably told you what's going on with me."

"Not really," Agnes says.

"I get anxiety sometimes. Especially at school." Ruby looks quickly at Agnes and then back at the dirt. "But it's nothing basically. It's not like an actual problem."

"What are you anxious about?"

Ruby just rolls her eyes.

"I'm not anxious *about* anything," she says. "It's just anxiety."

"Sorry," Agnes says.

They dig again for a moment, but Agnes can feel Ruby vibrating next to her, wanting to say more.

"I just get bored," Ruby says. "And my brain starts racing. Lately it's diseases. I'll be sitting in maths and, like, I've done all the problems in my head already, and I'll start thinking about all the things that could kill me. So like just now, I saw this spot on my arm, I know it's actually just dry skin but part of me thinks, 'What if I have skin cancer?' And I'll know, logically, I probably don't, like, it's really unlikely. But my brain is just going, going, going, and it won't stop. Does that make sense?"

Agnes remembers those trips to the cardiologist, the silence in the car with her father, the terrible sound of her heart squelching on the echocardiogram, the waiting and waiting. And what would happen if it did not come, the smile, the "Everything looks good," the "See you this time next year"? Agnes would imagine disappearing on the spot, being invisible and inaccessible to her father, still conscious but trapped in a void of blackness, bodiless and howling.

"It makes sense," Agnes says. "I used to be scared of dying too."

"You used to?" Ruby asks. "How did you stop?"

Agnes has never spoken it aloud, the story of how her life started to take shape. She is not sure how to begin.

"My, ah, my mom died," she says.

"God, I'm so sorry," Ruby says. She looks confused and a little panicked.

"No, that's not what I meant. I mean, she did die. But when I was a baby. I didn't know her. It was a long time ago."

"Okay . . ."

"Anyway, my dad," she tries again, "I think he wanted to shield me. For a long time he wouldn't tell me what happened to her, he just said she was 'gone.' I kept asking when she was coming back, so finally he had to tell me the truth, but he wouldn't explain what it meant, to die, to be dead. My dad explained everything else to me, I knew how bad it must be if he wouldn't talk about it. I was so afraid."

"That's terrible," Ruby says. "I mean, I get it, he was sad about your mum. But he's the parent, he's supposed to talk things out with you."

Agnes smiles. Such assurance, in someone so young, of how people ought to behave. She's jealous.

"I guess," Agnes says. Impossible for her to imagine her father doing anything other than what he did, and does. "Anyway, what I was going to tell you—one time, I think I was nine, I found a dead bird in the backyard. It had slammed into the kitchen window."

A house finch—she knows that now, although she didn't then. Palm-sized, its blunt beak and red head. The little legs drawn up against the belly.

"I had this feeling that I shouldn't go get my dad. I just stared at it for a long time. I wasn't disgusted or scared, I wasn't even sad. After a while I found a trowel and I scooped the bird up and I hid it behind a rock, in a corner of the yard where my dad didn't usually go. And then every day I would just go check on it and watch it change."

First the ants, eager and swarming, then the flies circling about and investigating the soft parts of the breast and belly. Then the pale and busy maggots—the body at this point teeming, wild with life. And then the ebb as the insects took what they could, bore it away, and transformed it, the feathers loosening and falling from the skin, the skeleton exposed, so fragile and elegant it made her breath catch in her throat. The gravesite peaceful, the body reduced to its essence, perfect and complete.

"I just kept thinking, this is it? This is what they wouldn't tell me about? And after that I wasn't afraid anymore."

"Really?" Ruby says. "That was it?"

It was not entirely so simple, the process of losing her fear of death, it was slower, when she took her first biology class, came face to skull with her first model of a human skeleton, dissected a squid and then a pig and then a cadaver, with each encounter it was as though a part of the darkness was illuminated, until what had been void was a busy and various terrain over which she could move freely and comfortably, navigating without a map, the landscape of death becoming as or even more familiar than the living world.

"Pretty much," she says.

Ruby seems more relaxed now, her shoulders looser.

"So what you're saying is I should find some dead animals to stare at."

Agnes smiles. "Couldn't hurt. Mostly what we have here are dead plants, though."

She hefts a trowel of peat, black and crumbling. But Ruby's eyes scan wide, taking in the whole moss.

"What are we looking for here, exactly?" she asks.

Agnes breathes out. It's hard for her to remember sometimes too, so far are they from the body itself.

"Grave goods," Agnes says. "Hair or fiber. Fragments of bone. Anything that could help me—ah, help us—determine a cause of death."

Ruby nods. Agnes thinks she sees a concentration gathering in her face, a great diffuse energy narrowing and focusing to a point.

Time of recognition

A colony of moss does not acknowledge the arrival or departure of other living things. Imagine how exhausted we would be: We have seen so many come and go.

But if a colony of moss did experience, from time to time, a desire to greet a human being—perhaps someone of importance to us, whose actions will be pivotal in their time—how might we greet such a person? We would greet her in the same way that we meet the day's first sunlight: green and brilliant, perfect in our order and cohesion, inviting it to feed us.

April 2018

There is so much waiting during the excavation, much more than Agnes expected. They dig, they sift the dug-up earth, they dig some more. Now they are also waiting for the pathologist to come and examine the soft tissues. Agnes had thought that once the obstacle of the protest was removed, the investigation would proceed easily, but the days inch by with no progress. The body lies frozen in her quiet drawer.

A dry spell has come over Ludlow; the land is starved for rain. The fibrous dirt resists Agnes's trowel a little more every day. And yet with the peat-cutters gone, the moss seems to be making something out of next to nothing: deep in the furrows are bright patches, pockets of vivid green. The dig site stands out for its barrenness, an open wound on the reviving land.

Finally on the ninth day Oliver stands up from the dark trough of the dig, holding something in gloved hands. Under the good lights in the research tent, it looks like a piece of wood or bark, paper-thin but rigid. But when Agnes pokes it with a metal pick, she feels a kind of hardy give, like leather.

"What is it?" Agnes asks.

"Do you think it's part of a waterskin?" Oliver asks eagerly, his head and shoulders pitched forward.

He's not much younger than Agnes—twenty-two, maybe twenty-three—but he seems callow to her, fresh and unpracticed in this world. Is this how she was in graduate school, she wonders, this combination of confidence and inexperience?

"It could be," Sunita says. "We'll have to clean and date it to tell much of anything. But look at this."

Sunita points to the upper right-hand corner of the scrap. Something greenish peeks from beneath the mud's dun crust.

"Berry juice?" Oliver says. "I'm thinking of the Jutland Queen."

"It's not a bad thought," Sunita says, teacherly—she sounds more at ease, Agnes thinks, with this young man than with her daughter, perhaps less is at stake. "But let's not get ahead of ourselves. Jesper Claasen, at Oxford, he's great with materials like this. I want him to take a look."

"Who's, ah, who's the Jutland Queen?" Agnes asks, a little embarrassed. The many names and histories, she still can't keep them straight in her head.

Sunita gives Oliver a nod of encouragement.

"She was discovered in Denmark in the sixties," he says. "She was really tiny, even for the period. Like under four feet tall. Her leg bones showed signs of osteogenesis imperfecta—she probably wouldn't have been able to walk. But she died in her forties, so it's likely she was cared for, even revered."

Agnes smiles to herself—he knows so much more than her, she is callow still. A deficit, surely, but also a world yet before her, opening into flower.

"Revered?" she asks.

"She was buried with a really striking number and variety of grave goods. Decorated waterskins and meadskins, that's what made me think of it. Food. A fur cloak. Arm-rings, necklaces, even a sword that looked like it was sized for her."

The excitement in his voice, how he loves this story. Agnes thinks of the year she took anatomy at the community college, all that spring and summer how she saw the people around her in a new way. She understood their limps and wobbles, the way their bones turned cleanly in the joint or hitched and scraped at their swollen housing. An X-ray vision, she was giddy with it, a second sight.

"Was all that stuff supposed to be for the afterlife?" Agnes asks. "I know Stilwell—"

"Right, that's her theory," Oliver says. "That the bogs were seen as liminal spaces or portals to another world. But there are other possibilities."

He looks at Sunita, deferential.

"Some people think the bodies were put in the bog specifically to preserve them," she explains. "There's evidence of Iron Age Celts saving butter and other foods in bogs to dig up at a later date, so they knew the peat had these properties. It's a little silly, and not the kind of thing you could ever prove or disprove, but sometimes I like to think they buried people in the bog so that one day, someone would find them."

Waxing Crescent, Third Cycle ☽

I arrived at the king's compound on the back of his guardsman's horse, my cloak dirtied, my spirit shaken, and my pride significantly wounded. The king met us at the gate, alone and in ordinary clothes, a tunic and breeches like the men of my village. I turned my eyes from him as he conferred quietly with the guard, hoping to hide my relief and embarrassment.

"So," the king said finally, "you've seen some of our city."

"I have," I said, accepting his hand to help me dismount. "I found myself in a difficult situation, from which your guard was kind enough to deliver me."

"I would have preferred to show you around myself," the king said. "It might have been safer."

I drew myself up, attempting nonchalance. "You were busy this morning," I said.

"I was," he said. "Will you walk with me?"

He led me back to the great house, where now a half dozen women seemed to be making preparations for dinner, laying cushions and stoking the fire. The bathtub had been carried away but the orange robe lay where I had left it, neatly folded on the floor.

"I should have taken better care to explain my gift," he said. "These robes are worn by the highest of Roman priests, the flamines. I thought it would be a fitting recognition of your station."

He bent to lift the cloth and offer it to me himself. I took it from his hands; it was light as spider silk.

"If you'd prefer to wear your own clothes, of course I understand."

"No," I said. "Thank you for this gift."

One of the women led me to a painted screen, behind which I unfastened my dress and cloak, and over my shift wrapped the golden robe, fixing it at the shoulder with a brooch inlaid with green stones, given to me by the woman. The fabric slid smooth over my arms and legs and smelled of festival fire. When I stepped out from behind the screen the king bowed to me, and held my gaze as he lifted his head.

"The flamines are not ordinary priests," he said. "They live by a very specific code. They may not handle money or animals. They do not prepare food. It is considered bad luck for them to touch iron."

"Sounds like a dull life," I said.

"But the flamines are also present for every important decision of the empire. The emperor himself must consult them before he moves troops, before he raises taxes, before he makes an official visit or embarks on a journey. Even before he takes a mistress."

"And do you plan to consult me in such matters if we enter into an alliance?"

"Do you plan to advise me?"

"If I did, I would tell you never to send cavalry into the White Forest, never to collect taxes in winter, and never to undertake a journey without making offerings to the gods."

"And on the matter of the mistress?"

When I got my first blood, my mother had instructed me about my future. Nothing in our laws prevented a druid from marrying or taking a man to bed, if she chose to do so. But my mother cautioned me against becoming pregnant too early in my tenure, because I would struggle to earn the villagers' trust if they saw my attention occupied with a child. She explained to me several ways of avoiding the problem, which I employed when our neighbor the huntsman's son came to visit me at night, placing into my hand fresh rabbit skins, the fur still warm.

But my mother also told me of another vulnerability, this one harder to avoid: that a man might charm me, either unwittingly or with intent, and cause me to abandon my judgment. I had previously paid little mind to this warning, but now, as I walked with the young king of Camulodunon, his head bare, his face fierce and humorous, I saw how it might happen.

"I would tell you," I said, "that even a king does not simply take a mistress. He wins her."

The king smiled, shaking his head.

After she had delivered her warnings and wrapped soft linen for me to wear under my skirt, my mother had told me that I, too, would in time gain the ability to bend a man's judgment, and that I would have to learn how to use it.

"Come," the king said, "if you're not too exhausted from your morning's journey, there's something I want to show you."

I walked with him through the garden and past the great house to a more modest building just past the crest of the hill. This structure was windowless, with a tree growing before the doorway that bore waxy, sweet-smelling flowers.

At first the room into which we stepped appeared ordinary, a kind of pantry with shelves lining the wall, a scent of soot and bitter oak bark. The shelves were stacked high with rolls of stripped sheepskin, some appearing marked or stained, and it seemed we had entered a kind of scullery for storing rags. I wondered if this was some trick or stratagem to belittle me, and I turned to the king with irritation in my voice.

"Where are we?"

In answer he only selected one of the sheepskins and unrolled it on a table in the center of the room. It was painted in bright red and blue, and I took it for the king's banner, to fly ahead of his troops in battle.

"Very impressive," I said. "Intimidating."

The king shook his head. He pointed at a kind of red blot near the top of the skin.

"This is where we are," he said. "Here is the water your mother crossed. Here is Rome, where the queen was born."

He was pointing at another red blot, this one longer and thinner, that extended into an area of blue.

"I have visited Rome myself," he went on. "It makes Camulodunon look like the smallest village on one of the northern islands, a few meager huts, inhabited by primitives."

He continued talking about Rome and what he had seen there, but something else was happening in my mind. The blots on the sheepskin were coalescing and ordering themselves before my eyes. They were information, like the laws my mother had repeated to me until I knew them by heart, or the dozen complex steps of a divination. I saw my home, and my mother's country, and the water between, as I had always imagined them, the gray waves, the boat where my mother stood facing the sunset, and I saw how each place in my imagination had its own line and color on the sheepskin before me, and indeed how any place could be set down there, each corner of the world had its counterpart in the miniature world I now traced with my fingertips. I felt my spirit expand within my body, I was laughing, the king was laughing too, I could see in his face not only amusement but recognition.

"Do you want to keep the map?"

I did want it; I wanted to understand it. In addition to the shapes and colors, it was covered in strange markings I could not decipher, and below the red regions of Britain and Rome was a whole yellow swath of land I had never heard of or imagined. But I did not answer the king right away. I remembered what the queen had told me. I looked the king in the eyes, and let the silence lie between us.

"My lord," I said finally, "you flatter me, you give me fine clothes, you show me wonders. You make me forget myself. But I cannot forget what you ask in return: that I should rally fighters against my oldest friend."

The king rolled up the map.

"I understand it's difficult," he said. "But think of your constituents. Your people would have all the knowledge of the world at their fingertips. And you—you could travel to Rome, to Athens, to Carthage to study with the priests and doctors. You could surpass even your mother as a druid, and be remembered for generations to come."

"I'm not sure anyone can surpass my mother," I said. But still I was intrigued. I had hoped to visit my mother's country one day, but I had never dreamed of traveling to Rome, let alone Carthage. I thought of all the herbs and instruments in the doctor's house, and all I could do for our flocks and our people if I understood the function of every powder and ampule.

"You don't have to decide now," the king said. Then he lifted his eyes to mine. "But consider: Does your loyalty to your old friend serve you both, or only Sego?"

April 2018

Agnes is leaving the dig on the tenth day feeling unsettled in her mind—a scrap of something sleeps in a stranger's lab, the pathologist has pushed back their appointment again, Agnes cannot remember the last time she had to rely so much on other people to discharge the most sacred responsibilities of her life—when she spots Nicholas kneeling in a trough on the eastern side. Agnes is not sure if they are friends still, if they were ever, she is anxious about approaching him, he may be angry with her, or simply annoyed that she is bothering him. And yet, she finds, she is approaching him, he wears a dark-blue hooded sweatshirt and black work boots, light mud-stained jeans, his body at work broad and solid, fully and vitally in the world.

"It's coming back," Agnes says, pointing to the green.

He looks up, surprised to see her there. "It is."

"I don't know anything about sphagnum," she says, kneeling. Up close, the flat mass resolves itself into individual clusters, each one the shape of a star. "Are these the leaves?"

"The part you see is the capitulum," he says. "That's where the new stems grow."

"And the stuff that makes the peat," Agnes asks, thinking of the brown thready matrix she punches through with her trowel, "that's the dead growth?"

"Kind of," Nicholas says. "You could argue the sphagnum never dies, not really. The older leaves just kind of hang out under there, getting pressed down and pressed down until they turn into peat. The peat is really what creates the bog environment, it holds on to water so the new growth can survive in dry seasons. And the whole organism, it's clonal, I assume you know what that means?"

She nods. He is looking at her closely, he does not fully trust her, perhaps he is trying to suss out her motivations. But also, she thinks he is not angry, he is glad that she is here.

"Right, so this patch here, for example, even though there are a number of individual stems, they're all genetically identical. You could say they're all part of one organism. Which means— this is kind of my favorite part, actually—"

Agnes recognizes something in him, it is not merely excitement at his subject matter. The acuity of his gaze on the greenness at their feet, the way it draws his body down—she can see that he feels for his charge what she feels for hers, a love.

"Because they're clonal," he goes on, "they're interconnected not just across space, but across time. So this little patch here, functionally it's the same organism that's been here, in some form, for tens of thousands of years."

"It's not the same," Agnes says.

She has forgotten her anxiety, her uncertainty with him.

"What do you mean?" he asks.

"It's not the same organism, not really. I mean, the individuals still die. The ones who were here two thousand years ago, when the body was buried, they're down there in the peat, they're dead. The new ones up here, those are different individuals, even if they're genetic clones."

"Sure," he says, "you could think of it that way. But why draw the line at the individual when what matters to this species is the colony? Like, as long as a tiny part of the colony survives, the organism is passing along its genes. It's still alive, whether some individuals die or not."

"I get that," Agnes says. "But the dead individuals, they're playing a role too, right? They're the ones that make the bog a bog."

"I suppose to me it's all part of the same system. Every individual has a role to play."

Agnes smiles. She feels, if not an ease with him, then some kind of interchange, a buzzing of particles back and forth.

"I just want the dead to get some credit," she says.

He smiles too, now, and pushes to his feet. His face: She likes the changeability of his features, the way they can be sharp or soft.

"Glad they have someone looking out for them," he says, and then, courtly, he extends his hand. A little irony in the gesture, she thinks, it is a joke and not a joke.

"I'll walk you to your car," he says.

She puts her hand in his, left in left, and he pulls her to her full height. He looks up at her, her eyes and mouth, what is he seeing? He keeps hold of her hand a moment longer before letting it go.

She doesn't tell him she doesn't have a car, that she'll have to call a cab or walk a mile into town to get the bus. She doesn't want to seem childish, out of control of her life.

"Thanks," she says.

It is early evening; the light slinks away out of the furrows toward the west. Their feet follow the moss, twinkling islets in the black.

"How's the, ah, the investigation going?" he asks.

"We found something," she says. "Some kind of skin or textile. If we're lucky, it might tell us more about who she was."

"Who do you think she was?" he asks.

"We can't say much yet. But people buried in bogs were often unusual in some way. My colleague was telling me this story about a body called the Jutland Queen."

"So your body here is the Ludlow Queen?" he asks. "I like that."

"We don't know that she was a queen," Agnes says. "She could have been a military leader, there are other examples from the period. Or she could have been some kind of outcast, a criminal. What we know right now is that she was wounded, in the head and the abdomen, and sometime after that she died and her people decided to bury her in the moss."

He nods. He is watching her again, she is conscious of her own body moving over the mulchy ground, the strength in her calves, her narrow shoulders, the slight inward turn of her left foot.

"How did you come to this?" he asks. "This work, I mean? What made you think, 'I'm going to dig up bodies'?"

"I don't really dig up bodies," she says. "I mean, not usually."

"So what do you do, usually?"

"Usually law enforcement or a member of the public finds a body, one that's fully or at least partially skeletonized, and they call the county coroner's office and the coroner's office calls me."

"Okay, then," Nicholas says. The sky overhead going lavender, then indigo. "How did you come to that?"

"I did biology in college," Agnes says. "I loved anatomy, and I was especially interested in bones, I think, because they last so long and they can tell you so much. Like, you can do a strontium analysis of someone's tooth enamel and find out where they were born."

"That's wild," he says. He is impressed with her, she thinks. He keeps his eyes on her face and does not drop them until she turns away.

"And then I got into forensics kind of by accident," she says. "I got called in on a case, and I enjoyed it, and I just wanted to do it again."

"A case, like, a dead body?"

"Yeah," Agnes says. "A man, Edgar Durand. He was killed and his body was disposed of in the desert."

"Wow," Nicholas says. "That's extraordinary."

"That he was killed? It happens every day."

"No, that you went in and had that experience, and you thought, 'I'll do this again.' Not everybody could do this kind of work. I'm not sure I could do it."

It is not disgust she feels from him, she thinks it might be awe. And isn't this part of her pride in what she does, if she's honest with herself? That she can do a job few others can, that she is called to do it.

"You could if you wanted to," she said. "You have to recognize that dead people are just people. If you can do that, there's nothing to be afraid of."

"Simple as that," he says, smiling in the fallen night. They are near the western edge of the moss now, the stand of trees between the mud and the main road. "If you're not afraid of death, what are you afraid of?"

She has not asked herself this question, not when she sits awake at night looking at the job boards on her computer, or when she stares at the CT scans of the body, seeing and unseeing signs of sepsis in the heart. To be asked it now feels like a door opening inside her mind, letting in a bright light.

"Failing," she says. "It was hard for me, coming here. I think I thought, 'I'm going to have something to show for it. This is how my life is supposed to be.' And now my postdoc's almost over, this is the last case for me. If I can't determine how she died, if I can't determine *something*, I guess I'm scared I'll just be back where I started. Does that make sense?"

"Of course," he says. "I'm scared of failing all the time. Tomorrow I have to testify in court, for example. I'm terrified of that."

He walks slightly behind her, so she no longer sees him but only hears his voice in her ear.

"You don't seem like you'd be scared of something like that," she says.

"Thank you, I think. I am, though. I've never actually done it before. I'm used to a, ah, friendlier crowd."

Agnes is surprised to find an area in which she is more experienced than he is. She has served as an expert witness in three criminal cases, each of which she found less stressful than most social situations, because the expectations of her were entirely clear.

"It's really easy," she says. "You just answer the questions."

"Oh, is that all?"

She feels he is mocking her, and pulls away. She has misjudged him, she thinks. He finds her strange after all.

"I didn't mean to be flippant," he says. "It's just, there's so much riding on what I say tomorrow. If we lose—I mean, it's literally life or death for the plants and animals here."

She turns around to face him. What does he think of her, of her work, that it is immaterial?

"What I say in court is important too," she says. "I have to tell how someone died."

He drops his eyes. "Of course," he says. "I'm sorry. I can get kind of stuck in my own head sometimes. It's a bad quality."

They walk on in silence. Agnes is wary.

"What's your advice?" Nicholas asks. "For not getting nervous, I mean."

She looks at him; he is really asking. She has to think about her answer, and in the thinking her body begins to loosen, the knots in her neck unstring.

"I don't get nervous in court," she says finally. "And when I do get nervous"—she thinks of teaching, a roomful of people relying on her completely for direction, and invariably disappointed with the direction she offers—"I don't always do very well. But I guess, for you, I would say not to think about the outcome too much. Just try to go in and do your job."

"That's good advice," he says. "I'll try that."

She wonders if he will. As they cross through the oaks he puts a hand on the center of her back, where her spine is.

"You shouldn't be scared," he says.

"What?" She is confused.

"Of failing, I mean. An unusual woman, a queen or a warrior or whoever she was. Someone who wasn't like anyone else in her time and place—it seems like you might be the best person to figure her out."

And then they are through onto the dark road, with just one car parked on it, in which a man sits smoking a cigarette.

"Where's your car?" Nicholas asks.

"Oh, I left it up by the stables," she says, and takes off walking very quickly, almost running, turning back only to wave and shout goodbye.

Waxing Crescent, Third Cycle   ☽

That night I sat by the king's side as the festivities began. All day I had been turning the king's words over in my mind. I thought of Sego's absence on the road the day we left for the city. How long had it been since he had visited me in my mother's house, or brought any offerings for festival days? And yet here I sat now in the house of a great ruler, with priestly robes on my back, and the promise of the world before me. I wanted Aesu's counsel, but I could no longer find his face amid the fine, strange people in the room. I thought he must have gone off somewhere with the woman he had met the first night, and I was glad. Perhaps she would help moderate his mistrust of this place so he could advise me more dispassionately.

Just as I had given up looking for him I heard a great commotion at the door to the house, and two men entered bearing a whole goat carcass on a spit between them. A hush fell over the room then, and I saw that the eyes of the crowd were not on the glistening goat meat, but on a third man, small and bald-headed, who bore a silver platter, covered with something dark and soft-looking.

The king leaned toward me, excitement in his face.

"I want you to see this," he said. "This is Comitinus, our haruspex."

Before I could ask what the word meant, the small man approached the throne and laid the platter at the king's feet. It was strewn, I saw now, with the raw entrails of the goat: the black kidneys with their yellow crowns; the spongy mass of the brain; the heart, slick and small, leaking its last blood onto the metal.

The small man bowed quickly before the king, and spoke in a matter-of-fact tone that made me think he must enjoy high status in the court.

"Today, at your request," he said, "I'll be dedicating my energies to Mars. We've been making offerings to him daily, so hopefully he is well-disposed to us."

The haruspex drew out the lungs from the pile of organs and laid them side by side on the platter.

"The left lung is larger than the right," he began, "which is always a difficult sign with Mars. It can mean his energies are out of balance, that he's angry and needs to be placated. Or it can simply mean he favors one side over the other in a conflict. As we move on, hopefully we'll see which it is."

My mother had taught me many types of divination, and I could read not only birds but also the movement of clouds and even the pattern of milk or grain spilled on a floor. But this I had never seen: the extraction of knowledge from the basest parts of the animal, those that, except for the kidneys, we would feed to dogs or bury for the crops. I wanted to sit beside the haruspex and learn his method, but I sensed that his divination was not to be interrupted.

"The heart is slightly enlarged for this size of animal, which is a sign of intensity, either of favor or disfavor. Here we see the main heartstring is exceptionally large and well-formed, which indicates that Mars favors a direct approach in battle, rather than any sort of ambush or approach from a flank."

"Is 'Mars' one of your local gods here?" I whispered to the king.

He smiled. "He is a god of the entire Roman Empire, from Byzantium all the way to Camulodunon, and beyond."

I did not know where Byzantium was, but I could tell it must be far away, and I did not understand how one god could inhabit so many places at once.

"But where does he live?" I asked. I thought of the map the king had shown me. "Does he live in the water?"

Before he could answer, the haruspex began speaking again. "Now," he said, "most importantly, the liver."

He held up a purple mass, evil-looking, dripping something that was not blood.

"As you can see, the head of the liver is intact and pronounced," he said, pointing to a kind of fleshy knob at the top of the organ.

"The visceral side, facing inward toward the body, is smooth and unblemished. And the organ as a whole is well-proportioned, firm, and free from fat or gristle. From this, coupled with the enlarged heart, I think we can say with confidence that Mars looks upon your campaign in the southwest with intense favor. We should, of course, continue the offerings . . ."

The king held up a hand.

"Can you tell me a little about the north?" he asked. "If I needed to establish a presence near, say, Bereda, what location would Mars favor?"

I stiffened at the question, not least because I knew what location I would favor: the rise above the moss, where a sentry could see men coming either by water from the south or by land from the north, and a large force could shelter easily in the trees behind. It was a strategic vulnerability about which Aesu had warned Sego in the past, but Sego said the gods themselves could protect the moss and there was no need for men to guard it. In truth I believed he was afraid of the moss, of the strength of the gods' power coming through that place, because he frequently found excuses to avoid festivals and other events that took place near it.

The haruspex paused. I thought perhaps he would refuse to answer, or offer some platitude. It was a difficult question, specific, of a kind that diviners would often refuse to answer for fear of being wrong. But the haruspex drew a small knife from his belt, sliced into the liver, and spread it open like a pair of butterfly wings.

To my eye the inside of the liver was smooth and shiny, but the haruspex traced a line down the left wing with his fingertip.

"These striations would suggest to me that Mars supports a riverine location, in keeping with your strongholds in the south," he said.

Then he flipped the organ over. "And the fact that we don't see them here, on the outside, suggests a preference for isolation, high ground."

He took up the knife again and separated the two halves, then squeezed one over the platter. A small amount of black liquid came trickling out.

"The liver is also relatively dry," he concluded, "which suggests to me that while Mars favors proximity to water, the element of earth is desirable as well. Perhaps not a river, after all, but a pond or marsh? But of course these are decisions for the king."

I stared at the haruspex. His skin was sallow and wrinkled; his eyes were small and drab. He bore no outward indication of his own power or that of his god. And yet it certainly seemed that this Mars knew the strong and weak points of our land, as well as I did myself.

I looked at Crab. He met my gaze with wide eyes, and I could tell that he too understood the import of the haruspex's words.

The king, of course, could not see what we saw. He merely thanked the haruspex, promising additional offerings to Mars as well as rewards of gold and silver to the man himself should the campaigns turn out well.

"Just one more question," he added. "We are hoping to form an alliance here today between the crown at Camulodunon and the druidic seat at Bereda. Can you tell me how Mars would look upon such a friendship?"

The haruspex nodded. He rotated the remainder of the liver several times on the platter, then cut away three pieces, each the size of a thumb.

"If I may," he said, approaching the throne. He placed one of the pieces in the king's open hand and offered another to me.

"If the liver is sweet in each of our mouths," he said, "then we can assume Mars welcomes the alliance. If anyone tastes bitterness, however, it is a sign of his displeasure, and we will need to perform more tests to determine the reason."

I looked at the purple lump oozing in my palm. When I lifted my eyes, Crab was shaking his head vehemently at me. None of us would ever eat raw goat meat, least of all the liver, which we knew to be the source of many fevers and distempers. The king, however, did not hesitate, but popped the piece of flesh in his mouth. The haruspex did the same with the third portion.

"Sweet as honey," the king said, swallowing.

The haruspex smiled wanly. "I wouldn't quite say that. But yes, a pleasant taste. No bitterness at all."

Now all the lords and ladies of the court, the queen with her calm arching brows, the doctor turning a piece of fruit nervously over in his hands—all their eyes were on me. But it was not only their influence that made me bring the slick jiggling morsel to my mouth. I, too, wanted to know what the king's god would say of our alliance, if I would have his strength at my back if I accepted it.

I took a breath. I placed the liver in my mouth.

Once when we were very young, Aesu and I got into a fight. I started it—I was angry for some reason or no reason, and I took his favorite toy, a stick carved into the shape of a horse, and threw it in the river. When I laughed to see it float away on the current, he hit me with a closed fist, the first and only time, a glancing blow to my left cheek, and I tasted blood in my mouth. I remember it was salty, bright, it frightened me, I began to cry and Aesu began to cry too, we held each other there by the river sobbing until it began to rain. That was the taste I thought of as I swallowed raw flesh in the house of the young king at Camulodunon. I turned to the haruspex, then to the king himself.

"Sweet," I told the assembled company. "It's sweet."

April 2018

"Are you okay?" Agnes's father asks.
"What?"
Agnes is trying to repair a broken coffee table she found on the street in front of her building. It is perfectly good except that one of its legs is snapped nearly in half. Agnes is very proud of herself; she has ordered wood glue and a clamp and she has followed the instructions she looked up on YouTube. She has left the glue to dry overnight and it is time to remove the clamp.

"Your case," he says. "I read about it on BBC.com."

Over the last week, the crowd on the moss has multiplied. New protesters come every day with signs and sleeping bags; some set up a drum circle; some smoke strong, sweaty weed; one is dressed as the Grim Reaper, one all in green with leaves and flowers woven through his beard. In addition to environmentalists, a dozen neo-pagans have arrived to pay tribute, it seems, to the body. In the early mornings they often join hands in a circle around the dig site. Agnes has heard American accents and Australian, and a language she thinks is French. In addition to Grace's, she has seen at least two other camera crews, and once a reporter came grinning at her with a microphone, but she turned and walked swiftly the other way.

News coverage makes Agnes anxious—the more people find out about the body, the more likely it is that someone far more senior will show up and try to publish before she can. Agnes does not want to be scooped, but more than that, she does not want someone else to understand the body's death before she's had the chance to do so.

"What did it say?" she asks.

"That there's 'a battle raging between scientists, environmentalists, and corporate interests over a thousand-year-old body,'" he reads.

"She's two thousand years old," Agnes says. Strange to hear her life described like this, as from afar, when daily it is dirt, bone, flesh, and waiting.

"It says the environmentalists are suing," her father says. "'On a recent afternoon, some two hundred protesters were gathered at the dig site.' It sounds like a nightmare."

"It's fine," Agnes says. "I don't think there are really two hundred."

Agnes unscrews the clamp from the table leg. The joint looks a little crooked, she can see where the straw-colored glue has dripped out and dried along the side. But the leg holds up, she pushes the coffee table into the middle of the room and it stands nearly plumb on her bare floor.

"Sweetie, I'm proud of you for sticking this out as long as you have. But I know you don't like attention. You should think about coming home early."

"I can't just leave, Dad. I'm working. We're supposed to meet with the pathologist tomorrow."

She places her students' anatomy textbook on the coffee table. It holds.

Her father goes on, as though she has not spoken. "These protests, and whatever's going on with this peat company. Being in the middle of all this, it would tax anybody to the limit. And especially for you—"

Agnes stacks her forensics book on top of the anatomy book. "What do you mean, 'especially for me'?"

"I read something recently, about sunflower children and orchid children," her father says. "Sunflower kids, they flourish no matter what happens to them. Just like a sunflower growing in poor soil. But orchid children, they need a lot of special care and attention. If they don't get it, they wilt. But if they do, then they'll be more beautiful than any sunflower."

Agnes puts a pile of her students' exams on top of the forensics book, and a can of beans on top of the exams. The table leg creaks, then splits along the joint, sending the bean can rolling across the uneven floor.

"There are no orchids or sunflowers here," she tells her father. "Just moss."

○

The pathologist, Danielle Muller, enters the exam room with the stiff and shuffling gait of someone badly injured. Sunita asks permission before hugging her.

"Of course," Danielle says, "I'm fine. I'm doing so much better."

"I wish I could meet your OB so I could strangle him," Sunita says.

"It's hardly his fault I had placenta previa." Danielle sinks into the hug, her shoulders loosening.

"No, but the infection."

"That wasn't his fault either. Anyway, I'm okay, Sabine's okay. We're all okay. Let's take a look at this, shall we?"

Agnes opens the cold case. Danielle bends; her fine tall wounded body greets the body curled in the dry ice. Something passes between them that Agnes is not party to, Danielle bows her head, she is whispering. When she looks up again her eyes are far away.

"She is a wonder," Danielle says quietly. Then she goes to work.

For a few minutes they are all three silent as Danielle circles the body, going back and forth between it and the CT images on her laptop screen. Finally she zeroes in on the wound. Its edges are shiny and tight with healing, but its center is pitted, soft-looking, as though still wet and open when the body died.

"Ouch," Danielle says. "Okay, I need to take some samples."

She pierces the wound with a biopsy needle, once at the margin and once right in the raw center. Agnes imagines what might have wrought this harm on living flesh, a knife or sword, a wooden stake. Did the woman lie in pain a long time, bleeding on the wet ground, or was she carried to a house and bound with clean bandages, supported on pillows? Did her wound puff and curl with gangrene, did she die sweating and raving with fever? Did someone tend to her, changing her dressings, wiping her brow, or was she alone?

"Now I will take from the lung," Danielle announces.

"The heart looks especially odd to me—" Agnes begins, anxious about contradicting, anxious about not doing so. She is good with soft tissue; the pathologist in Las Minas, a brusque and overworked woman, developed a grudging respect for her. And yet Agnes is conscious that the vulnerable heart, the delicate branching pathways of the lungs, are not her specialty.

"The lung tissue will tell us more, I think, if we are looking for systemic infection," Danielle says. "The left is exceptionally well-preserved. It is amazing, really. It is a once-in-a-lifetime discovery."

Agnes wants to ask her what she means by that, "once-in-a-lifetime." Agnes thinks about what Sunita said, that the people who buried the body might have wanted her to be found. If the body is a message, sent to her across the centuries—how great, how weighty is her responsibility then?

Danielle pulls up an image on her laptop, then measures along the body's back until she comes to a spot several inches below the bottom rib. The needle is inside the body a long time. She removes it carefully, in a way Agnes appreciates, doing no more damage than is absolutely necessary.

"How long do you think, for the analysis?" Agnes asks.

Danielle stands back to see the body whole.

"I should have a report for you in three to four weeks."

Four weeks will be mid-May, and Agnes's lease is up in June; this is also when the university will stop paying her. She has not truly faced the reality that she might have to leave this place without an answer. Agnes knows that for many bog bodies, the cause of death is still unknown. And yet *she* has not worked on those bodies; *she* has not failed to identify how they died. She has not slunk home defeated, forced to admit that when she ventured out into the world without care and coddling, she could not succeed.

"I hate to ask this," she says, "but is there any way to expedite that? It's just, we're working on a tight timeframe—"

Danielle turns to Agnes with a cold, bright anger.

"I also have a timeframe," she says. "My daughter is still at home with me. She does not take a bottle. I am nursing her approximately six to eight hours per day. The rest of the time I am playing with her, I am bathing her, I am doing other things to care for her, and also I am going to my doctors' appointments and doing physical and psychotherapy because I had a traumatic birth and nearly died. For three hours per day, my daughter naps. This is the time when I will work on your analysis. I think this is very quick, given the circumstances."

Agnes is cowed. She bends her head to make herself small before this woman, whose suffering she does not understand.

"I'm so sorry," she says. "Whenever you can do it is great. Thank you for doing this for us."

"I am not doing this for you," Danielle says. "If it was for you or anyone else, I would have said no. I am doing it because I want to do it, and so you can be assured I will finish exactly as quickly as I can."

On the bus home that day Agnes cannot stop thinking about her own self-centeredness—of course by "once-in-a-lifetime," Danielle meant her own life, not Agnes's.

○

"Why did you run off the other day?" Nicholas asks.

He catches up to her in the shallow woods to the west of the moss in the late afternoon of the twelfth day of the dig. She has been avoiding him; the reason for her flight is so stupid she cannot begin to explain it. And yet also, she has been consistently aware of him, where he is on the moss, what he is doing, speaking to a journalist, setting up a tent, when he enters her peripheral vision her attention is divided until he leaves again, and even then sometimes she follows him with her eyes.

"I just, ah, I had to get back," she says. "Grading."

In fact she is weeks behind on her grading, her students are starting to send her emails.

"I thought you might be trying to get rid of me," he says.

How he looks up at her, hanging on her answer. At the collar of his sweatshirt she can see his throat.

"No," she says. "How did it go in court?"

"It went okay," he says. "Or, I think it went okay. The peat company has their experts testifying next, so we'll see how that goes. But I tried to take your advice."

"Did it help?" Agnes asks.

"The thing is, my job is persuading people. So I can't just forget about the outcome entirely."

"That makes sense," says Agnes, disappointed even though she did not think much of her advice to begin with.

"So instead, I pretended I was talking to you."

He looks away when he says it, across the woods where the oak shadows lie long and stark in the orange light. Not a joke, Agnes thinks.

"Did that work?"

"Not at all," he says. "You're much more terrifying than the judge. I think I muddled through all right in the end, but if we lose it'll be on your head."

He is smiling now. A breeze in the trees; a far-off argument of thrushes. She never would have guessed, before she left her home, how strange and huge the world is, what surprises it contains.

"I accept responsibility," she says.

"Good. You want to see something?"

He leads her to a spot behind a tall oak where last fall's leaves lie dark and papery, shriven by frost and thaw. Gently he brushes them aside to reveal a tiny, speckled pod. At first she takes it for some seed casing, but then she sees along its length unusual, delicate groove marks, and all over a protective covering of spines.

"What is it?" she asks.

"It's a green hairstreak chrysalis," he says. "It should hatch any day."

"Those little butterflies?" Agnes asks. She's noticed them in the grasses at the edges of the moss, their brightly snapping iridescent wings.

"When I was a kid they were all over," he says. "Now there's fewer and fewer every year. I try to look for the pupae, to keep a count. This year I'm at four."

She can feel the sorrow of it, that dwindling. For one individual to die is no tragedy, only a cycling out of one kind of existence. But for an entire species to disappear, she thinks this is a true loss for the world, an impoverishment of the whole. She envies him a little, being able to see this at a young age.

"How many were there when you were a kid?" she asks.

He smiles, she thinks she reads embarrassment on him.

"I wasn't into that then," he says. "I liked cars and football. Whatever my mum wasn't into."

"What changed?"

"My second year at university I did a study abroad in Brazil," he says. "There was a man there who studied trees. He and his team would wrap a tape measure around a tree trunk, basically, and measure how much bigger it got on any given day. And what they found was, as the days got hotter in the rainforest, the trees grew less. Until at a certain point they weren't growing at all. And of course when the trees stop growing, they don't absorb as much carbon dioxide, so more of it stays in the atmosphere and the rainforest gets even hotter."

"A feedback loop," Agnes says. She's familiar with the research.

"Exactly," Nicholas says, "Anyway, I raised my hand and I said something, like, 'This sounds very bad, how do we convince people back home to do something?' And he just sort of looked at me blankly and said, 'My job is to present the science.' And I thought, 'Huh, this is something I can do.'"

His voice has that quality of youth she heard over the phone, he speaks quickly, she can hear his breath.

"I always had this ability—I don't want to call it a talent, it's not like it comes naturally, I kind of have to turn it on—but anyway I'm a good talker, or I can be. It's like, when I was growing up, I wasn't the smartest, I wasn't the fastest, I was a Black kid with a weird hippie white mum, it wasn't automatically easy for me to fit in. I needed, like, a hook, and I learned I can tell stories, tell jokes, I can make people pay attention. For a long time I didn't know what to do with that. I didn't want to run for office, I always hated everybody in student government. I didn't want to sell cars, or houses. And then when I heard that guy talk it was, like, 'Right, this is my niche.'"

He is smiling but also she sees anxiety in his face. More terrifying than the judge, she thinks.

"It doesn't make me look very good, does it?" he asks. "That it was all about me, in the beginning. I'm not like you."

"What do you mean, you're not like me?"

"The way you talk about your work. I don't have this higher calling. Or I didn't, at first. I kind of backed into it. It's different now."

Agnes is only half listening. She is thinking about herself, and about what pulls or pushes her through her life, guiding her feet on the earth and her hands around the trowel.

"I'm not sure it's higher," she says.

"What?"

"The calling. Or whatever. I'm not sure it's higher. I used to think everything I did was about serving, like, caring for people after they die. Now I'm not sure."

"Look," Nicholas says.

At first Agnes sees only still earth where he's pointing, but then, so subtle as to be almost imperceptible, the chrysalis moves. She never would have noticed if not for him: a wobble so tiny that her eye, untrained on living things, would have seen right past it. They bend close to get a better look, she smells forest in the dirt, she thinks she sees, within the delicate pod, the strainings of a creature trying to get out.

First very gently and then with more force, the chrysalis splits along its seams. Agnes sees a translucent membrane, and then a clutch of struggling limbs, tensile and alien, the metallic parts of the most intricate and finely made machine. The legs push out, she sees the creature's knees flex and its filamentous thighs push outward, here is its tiny ciliated head, its compound eye, the curl of its tongue, and then the wings, folded like sails in calm weather, dun-colored, then emerging curved from their curved home, wet with a bloodlike liquid, rising arthritically at first—is something wrong?—and then, snap! The green shining in the slanting sun, bright as gemstone.

The creature clings to its empty pod, its slick wings drying, its sharp efficient mind adjusting to the shock, the light, the need still to constitute this new body, chemical signals on the wind, this light, light, light, light, light.

And Agnes and Nicholas are laughing, laughing, as though all this was for their benefit alone.

○

Sunita has her laptop open, and Agnes peers at the image on the screen. The scrap is lighter with the outer layer of peat removed, a tannic orange-brown. Across its surface is a kind of design or pattern in greenish-black—a square, or off-square, with a curved line at the top and a straighter one at the bottom, and clusters of spots or smudges bounding either side. Filling the center of the square are whorls and swirls, trailing up the left side and snaking across the top before coiling in the lower right-hand corner around a large mark that looks pointed at its base, a rough triangle.

The image jogs a feeling in Agnes like the opposite of memory, like something she is going to see in the future but has not seen yet.

"What is it?" she asks.

"Parchment," Sunita says. "Maybe calfskin, but probably sheep."

Agnes buzzes with a fragile happiness this morning, she let Nicholas walk her back up to the main road after the butterfly hatched—"I took the bus today," she said, no need to explain more than that. When they reached the road she said, "See you tomorrow," and he held her eyes with his eyes and said, "Good."

Sunita, though—her voice is clipped and weary. She hunches over the laptop, heart sunk between her shoulders, brows brought down low over her eyes.

"I mean the pattern," Agnes says. "What do you think it's supposed to be?"

"Well obviously that's the big question, isn't it?" Sunita says, her tone is mean and hard, Agnes steps back from the table into the mildness of the day.

"Sorry," Sunita says immediately. "I didn't mean to snap at you. I'm just having a hard morning."

"It's frustrating," Agnes says. "I do think it has to be sepsis, though. Once we have the pathology report—"

Sunita waves her hand. "I don't mean the case," she says. "It's this thing with Ruby. She keeps refusing to go to school. She says her mind races when she's there; I told her I *wish* my mind would race. That probably wasn't helpful."

She gives a rueful laugh.

"My wife is staying home with her today, but we can't keep doing this. We're trying to get her into therapy, but of course there's a huge waiting list."

She digs in her backpack, finds a tissue, and blows her nose. "I'm sorry," she says. "I'm going on and on."

"No," Agnes says. "I'm sorry about Ruby. School was hard for me too."

"Yeah?" Sunita says. Her eyebrows lift, her face softens.

"I didn't like it," Agnes says. "I didn't fit in."

Sunita is looking at her intently. "What did you do?" she asks.

"My dad put me in classes at the community college," Agnes says. "Science and math. So I only had to go to school in the mornings, and then I did college classes in the afternoon."

"And that helped?"

"I mean, no," Agnes says. "I still don't fit in. But it helped with the school part, because I wasn't in school."

Sunita smiles.

"I can picture it," she says. "This little girl with a huge graphing calculator."

"I was five eleven already," Agnes says. "But yeah, I did have a graphing calculator. I still have it somewhere. I loved that thing."

The way her father presented it to her, as though it was an object of awesome power, a young knight's first sword.

Sunita looks away, her face folds into worry again.

"The thing is, I don't think school is what Ruby's afraid of. She has friends, her teachers like her. What she's scared of—sometimes I think it's her own body."

"That's what it sounds like," Agnes says.

Sunita's gaze snaps back to Agnes's face.

"She talked to you about it?"

"A little."

"I wish I could understand it better," Sunita says. She shakes her head. "I just don't think about my body very much. I never did. It's just, like, a structure to support my mind."

Does Agnes *think* about her body, she wonders. Unlike other bodies it is a blank to her, she has never seen it clearly. She remembers the ever-deepening mystery of her adolescence—into what was she transforming, into whom? The one photograph she had of her mother—those long hands, that mantid beauty—how she used to hold it up to the bathroom mirror at night, unable to see if she was a match or not. Death, however—she knows death, what it is to watch it crouching in the shadows, and then, to hold out a hand and invite it into the light.

"I think I understand," Agnes says. "People get sick all the time, they die. It's scary when you don't know how it all works."

Sunita shakes her head. "I think she does know how it all works. Sometimes I think that's the problem."

Waxing Crescent, Third Cycle ☾

In the morning the king and his court saw us off with gifts and well wishes. The sun was bright and high in the sky already; the solstice was coming.

The king gave to Aesu a special drinking goblet, heavily inlaid with gold and gemstones. To Crab he gave an arm-ring, intricately worked and glinting in the sunlight.

"For when we meet again," the king said. "I look forward to more of your wise counsel."

To me he gave two rolls of lambs' hide. The first was the map he had shown me the night before. The second was blank, and rolled inside it was a woven bag containing a stylus and three small bottles.

"Ink," the king said, "so you can make your own."

I thanked him, and he embraced me, speaking into my ear.

"You won't regret this," he said. "Your descendants will speak of your travels for generations to come. You will be the druid who opened the north to the world."

The doctor came forward next, and his gift disappointed me: I had hoped for some of the mysterious herb that had healed my aching head, or perhaps another of his potions and tinctures, but instead he handed me a small vessel like the one I had seen lighting his house.

"A lamp," he said, handing over now three jars of a thick orange liquid. "Fill it with oil and light it, and you can work at your maps or tinctures long into the night with no need to build a fire."

I tried to thank him earnestly, and indeed I was grateful, if not for this strange gift than for a glimpse into the medicines of other lands, about which I hoped I would soon enough learn more.

The queen spoke last, taking me by the arm and leading me from the group to a spot in the garden where the light came slanting through the leaves.

"I hope you've enjoyed your visit," she said, and I dropped my eyes from her long elegant face, embarrassed.

"I have, thank you."

"I'm sorry I don't have a gift for you," she said. "All I have is a word of warning: Your alliance will make you enemies at home, and for all his promises, the king cannot always protect you."

I was a little affronted that she thought I would need this counsel, that she knew the politics of my home better than I did.

"I will protect myself."

She smiled, I could not tell if kindly or unkindly, and began to lead me back to where the horses stood ready.

"Of course you will," she said.

I had risen uneasily that morning, my mind turning over and over with thoughts of Sego and my friends and neighbors in their small houses by the river. The queen's words, though unnecessary, only added to my anxiety. But as we set out on the road for home I felt strong again, and clearer in my heart: My mother, I knew, had not named me the druid so that I would cling to the old ways. She trusted me to act with boldness and courage, and I would do so, even if it meant breaking some old bonds. What was more, I thought perhaps Sego could be won over to the king's side. After all, he had never been to Camulodunon. To my knowledge he had never traveled more than a day's ride south of Bereda. Once I explained to him what the king and his friends in Rome could offer, I thought, he might agree to lay down arms and join the alliance.

Crab seemed to share my enthusiasm—he kept turning the ring around and around on his arm to admire the beautiful pattern. Even Aesu was in better spirits; he was quiet but seemed at peace as we rode through the forest, which had seemed so uncanny just a day before, but now felt familiar to me. I imagined it laid out on a map, with the great city nestled within it and the farmlands above, and then, far up near the top of the lamb's hide, our river and our homes, our lives. I could see it as clearly as if I had already set it down; I felt a kind of ecstasy; I imagined it was what the mystics felt when they took mugwort and communed directly with the gods.

We camped for the night in a small thicket of beech trees overlooking a meadow. The air was warm; we built only a small fire. We made a meal of fruit the queen's serving women had given us, and a delicious type of cold salt meat, like goose but leaner and sweeter, the taste of corn and summertime laid down in its flesh. When we were finished Aesu volunteered to take the first watch, and I slept and dreamed of great birds with long tails flying over the sea.

I woke in the deep night to Crab shaking me by the shoulders.

"Get up!" he was shouting. "There's so many of them!"

I rubbed my eyes. In the moonlight I saw Aesu with his sword drawn, and in the next moment, a man with a club swinging at his head. Three more men were running up at me across the meadow, and another two came from within the thicket; we were surrounded.

I wore a knife on my belt as a basic precaution, the way any traveler would, but as a druid I was not trained in combat. Crab and Aesu were more than enough protection from an ordinary thief or wild animal; I had never dreamed of a force that would overwhelm all three of us together. I drew my knife and assumed what I thought was a fighting stance, but my fingers shook on the handle. I was terrified.

In an instant the battle was all around us. The men sounded war cries like wolves on the hunt. I heard iron on iron, and my brother bellowing in pain, a terrible sound. I cut at the air around me with my knife; I tried to remember what I had learned playing war with my brothers when we were very small, and death meant lying on the soft earth with our eyes closed, waiting for a count of ten.

I felt a weakness, suddenly, in my right side; I lost my balance and fell to my knees. Then came the pain, a cold shock like walking barefoot into snow, all up and down my body. A man above me slung his sword, but I crumpled myself small and rolled like a hedgehog away from his blow.

Crab came raging forward at the man, and cleaved his skull with an axe, but two more men rushed in where he had stood, and I knew we were finished, we would die unless someone came to help us. Lying in the grass, I called on the gods one by one— the gods in the moss, the pine and meadow gods, my mother's austere gods from across the water with their strange tastes and beautiful names. It was only when I got to Mars, the Roman god, that I thought of the jars of oil in our saddlebags.

I forced myself to get up and run, or hobble, my right side numb from rib to foot. Crab and Aesu kept the men at bay long enough for me to reach the horses and gather the three jars into my arms. From there I limped to the embers of our fire, took a breath, and cast the first jar in.

It was better than I had hoped. The flames leapt as high as my waist with a roaring sound and an acrid stink.

"You have provoked the anger of Mars, the greatest of the Roman gods," I shouted.

The clash of iron and wood went silent. I saw one man's face in the orange firelight; he looked like a lost child. I threw the second jar into the fire.

"Mars is everywhere and nowhere; he rules this land and all others with lightning and flame," I shouted. "He will burn you to your bones."

The fire leapt again. Crab swung his axe; the man's head fell away. I found a thin log, dipped the end in the third jar, and lit it aflame. I thought of the warriors of the old days, when gods fought alongside men, as I rushed forward with the flashing brand in my fist and the fire at my back, devouring.

In what happened next I cannot separate moment from moment; I remember only the war cries and the swords whistling, the crunch of bone and smell of burning flesh. When it was over we three stood alive, and the men who had attacked us lay dead, except for one who went fleeing in the dark, bearing the bad news back to his kinsmen.

April 2018

On the fourteenth day, Ruby is already at the dig when Agnes arrives. She sits under the tent, her body curled around a book, while her mother and the postgrad students work nearby in their white jumpsuits, silently picking and brushing. Away across the moss Kieran's team too is digging; they are listening to something, maybe a soccer game, on the radio. Over the mud comes the sound of cheering as Agnes reaches Ruby.

"What are you reading?" Agnes asks.

Ruby shows Agnes the cover—some Latin words Agnes doesn't understand. Agnes shakes her head and holds up her hands in a shrug.

"Oh, sorry," Ruby says. "*Ab Urbe Condita*. I finished the textbook so my teacher's having me translate from the original."

"How is it?"

"Good," Ruby says. "Fun. More fun than school, anyway."

Agnes looks at the book, blocks of text in small dark print, incomprehensible.

"This is fun to you?" she asks.

Ruby shrugs. "Yeah, it's like a puzzle. It's not like English, the words can kind of be in any order. So you have to use the case and put it all together to figure out what it says."

"That sounds hard," Agnes says.

"It can be. I like it. It's like it uses my whole brain, and I can't think about anything else."

Agnes thinks of the hardest class she ever took, discrete math, remembers being asked to tile an infinite plane. Mostly she found it frustrating; it cemented her decision not to become a mathematician. But there were moments, too, deep in a problem that was just barely within her power to solve, when she would seem to leave behind her self entirely, and on finishing (or getting stuck) she would be almost surprised to find her body in the chair where she had left it. It was not the same as what Ruby is describing, but it was not so different either.

"I think I get it," she says.

"I asked my teacher about Romulus and Remus," Ruby says as Agnes turns to leave.

Agnes smiles. She knows the story now; she will never forget it.

"And?"

"He showed me a third version, by Ennius, who lived, like, two hundred years before Livy."

"What does Ennius think? Birds or walls?"

"Birds," Ruby says. "But his is different. Livy just says Remus sees six and Romulus sees twelve and then they fight. But Ennius says Romulus sees twelve, and that makes him the rightful king."

"And then what, Remus just surrenders?"

"Oh no, they still fight," Ruby says. "Romulus wins, Remus dies."

"I don't get it," Agnes says.

"The difference is, in Livy's version, the birds are just birds. Remus sees one thing, Romulus sees another, you don't know who's right. But in Ennius, Romulus is right. The gods made him king, and the birds prove it. Everything that happens after that is just part of their plan."

◯

In the cold the mud is hard to dig, the strands of peat stiffen and resist the trowel. But the chill seems to change the structure of the peat as well, or make it more distinct, so that Agnes can see more clearly the layers within layers, and variations of color and texture—here a tight pack, there a more open matrix, like bands of tissue within a sample of bone.

Some of Agnes's grad school classmates described excavation as meditative, even calming, the rhythmic brushing and digging, the feeling that methodical work will eventually be rewarded. Agnes has always found digs confusing, she has no instinct for the inert soil, her mind loses its way without the focal point of a body.

The moss, however, has a logic she is beginning to understand. Each tight layer sandwiching a loose layer, each loose layer capturing and holding the small objects that naturally accrue to any open place: sticks and branches, stones, once, beautifully, the partially skeletonized wing of a bird. When she understands this, she learns to focus both her digging and her gaze, and to feel a kind of purpose in her work, and she is not entirely surprised when, just as the cold of the afternoon begins to soften into rain, her brush uncovers something in the mud that is not mud.

The object is long and thin, about the size and shape of Agnes's index finger, and covered in a thick, red-brown crust that makes Agnes think of shipwrecks, the way masts and rigging become a substrate for tiny living things to build their cities of crystal and bone. In her gloved hand it is heavy and substantial; she handles it carefully but it feels unfragile, like it will endure.

"What is it?" Ruby asks when Agnes carries it back to the tent.

Something is happening across the moss, at the other dig—a gathering of voices, men shouting to each other across the furrows. A small portion of Agnes's attention snags there, watching.

"Too soon to tell," Sunita says. "We've seen medical instruments from the period that look like this. In Scotland they've found long, thin tools that might have been used in divination. But we haven't dated it yet—we don't know if it was hers."

Agnes gazes at the object, lying now in a plastic tub. It could be a car part, she thinks, a shard of peat-cutting equipment, a piece of rebar from a decades-old construction site. But she thinks, too, of the wound in the body's side, the shining fresh hurt tissue barely closed over the vulnerable guts. A medical instrument, a relic of an ancient surgery gone wrong. A divining rod left over from a failed prayer.

Sunita is still speaking, but Agnes holds up a hand—*wait*—because the men of the other dig have all converged now on a single point, Agnes cannot see their faces, she cannot see what they see as they squat down into the dugout earth, but she knows, of course she knows, what they have found.

Time of release

A colony of moss has no concept of the sacred or profane, good, evil, accident, or crime. But if such a colony could speak about what it had witnessed, it might say this: Across time, many human bodies have been given into our care. Some were lowered into our embrace with great ceremony; others tumbled into us in a storm; still others were violently thrown. We receive all of them, however, as fellow organisms that join and, for a time, become part of our home. Some we preserve, some we transform. Some are acted upon by forces outside our or their control.

We do not know what the humans expect, when they entrust a body to us, nor do we care. We give each one our kinship, our sanctuary, and when the time comes, we let it go.

May 2018

"I'm sorry," Nicholas says. "I really am. I know how important this is to you."

"It's not important *to me*," Agnes says. "It's just important."

They stand at the edge between the forest and the mud, a bright morning. At Agnes's feet is a pocket of living moss, incandescent green.

"I know," he says. "I know it is. But this was always the plan, this is what we talked about. And you already have a lot to work with, right?"

Across the moss Agnes can see the dig site, a two-foot-deep trench in the tilled mud. It is lighter in color than its surroundings, the bronzy peat threads exposed under the top layer of black muck. A scar within a scar.

"We're not even close to finished," Agnes says. "We have no idea how she died."

Ordinarily Agnes would be inside the trench already, digging. Instead a dozen protesters encircle the dig site, dressed in white, the bottoms of their pantlegs darkening with mud. They seem to laugh and talk with one another now, but when Agnes approached they joined hands and stood silent with their chins thrust forward, as though they were blessed with holy purpose.

"You have the body still, don't you? Aren't you studying her?"

"Of course," Agnes says, "but we need the grave site too. Just yesterday we found something—we haven't even been able to identify it yet, but it could help us. We can't stop now."

Washed of its outer layer of mud, the object Agnes found looks smaller and more delicate. Its color beneath the peat is a dark brownish-red. Most interestingly, it is hollow; when Agnes holds it up with a gloved hand, she can see a pinprick of light on the other side.

"Neither can we," Nicholas says. "The suit—our lawyer isn't feeling very optimistic, honestly. But public opinion is with us right now. The more we can present the moss as a wild place, a place where things are growing, the more we put pressure on the court to rule in our favor."

At the northern boundary of the moss, closest to the rise, Agnes can see protesters with plastic buckets. She knows they are full of rocks. The blond dog darts among them, its body joyful and intent, as though it is chasing something.

"Can't you just leave a space for the dig site?" Agnes asks. "Flood the parts around it, or whatever?"

"That's not really how the drainage system works," Nicholas says. "And even if it was—Agnes, a lot of people here have issues with your project. It's not just about rewilding the moss. They want you to stop digging."

Agnes has a frightened realization. All this time on the dig she was being watched, people were forming opinions about her and her work. She should have known—her father, in fact, had tried to warn her about it—but she had forgotten to pay attention, she thought she could work and think and get to know people, and open herself to the world without penalty.

"What issues?" Agnes asks.

"The body, for starters," he says. "Some of our new arrivals feel we should be more respectful of the customs of her people. The phrase 'digging around in her grave' has been used."

"We don't know what the customs of her people were," Agnes says. "What if they would have wanted us to dig?"

"I've raised that," he says. "But it's not just about her. You have to admit, Agnes, your excavation is damaging an already damaged ecosystem. You've dug this big hole, you've extracted who knows how many pounds of remaining peat. I've been explaining that we made an agreement, but there's no way I can keep selling it. People are asking me who exactly benefits from your dig, and I don't have a good answer."

"The body benefits if we find out how she died."

"Does she? Agnes, she's dead! She doesn't care how she died anymore. You're the one who cares."

Occasionally when Agnes was a child she would feel within her a bright rage, nameless, and she would lash out at her father, screaming at him and once, pummeling him with her fists. He only held her tightly and whispered to her until she calmed, and her anger went out like a match in a bucket. With Colin, in the early days, there was something: a challenging, a sharpness, boxers dancing around each other in the ring. Once theatrically she whipped her T-shirt off and threw it in the trash can because he said it was too big for her. But by the time he moved in they had all three settled into a static triangle of protection: No one was to do anything to upset her, and also she was not to be upset.

And so it has been years since she last felt this way: the sick excitement of it, how her body primes for fighting, how her mind goes black. She is angry at Nicholas—that he is wrong, that he is right. She is angry too at the recalcitrant earth that competes with her, that holds her rightful knowledge fast within itself and will not give it up.

These thoughts are available to her, but only as inarticulate impressions, they do not coalesce into language that she can share with another person, whatever expressive power she has rests now in her body, and so she reaches down, she digs her fingernails deep into the green, as she pulls the moss holds together, those soft stars locked together in a doomed embrace, so that the entire bright carpet of it comes away, a flag dripping dirt and water, a month's careful husbandry, a single quivering kill, which she holds in the dry air for a moment before flinging at his feet.

Time of minor violence

A colony of moss does not feel pain, or suffer when a part is separated from the whole. The moment we experience the change in electric potential, we have already begun to heal.

If, however, a colony did choose to react in any way to such an injury, it might say this: We are amused. That anything so weak as the human hand could damage us, when we have seen whole tribes of humans rise and fall—the idea would make us laugh, if we could laugh.

And as for any punishment we might enact, any revenge? Well, our revenge is here. All you who seek to damage and disturb us, we might say (if we could, or indeed bothered to, speak), your every move is known to us, you exist inside our design.

Waxing Crescent, Third Cycle ☽

We left that place quickly, but not before ransacking the bodies for what weapons we could carry. I was the first to see the image, stamped into the pommel of a sword: two interlocking rings, Sego's mark.

"Why now?" I asked Aesu as we rode, the morning just beginning to silver around us. "Sego doesn't know what we agreed to with the king. What's changed since we saw them on the forest road?"

Aesu had sustained only small wounds, gashes to the leg and arm. But he was as troubled as I had ever seen him, his brow heavy with the knowledge that our old friend had wished us dead.

"He must have known what the king would ask of you," he said. "He didn't want to risk you saying yes."

"Surely you understand that he is our enemy now," I said, "whatever friendship once existed between us."

Aesu nodded. We rode along together in silence, and though it had come at such a cost, I felt relief that my brother and I were of one mind again, and whatever came we would face it together.

We rode all day and all night to reach our home, partly because we could not risk camping again, and partly because my wound would not allow it. Crab—still reeling himself from a club to the head—had dressed it under my direction, with the witch hazel and comfrey that I carried with me, but the bleeding had not stopped, and in the afternoon I began to feel drunk with fever, the road sliding away from my eyes to reveal the king's hearth, or the moss, or the house where I was born. I knew I needed better medicine than what I had added to our saddlebags before we set out, medicine only my mother could provide.

We arrived in the village near sunset, when the men were bringing in the wheat. At first I felt our homecoming like a warm cloak around my body—the light on the sheaves; the voices of my friends and cousins calling to each other as they worked; the children running to welcome our horses, their hair falling into their eyes. But as soon as Crab and Aesu helped me dismount, a wave of ill-feeling came over me—the air seemed to take on a green cast, the women to look askance at me from their doorways, and I bent double and vomited in the dirt.

May 2018

"I worked very quickly as I know you are in a rush," Danielle says.

Her voice from Sunita's phone fills the bright room, cool and clipped, a relief to hear. Agnes and Sunita sit in metal chairs next to the sink in the lab room; Ruby is in the adjoining office, ostensibly doing her homework.

"Thank you so much," Agnes says.

She is thinking several steps ahead: To confirm death by blood loss, she can look for markers in the marrow. For systemic infection, there will be lesions in the long bones.

"I don't know if you're going to like what I found. Did you get the images I sent?"

Sunita opens her laptop. The grayscale lattice of a tissue section fills the screen. Agnes recognizes the marbling of skin and epithelial cells, a structure that might be a hair follicle. And yet parts of it are entirely unfamiliar: for example, a block of tissue in the lower right-hand corner in which the cells are strangely regular, almost rectangular.

"I took this from just inside the lesion," Danielle says. "Now, I'm sure you are already familiar, but just in case you're not, when we look at wound age we are looking at a few things, and one of them is inflammation. In this case inflammation is good news, right? It means healing. So here we are looking for inflammatory cells."

"On the left," Sunita says, pointing for Agnes, who sees it right away: a section of smaller, more densely packed structures, like a tighter weave in fabric.

"That's right," says Danielle. "This tells me the wound is not new. Indeed the body is well on its way to closing it up. The inflammatory processes are working as one would expect, and if this were a living patient, I would say, 'This patient will recover.'"

"Can you tell us how old the wound was," Agnes asks, "when she died?"

"Not precisely," says Danielle. "But with this level of inflammatory activity, I would say minimum two weeks. Probably more."

"So the wound was healing," Sunita says.

"It was definitely healing," Danielle says. "Your decedent, she did not die from this wound."

"What about a secondary infection?" Agnes asks.

"This is a more complicated question," Danielle says. "It is difficult to confirm or disconfirm sepsis, even in a recent decedent. I'm sure you already know this. Still there are tissue changes we can look for in the kidneys, the liver, and especially in the lung. This is why I took so many samples."

Agnes hears in the background a single high-pitched mewl like the call of a hungry cat.

"One minute," Danielle says, and then she pulls away from the phone, clucking her tongue and speaking quietly, as though telling someone a secret. All the hard edges of Sunita's face go soft.

"Is that her? Hi baby, how are you?"

"She's just waking up," Danielle says, her voice now warm and full of feeling. "Say hi to Auntie Sunita? Okay, she's trying to eat the phone."

Agnes hears sounds of rummaging, a tinny lullaby playing from a toy. She imagines the baby's watery vision, pools of light coming in from windows, the soft overwhelming shape of the mother bending to kiss her head.

"Now you are in your little chair," Danielle says. Her voice goes crisp again. "Okay. Sorry about that. So. To confirm sepsis, usually we are looking for vascular and alveolar damage in the lung tissue, and there are some markers in the kidneys as well. I did not find any of these markers in the samples from your decedent."

Agnes hears a disorderly preverbal moan, a shapeless chain of vowels. She can taste the baby's frustration, she wriggles helpless in her body, her desires cannot be expressed.

"Shhh, hush, sweetie," Danielle says. And then to Agnes and Sunita, "The lung tissue does have some unusual characteristics—there's some evidence of pulmonary edema that I can't quite explain. It's not consistent with, for example, drowning. It's possible your decedent had some kind of heart condition. More likely, I think, is that the tissue became damaged postmortem in a way that mimics premortem edema."

Agnes feels panic creeping up the back of her throat. The baby cries again.

"A heart condition," Agnes says, grasping. "Did you see any other evidence of that? Or anything else abnormal in the tissue samples?"

Danielle's voice is curt. "This body has been submerged in peat for two thousand years," she says. "There are many things that are abnormal." Then she softens. "But I understand you want a cause of death—I am curious too. I did not see in the samples any sign of liver or kidney failure, or of advanced respiratory disease. Of course there are many other possibilities—a heart attack, a stroke, there are types of cancer we might not be able to detect so long after death."

She sighs, she shushes the baby. That one familiar sound down the frightening tube of the world.

"Agnes, I hope you learn what caused this person's death. But if you don't, at least now we have found her. People will be studying her for decades, maybe centuries to come. Whatever we don't find out, one of them will discover."

○

"Who died?" Ruby asks.

She's sitting cross-legged on Sunita's chair. On the desk is a photograph of the four of them, Sunita, Tianna, Ruby, her little sister, Maya. The photo can't be very old, but in it Ruby looks so much more carefree, her cheeks full, her eyes unclouded.

"Not funny," Sunita says.

"Sorry," Ruby says. "You guys just look depressed."

"We've had some setbacks," Agnes says.

"Mum told me they found her body. The other woman, Isabel Something? What is it like?"

It took the coroner's team just under a day to excavate and clean the remains of Isabela Navarro, who died in 1961 at the age of twenty-one. Based on measurement of her right femur, she was five feet, four inches tall at the time of death, with a weight between 120 and 150 pounds. Her left foot had the beginnings of a bunion, probably brought on by prolonged use of high-heeled shoes. Her left ulna showed evidence of a long-healed injury, likely a break sustained in childhood. She had a gold filling in her right bicuspid, and the corresponding cuspid showed signs of untreated decay. Her parietal and occipital bones were shattered, consistent with a fatal blow to the back of the head.

What is the body *like*? She is like an armload of driftwood, Agnes could say, rubbed clean and silvery by the sea and sand. She is like a dried flower. She is like a pearl. She is someone at rest in a final state, as final as is possible on this turning Earth, whose cycles are ushering us ever into wondrous new forms.

"The bog didn't preserve her body in the same way," Agnes says carefully, a beginning. "The Iron Age body, she entered this unusual state because of the environment of the peat. Isabela, her remains followed the more typical course."

"Which means what?" Ruby asks. Her face is on a razor's edge between fear and eagerness. "She decayed?"

"Ruby, we don't need to talk about this," Sunita says.

"It's okay," Agnes finds herself saying. "She did decay, at first. That part of the moss, at the edge, it's an aerobic environment. The ecosystem relies on decaying organic matter. She would have become part of that. She's part of it still. And also, the part we have of her now, the part that we'll send home with her niece—that part is bones."

Ruby nods, quiet, her consciousness seeming to turn inward. What is she doing with this information, Agnes wants to know, does it frighten or calm her, or function in some other way that Agnes cannot begin to understand?

"So what's the other setback?" Ruby asks finally.

"The pathology report didn't reveal much," Agnes says. "There's some sign of pulmonary edema, but the wound—"

"All right," Sunita says. She is looking sternly at Agnes, and then at her daughter, with concern. "Agnes, we can discuss pathology later. What's the story with the protesters? Have you talked to them? They can't really expect us to stop digging now."

"Unfortunately, they do," Agnes says.

"So, what then?" Sunita asks. "We could try to sue, but I'm not sure the university will back us—"

Agnes thinks of her outburst on the moss, how ineffectual and childish. And yet there is a power in her hands still, if she is willing to use it. She thinks of the greenhouse smell of the peat plant, the strange familiarity of that place.

"I might have an idea," she says.

Waxing Crescent, Third Cycle   ☽

I was half-awake as they carried me to my mother's house. I saw the world in discrete moments: my older brothers and their wives whispering at the doorway, a bed of furs laid out for me near the hearth, a draught of water steeped with bitter leaves. Only then my mother, taller even than I remembered, her iron hair long down her back, shooing everyone else away.

For many days I lay by my mother's fire, plagued by dreams and hallucinations. Of that time I know only that she packed my wound with herbs and bound it in clean wool, and that she did not allow anyone to visit me, not even her husband, who had been like a father to me since my own father died.

Finally I began to regain my strength and could sit upright, and drink a broth made of roots and bones. It was then that I asked my mother for my satchel with the lambskin and pens inside.

For three days I slept and drew, translating the places I had seen and that I knew from shimmering pictures in my mind to stark lines on the tough leather. At first my work frustrated me. My hand was clumsy, the pen a temperamental and difficult tool. Even when I learned how to avoid ink leaks and blots and how to lay down a steady line, I still felt a chasm yawn between the intricate and beautiful maps I had seen at the king's house and the rude scrawlings I produced. And yet when my mother sat down with me, her eyes grew wide and her body went still, as it always did when she was listening very closely.

"This is us," I told her, pointing. "This is the Small Rock and the Large Rock, and here is the river. This is the Gray Hill, and the town where Crab's brother-in-law comes from. This is the long road south. This is the great forest. And this is Camulodunon, where I visited the king."

My mother looked at the map a long time without saying anything.

"What's over here?" she said finally, gesturing to the empty swaths of lambskin to the east and west of our town.

"I need to travel there to fill it in," I said. "When I'm finished, you'll be able to see our whole village and everything for days in any direction, just by looking here. Then I'm going to do Aremorio, and Belgia, even Rome. Anyone who has these, they'll be able to see the world."

My mother wrapped her arms around me then; she held me as she had when I was a little child.

"Little one," she asked, "do you remember what I said when I named you the druid?"

"You said the gods had put their faith in me."

"I did say that. But the truth is the divinations were favorable for several of your brothers too. The gods' preference was not strong. I chose you because you're farsighted. Your eye is on the future, on the horizon. Someone like that is good for the people—you can see problems before they happen, you can see opportunities. And I think a part of me was selfish. I wanted someone like me as my successor, who would continue the work I'd started. I imagined you'd go to Aremorio one day, that you'd strengthen our relations with the Belgae, bring back new herbs and divinations. The south, Rome, I didn't foresee any of that. Maybe I'm not as farsighted as I thought."

I pulled away to look her in the eye.

"Have I disappointed you?" I asked.

She thought for a moment, then shook her head.

"Your time is beginning and mine is ending. I trust you. But listen: You can't keep looking at the horizon all the time."

I must have looked confused.

"My love," she said, "I don't have to tell you you're in danger. You're home now, but remember this is Sego's home too. He has a lot of allies here."

"Even after he tried to kill us?" I asked.

"Of course no one wants to see you hurt," my mother said. "There are many gifts for you, even from Paltucca, though I threw her oat cakes right into the fire."

It hurt to laugh.

"But even if they disapprove of what his men did, many of our neighbors are still loyal to him. They're skeptical of your journey, they know nothing of this young king in the south, and they certainly don't trust the Romans."

"I know they don't," I said. "But if they could just see what I've seen—"

My mother rose and took a walking stick of polished oak from a hook on the wall.

"Go and show them," she said.

May 2018

At midnight in her flat Agnes rereads the pathology report, hoping for something she has missed. On her flimsy coffee table sits a letter from her landlord; she has a week to renew her lease, or else she will have to leave at the end of June. Also on her coffee table is a stack of her students' lab reports, ready for grading.

Spring has opened on the campus; the breeze is warm. Her students, especially the ones in their final year, have come to class for the last two weeks with a wild-eyed energy, twitching this way and that, they see the gate standing open, they do not know which way to run.

Agnes feels it too. On her laptop are the images Danielle sent, what the body has given up—what they have taken—that they may understand her. Agnes has not entirely despaired of this. She looks at the lung, the kidney, the lung again. She wishes she had talked more to the pathologist in Las Minas; at that time she believed there was nothing her mind could not do on its own.

A few minutes after one, a dog howls. A drunk man yells in the street. Something in one of the skin samples catches Agnes's eye. Next to the round egg of the hair follicle, that unusual structure, segments stacked neatly one atop the other, plantlike, she thinks. A fungal growth? Such a thing would be unlikely to kill a healthy young woman, but nonetheless, it's something for Agnes's mind to grasp and hold to—she writes an email to Danielle to ask what the structure is, debates waiting until the morning to send it, and sends it anyway.

The next day she takes the long way to the processing plant. She avoids the rise, instead walking along the eastern edge of the moss, a narrow path marked with hoofprints and horseshit. The land lies low on this side, here the meager mists and drizzles have trickled downward to form shallow pools. Agnes has not walked this place in weeks and she is surprised to see it now: from green beginnings how shy grasses sprout and spread, among the tender stalks how tiny flowers bud and bloom. Overhead wheels a silver-feathered bird keening a high thin cry, and at Agnes's feet something rustles, a swift tiny creature fleeing beak and claws.

Agnes hardens her heart against all this life. This place is not her business; these creatures are not her responsibility. She has one small life, and she must use it correctly, she must be sharp as a scalpel that delves through thick tissue to the bone. Agnes imagines a funeral procession crossing the bleak moss, the men in front bearing a long bundle wrapped in burlap, and in the back, perhaps, two young girls, one cries because her mother cries, the other keeps her eyes trained on the horizon. Is it grandiose to imagine that they counted on someone such as her in the years to come, that in fact only she possesses the combination of knowledge and commitment necessary to fulfill their wish? If it is grandiose so be it.

When Agnes was in fifth grade she was assigned a group project: a simple experiment. She and two boys were instructed to fill two bowls with water, one with salt and one without. Then they were to place the bowls in the freezer and record how long each took to freeze. Afterward they would make a presentation of their results. Agnes still does not know who mixed up the bowls, but she knows that when Jason went to check them, he reported that the saltwater bowl was frozen solid and the freshwater bowl still slush.

Agnes knew that freshwater freezes before salt. And so she interrupted Jason during the presentation to tell the class that their experiment had been contaminated by error and would have to be repeated to get the correct result.

When she got a zero for "working cooperatively"—*Needs to learn how to resolve differences with classmates in a productive way*, the teacher wrote—she told her father she was sorry for what she'd done. Jason and the other boy had taken to ignoring her at lunchtime, as had most of the other kids in the class.

"You have a special mind," her father said. "Never apologize for being right."

She holds her face high to the spring wind now as she walks across the parking lot and into the plant.

Inside is a new sound, the reverberation of voices and mechanical creaks and clanks against iron and cement. Men walk the floor with purpose, with clipboards and walkie-talkies, one flips a switch and a portion of the assembly line rumbles to life, a great beast waking. Fiona wears a hard hat and is talking seriously with a man in a blue jumpsuit, but she turns when Agnes approaches.

"I thought you might stand me up," she says. A smile with a kind of admiration in it, as though she knows the resolve this walk required of Agnes.

"Here I am," Agnes says.

She follows Fiona into the office, the desk spread now with some kind of blueprint or schematic: a loop with boxes all along it, outside and inside, and an empty space in the middle.

"The plans from the developer just came in," Fiona says. "Have a look at this—it's a new kind of development. The affordable units are mixed in with the market-rate ones, so there's no distinction. The idea is to have a truly mixed-income community."

The map resolves itself under Agnes's gaze—a road paved through the south end of the moss, looping up to the rise before doubling back on itself again. Houses on either side.

"What's that?" Agnes asks, pointing to the space in the middle of the loop.

Fiona smiles again.

"The dig site, of course," she says. "I asked them to build it right into the design. It'll be open as long as you need it, and then when the excavation is finished—maybe a park? Maybe a small museum? You tell me. We'll need consultants, obviously, on the final design—no pressure of course, I know you're probably choosing between lots of offers."

Consultants, obviously.

"I don't know anything about design," she says.

"I'm not asking you to draw up the plans," Fiona says. "We have people for that."

Fiona opens a plastic container on her desk; Agnes smells vanilla.

"Do me a favor and take one of these?" she says. "My husband retired last month, and he's taken up baking."

Inside the container are four scones studded with blueberries. Agnes chooses one and takes a bite; it is slightly bad in a homey way, dry and oversweet.

"What I'm saying," Fiona says, "is you could help us figure out how to make this area a tribute to the body. Her place in history, her importance. A few months, maybe a year, all the attention around her will die down—I want to make sure she's remembered."

Agnes studies Fiona's face: The wrinkles carved between her nose and mouth, translucent skin at her temples revealing green veins. Her brown eyes clear and direct, the whites bright. Agnes thinks she is sincere.

"Why?" Agnes asks. "I mean, sorry, I guess I don't understand why you care about this—our work, the body."

"Oh, I don't."

Agnes is confused. The man in the blue jumpsuit, who has a thin face and a gray mustache, appears at the office door. Fiona nods and holds up a finger, and he leaves.

"Sorry, that sounded harsh," Fiona says to Agnes. "I'm very impressed with your discovery, and the way you've fought for it. I've been keeping tabs on you. But I'm not an archaeology person. School was never my thing, in general. What I care about is this town."

Fiona takes a scone for herself. She chews and sets it down.

"Jesus Christ, David," she says, shaking her head. "Someone has to tell him."

She opens her hand for Agnes's scone, wraps it in tissue, and throws it in the trash.

"You know, I'm not from here, Agnes. I'm from a little town in Wales, you won't have heard of it. But I've been here twenty years, and in that time I've heard the older generation—folks even older than me—talk about Ludlow. They have this sort of mythology around it. That it used to be a major trading center, even bigger than Manchester. The 'Gateway to the North.' It's a bit of a joke now, but to hear them tell it, it used to be true. And these days, what? A few shops, a Tesco, a Pizza Express. The steel mill closed down. The young people leave. Did you know the peat company is the biggest employer in town?"

Agnes shakes her head.

"When the peat's gone, there's nothing left. This development, that's another five years, fifty jobs I can save. But it's not enough. I'm hoping—and maybe this is crazy, but I'm hoping—this body could put us on the map again. If we play it right, if we build it out, we become a tourist destination, maybe there are documentaries, people coming here and spending money. I'll need help though, selling it to people. Why they should care. Why this body matters so much. And you're the expert on that."

"I can't sell anything to anyone."

"I'm not asking you to go door to door," she says. "I'm asking you to think about a way to memorialize this body, to show people how important she was. She is. I think I'm right that nobody cares about her more than you."

Fiona stands up.

"Anyway, think about it. You don't have to answer now. I'm just going to see what Tommy wants, and then you can tell me what you wanted to tell me."

Agnes sits in the warm office with the machines groaning in her ears. She sees what Fiona is offering her: a chance to bear witness to this body, for years if she wants, for as long as it takes, perhaps, to fully understand her. Never has she worked so purely for the deceased, served their memory so completely. And yet she feels her brows draw together, her shoulders hunch, she is not so sure now as she was before. She can't think straight, the noise, the smell—a garden smell, she realizes, of wild earth tamed and bagged up, made to bend to human will. She wishes she could call her father and ask his advice. She won't do it, she will hold firm, but she does check her phone to see if perhaps he has emailed her. Sometimes he still sends her funny links or stories about new astronomical discoveries, which annoy but also calm her, and make her feel less lost. Today she has nothing from her father, but instead she sees a message from Danielle, who has replied to her about the strange structure in the skin section. The email contains just one line:

"This, of course, is sphagnum."

And Agnes laughs, alone in the sweet-smelling room, and then she stands and walks, without saying goodbye, past the assembly line, the parking lot, and the chain-link fence and out onto the teeming moss, because of course her duty of care extends beyond the human woman lying cold in Sunita's lab, it extends here, to the living being who protected and transformed her, and whose body is intermingled with her body still.

First Quarter, Third Cycle

At first my visits to my neighbors went poorly. I was still weak, I became short of breath easily, and I found it difficult to speak at length. What was more, a cloud of fear hung over the village. Aesu and my older brothers, along with Crab and some of the other young men, were standing guard day and night at our perimeter, waiting for the day when Sego's men would attack again. And it was clear that many of my neighbors blamed me and not Sego for the situation—Narina took the fruit I brought her and ushered me out the door; Ria would not even let me in. Paltucca allowed me to show her the map I had made of our village and the road to Camulodunon, but only sat silently with her arms crossed over her chest as I explained it, while her baby daughter chewed the hem of my dress and her dog humped my leg.

Finally, when Tancorix said she would let me in but kept me waiting on her doorstep all afternoon while she "cleaned," I decided I needed a new approach. I remembered what the queen had said about the king, and how he knew what people wanted.

I left some fruit on Tancorix's doorstep and went to see Oconea—at least I knew she would talk to me. Indeed, she opened her door right away and ushered me inside. Oconea was a notorious busybody, and at first she alternated between inconsequential gossip about her neighbors and prying questions about my visit to the king. (Did I have a private audience with him? She wanted to know. Had I stayed overnight?) But instead of trying to steer her right away toward the topic of an alliance with the south and the Romans, I answered each question with a question, until Oconea finally began to excavate her own troubles, which centered on her two spindly and perennially unpopular sons.

"They're good boys," she said. "Not the strongest, maybe, but they work hard. Any woman would be lucky to have either of them. But just last week, Velua—who is missing three front teeth now, I don't know if you've noticed—laughed in Gavo's face when he invited her to come with him to the solstice festival. With a mouth like that, *she* laughed at *him*."

"Ridiculous," I said, and allowed her to lodge several more complaints about Velua's appearance and behavior before I asked, as gently as I could, "Have you ever thought of encouraging the boys to travel?"

"They go to the riverbend every half-moon and new moon to buy fish from Maccis. It's a whole morning's ride. They're such good boys, so hardworking."

"I'm thinking about somewhere farther than the riverbend. Perhaps even the south."

Oconea looked affronted.

"Why on earth would I send my sons to the south?"

"Of course it's your decision. But there are more women in Camulodunon alone than in every village from here to Lindinis. Beautiful women too, diligent and accomplished. Look at this material," I said, showing her the fine orange robe given to me by the king. "An ordinary butcher's daughter made this," I lied, "not even a professional weaver."

Oconea looked skeptical, but she was listening.

"Aesu and Crab both met women on our recent visit," I went on. "I wouldn't be surprised if at least one of them ends up returning south to marry."

"Aesu met a woman there?"

"That's right," I said, pausing for effect. "You know, I'd be happy to bring your sons with me next time I go to Camulodunon. I could take them to the king's court, introduce them to everyone. If you're interested, that is."

"Maybe," Oconea said.

I could tell she was.

"Of course, that's assuming we maintain our alliance with the king," I said, almost as an afterthought. "I know not everyone is convinced about that. Your husband, for example."

Oconea sucked on her lower lip. "I'll talk to him," she said. "He doesn't always know his own mind."

Then she went to her hearth and offered me warm porridge with berries and milk.

○

Winning people over was slow work, and I was not a natural at it. Most of my neighbors were not as easy to read as Oconea, nor were their interests as easy to square with the king's. Many of my kinsmen simply craved the lives they had always led, safe on their land, harvesting and herding, raising their children and growing old in peace and quiet. I tried to tell them that an alliance with the king would actually strengthen their security, but since our village had faced relatively few threats without his interference, they were largely unmoved.

On the third day of my campaign Aesu came to our mother's house, exhausted from the watch. Our mother gave him a bowl of nettle stew and then he asked to speak to me alone. She gave us both a long look. Then she kissed us each on the top of the head and left the house.

"How is your wound?" my brother asked.

"Better," I said. "It only hurts when I walk."

"Shouldn't you rest, then?" he asked. "I heard you've been visiting all around town."

"We have to be ready," I said. "If Sego's men come, I have to know the town is on our side."

"And is it?" he asked. "How are your visits going?"

"Slowly," I admitted. "There are some holdouts."

He nodded. He set his soup on the floor.

"Maybe it's a sign," he said.

"A sign of what?" I asked.

"You know the gods better than I do, of course. But if they're not turning our neighbors' hearts, then maybe they don't favor this new alliance after all."

I was angry, but more than that I was confused—that after all that had happened he still thought we could simply return to our old closeness with Sego.

"Do you remember who gave me this wound?" I asked. "Are you really my brother, if instead of protecting me, you tell me to beg for friendship from my enemies?"

"I have done nothing but protect you," he shouted. "Are you really my sister, if you can't see when our people don't support you?"

We stared at each other in the half dark of our mother's house, the house where we had both been born. My wound hurt. I felt the certainty that had animated my last few days leaking out of me, like blood.

If my neighbors truly could not be convinced, perhaps indeed I had been wrong. I had believed that an alliance with the south would be good for all of us. But home among my friends and cousins, far from the king's court, I had to acknowledge that my pride had played a role from the beginning—in my acceptance of the king's invitation, in what I said when I arrived in Camulodunon, and what I did. I knew from my mother that to speak with someone we trust can be a form of divination.

I answered Aesu in a soft voice now.

"I'll always be your sister," I said. "And you've always given me wise counsel, even when I don't agree."

He nodded, looking at the floor.

"Give me two more days," I said. "If I can't sway our neighbors by then, I'll consider making peace with Sego. But then we'll have to figure out the king and his men. They won't be happy."

Aesu's face had brightened.

"We'll deal with them if it comes to that," he said. "Those southerners with their soft cushions—they're not as strong as we are."

I smiled at him. When we were children we once used sticks from the fire to burn each other on the tender flesh of the inner arm, so that we would no longer be afraid of pain. I bore the scar still.

"No one is as strong as us," I said.

When Aesu left that day I felt calm, but in the morning I was frightened. No matter what Aesu said, I knew the king's armies were not weak, especially with the backing of the Romans. What was more, I was not sure what would become of me or my authority if I reversed my position now, and was forced to submit myself to Sego's protection.

In this mood of worry and uncertainty, I went to sit with Comux. I heard him shuffling to the door for several minutes before he opened it; Comux was the oldest person I knew. I usually addressed him as Great-Uncle, though I could not remember how or if we were truly blood-related. He seemed to have outlived death; his body was scarred by smallpox and the battles of his youth, he was bent and twisted with age, and I often thought there was nothing left that could truly threaten him.

"I don't know why you're talking to me," he said as he let me in. "I have no opinions on politics, and no one cares what I think anyway."

"You're selling yourself short," I said. "I know your daughters listen to you. Your granddaughters too."

"If my granddaughters listened to me, they wouldn't have married such worthless men," he said, but he was laughing. He gave me a plate of hard bread made with millet.

"I spoke with your daughter Senuna a few days ago," I said. "I know she's worried about changes coming to the village. She said something about her children speaking Latin."

"And they will be, by the end of their lives," Comux said. "If they can pay attention long enough to learn it."

This was not what I had expected. I stopped chewing and looked him in the eye.

"My son-in-law Andoco has gone south with his wool every year for thirty years. When he began he'd never heard of Rome.

Now everyone he trades with is allied with the Romans in some way. Those who held out, usually they met a bad end."

He shuffled to a pot over the fire and added a dollop of warm mutton fat to the remainder of my bread.

"It's not just that," he said. "When I was young our ships were little better than hollow logs. To cross the water you'd say goodbye to all your loved ones, sacrifice everything you owned to the gods. Most people would never attempt such a journey. Now the coasts crawl with ships. I've heard stories of the Roman vessels with their hundreds of oars. But it's not just them—the Danes, the Phoenicians—the world is growing, or shrinking, maybe? Anyway, the time when we could just be cozy here in our village is coming to a close, and if I don't see the end of it, then you will."

I stared at him.

"What?" he asked. "Just because I'm old, everyone's always so surprised when I know anything about the world. See how you like it when you're my age and everyone treats you like a baby."

"Sorry," I said. "But it sounds like, then, you're on my side when it comes to an alliance with the south."

He shrugged.

"I didn't say any of this was a good thing. Maybe we'd all be better off if we stayed on our land with our sheep and goats. Maybe we'd be better off if the Romans did that. I'm just telling you what I think is going to happen."

I left Comux's house that day uneasy in my mind, and I did not sleep that night. But in the morning I went to all my most resistant neighbors, repeating what he'd said. I told them Rome was coming; I told them we could fight and be flattened, or we could join and reap all the benefits the future held. I told them about the traders in the south and about the ships. I saw their faces darken over and heard them whisper among themselves.

None of them told me outright that they had changed their minds, but within three days even those who had avoided me the most assiduously were greeting me warmly in the clearing, and Tancorix, who had been the most skeptical of all, came to my mother's house with freshly dug spring onions from her garden, so sweet you could eat them raw.

May 2018

Agnes comes to Nicholas a proud, tall chaos, her hair wet, her eyes shining. She has been up all night; she is wearing her T-shirt from the day before. So she will not fulfill her responsibility to the body—she has a new purpose now. She has written a statement on the importance of preserving the Ludlow Moss as an anthropological site, along with a proposal for minimally invasive digging—in it she recommends a reduction in size of the current excavation site, along with restoration of the peat environment around it. Together the statement and proposal take up seven single-spaced pages on her laptop, but she can cut them down. When she presents them in court, she thinks, she will have to get some better clothes. She will need money; she will have to get a job outside her field. Something quiet, she thinks, outside in the open air, could she paint houses perhaps, she imagines the rhythm of it, the intoxicating chemical smell, the sturdy concrete comfort of making a place for a person to live.

At the southwest corner of the moss she spots him, near where the creek runs, that cool minerality in the air. The shy green in the black mud. He stands to greet her, a softness to his face, his eyes red-rimmed. In each of her hands she carries a flat stone.

"I'm sorry," she says.

"Sorry for what?"

"I didn't understand, and I was going to—" she begins, then stops, begins again. "I get it now, my job here and your job, really, they're the same. I think I can help you, I wrote this thing."

"Agnes," he says.

He doubts her, she thinks, he does not believe she can be useful to them.

"I can be an expert witness," she goes on. "I know this is a civil case, but it can't be that different—"

"Agnes," he says again, holding up his hand. "Agnes, we lost the suit."

"You what?"

"The court rejected our claim of environmental harm. Basically, they said this area was already so degraded that the peat company couldn't possibly hurt the ecosystem any more."

"But—" Agnes says, casting her hand impotently about the green patches.

"We showed photographs, we had projections for three and six and twelve months of undisturbed growth. It didn't matter. They're going to restart harvesting next week. They break ground on the housing development in the fall."

All night Agnes had chased them in circles in her mind, the possible consequences of her decision. Sunita would be angry, she would fight, probably, to keep the dig open, would they find themselves on opposing sides, Agnes and this weary keen-minded woman she was just beginning to understand? Oddly, Agnes has been unable to get in touch with Sunita for several days, is she somehow angry already? And Ruby, what would Ruby think, would she understand too that all the beings, the bodies, of the moss existed in relationship to each other, would she want to know them in their variety and commonality, would Agnes and Ruby even be able to speak or would they be lost to one another? But not even when morning dawned gray, then white, through the living room window, the light surprising her as she pressed Delete and drank the bitter leavings at the bottom of her teacup, not even then did she consider that her choice, the sacrifice of her own ambition, her subsumption into something greater, like leaping into a great body of water, like letting go, would have no effect at all, that she would find herself alone, drenched and dripping, on the shore.

"They can't just do that," Agnes says.

What is in his face? He receives her anger and frustration but instead of sharing them he looks at her as though from far ahead, as though he passed through the spot where she now stands many days ago, many years.

"They already are," he says, pointing east where men in hard hats are gathering, they plant red plastic flags in the growing peat, a new machine has joined the original three, a yellow contraption like the skeleton of an airplane, its wings skimming low over the mud. "They've made very clear that whoever's still here on June first will be arrested and charged with trespassing."

"What are we going to do?" Agnes asks.

"You'll be fine, I expect," he says, a hardness creeping into his voice. "Fiona's smart, she knows it would be a PR headache to mess with a 'historic find.' Although I'd watch out when the attention fades a bit. They'll find a way to quietly get you out of there."

Agnes thinks of the green space at the center of Fiona's map, her talk of tourists and documentaries. She grips the stones more tightly now.

"And the moss, what?" Agnes asks, vehement in her sleeplessness, her hunger. "We're just giving up?"

"No, Agnes, God!" he says, freshly angry at her now. "'We' are not giving up. You just got here. We've been working here for months. We'll appeal the decision, obviously, and we'll keep up a presence in the area as long as we can. It would be different if there was more to study here, another burial site or something. We could maybe make the case that the entire moss should be designated as a historic site. But as it stands—"

He lifts his hands to the empty air.

"We lost, Agnes," he says. "Sometimes you lose."

Agnes looks out across the mud field in the rising day and, as with an inner sight, witnesses it as it once was, a wild place, thick and teeming. Not bleak, the day they carried her across, wound in her burial shroud, but howling: the wind blowing a hard rain in their faces, the kites circling above, calling and crying. The rushes slapping at their shinbones as they walked, the woman looking back to see the two young girls come across safely. Pool on pool until they came to the one deep enough to lay her down.

Agnes holds her left hand out to Nicholas. The stone there is so deeply gray it is almost bright.

○

"So you're finished," her father says.

Agnes sits at her coffee table with a cup of tea in front of her. It is all the table can bear; she has fixed the leg and fixed it again, and now it holds as long as only a very small weight is placed upon it.

"I guess so," she says.

"What are you going to do now?"

Agnes has begun to receive emails from other anthropologists, people she vaguely knows and, in one case, does not know at all, asking to collaborate. But she has no idea what to do with these requests; she has ignored them. Meanwhile she still does not have a job. She has three hundred pounds in her bank account. Her left sneaker has a hole in the bottom.

"I'm working on it," she says.

A pause in which she can hear him open the refrigerator and remove what she knows is a can of Diet Coke. The pop of the tab, the sizzle of ice and liquid in the glass. All the familiar small sounds of that house, like a song she knows by heart.

"Come home, sweetie," her father says. "Just for a little while, to get your bearings. I promise, I'll stay out of your hair. You can stay here, save money until you can get your own place, apply for jobs again in the fall. What do you think?"

The blast of desert air on her skin, she can feel it already. The way it would be for him to pick her up from the airport in his car. Going through all the familiar motions: Lifting the breadboard and the broken radio off the seat so she can sit down. Leaning her forehead against the window as the air-conditioning kicks in. Back at the house, the tomato soup he'd make her from the can. The little crackers floating on the top. Agnes feels a catch in her throat. If she goes home now, she thinks, she will never leave.

"I'll think about it," she says.

○

"Sorry to pull you back into this," Kieran says. "I thought we were done."

The clutter and mementos on his desk, the photograph of the white-haired child who does not sleep, Kieran up in the middle of the night to rock her, small but heavy in his arms. The love and panic, Agnes can make out only their edges but she sees them on his face, in the slight stoop of his back as he leads her down the hall to the records room.

Dorotea sits very still on the pink love seat. She wears black, as always; today her earrings are tiny green stones. Her hands rest calmly in her lap, but her eyes dart with anger.

"I still don't understand," she says to Kieran, clearly continuing a conversation that has already begun. "Now this man is saying he did not kill my aunt?"

"No," the coroner says. "Mr. Bergmann is not retracting his confession. But he is saying there were extenuating circumstances."

"He pushed her down the stairs and buried her in a marsh, where she lay for more than fifty years," Dorotea says. "What extenuating circumstances could there possibly be?"

Kieran sighs. He scratches the back of his neck. He looks older than when Agnes first met him, they are all getting older.

"Ms. Navarro," Kieran says, "I know this is very difficult, which is why I recommended that we have this conversation with the social worker present."

"And the social worker is not available until Wednesday, but I want to have the conversation now."

He sighs again. "Mr. Bergmann is saying that Mrs. Bergmann—"

"Ms. Navarro. She did not take his name. She was Ms. Navarro when she died."

"Mr. Bergmann is saying that Ms. Navarro abused him during their marriage."

"*She* abused *him*?"

Dorotea's lack of expression is an expression.

"Mr. Bergmann says Ms. Navarro was an alcoholic and that she also misused prescription drugs."

"My mother always said Isabela didn't drink," Dorotea responds. "Neither of them did."

Kieran holds up his hand.

"I'm not presenting any of this as fact. I'm just telling you what Mr. Bergmann has reported so you can understand."

Dorotea moves back a fraction of an inch in her chair.

"Mr. Bergmann says that on the night of her death, Ms. Navarro attacked him during a drunken rage," Kieran goes on. "He says he pushed her down the stairs in a panicked attempt to defend himself. His lawyers have requested an autopsy, which they say will confirm that Ms. Navarro abused alcohol and drugs in the years leading up to her death."

Dorotea shifts forward again. Her eyes narrow.

"Can we refuse?"

"You can," Kieran says, "but then Mr. Bergmann will say the autopsy is necessary for his defense. The matter will go to court, it will be a long process, and you will probably lose. I understand this is not easy for your family, Ms. Navarro, but I personally suggest that you consent to the procedure."

Dorotea looks at Agnes as though seeing her for the first time. The look is at once respectful and accusatory; it is a look you give someone who bears responsibility. Agnes meets her gaze.

"What do you think?" Dorotea asks. "Should we do this?"

"Alcohol abuse can present in bone tissue, but the effects are unpredictable. Sometimes you'll see premature osteopenia, osteoporosis, even septic arthritis. Sometimes you'll see nothing. The largest effects come with decades of exposure, probably more than your aunt would have had."

Dorotea turns to Kieran, triumphant.

"You see?" she says. "There is no point in this test anyway. It will tell them nothing."

"Prescription drugs, however, are different," Agnes presses on. "Certain substances—benzodiazepines, for example—can be detectable in bone even many years after death."

"This procedure," Dorotea asks, "presumably it will be invasive to my aunt's body, you will remove something from her?"

"We would need to take a small sample of bone."

Dorotea nods. "I understand. And I am asking you again. Should. We. Do. This?"

Agnes sees now that she has neglected her most concrete and immediate duty in this place: to Isabela and to her family, who are alive. Is it because Isabela's case has seemed comparatively simple, because it does not test that within Agnes which she believes must be tested and confirmed? Whatever the reason, she has an opportunity, now, to offer some small remedy.

"Your aunt's bones might be able to tell us more about her life," Agnes says. "If it were me, I'd want to know."

○

"I'm sorry to call out of the blue," says a man's voice on the other end of the line. "I haven't been able to reach Sunita."

"Jesper?"

Agnes has never spoken to him before, she's not even sure how he has her number. She has not been able to reach Sunita either, she has now left several voicemails.

"Yes, hello. I'm sorry it's taken me a bit of time to get back to you. I just wanted to double-check the results because they're . . . well, they're a bit surprising."

Agnes has just finished taking the bone sample for Isabela's tox screen. She sliced away two one-centimeter sections from the thickest part of the left femur and placed the dark variegated coins in a plastic case for the toxicology lab. The technicians there will crush one section and run it through a spectrometer; the other they will examine under a microscope for traces of opiates or cocaine. Agnes will have the results in a few days.

"Surprising how?" she asks, taking off her gloves.

"Right. Well, I'll start with the lambskin. When I analyzed the markings, I found a mix of carbon you'd typically find in wood that's been burned for a long time at high heat. Essentially, it's soot."

"Okay," Agnes says.

"Right, this is not surprising. Now, are you familiar with gum arabic?"

"It's a food additive?" she guesses.

"Yes, today it is often used in candy and other processed foods," he says. "But in our period of interest, we primarily see gum arabic used as a binding agent. Mixed with soot or pitch, it was an early form of ink."

"Okay," Agnes says again.

"Now I want to turn to your second artifact, the metal object. As I'm sure Sunita mentioned to you, I took some samples from this object as well. And in several spots along the inside surface, I found traces of gum arabic as well."

Agnes sees the object in her mind, the hollow tube, meant of course for conveying liquid from one end to the other.

"It's a pen," she says.

"It's a pen."

"I thought the Celts didn't have written language," Agnes says.

"They didn't. And they certainly didn't have gum arabic, which comes from the sap of acacia trees in North Africa."

"I'm confused," Agnes says.

"Yes, it is very confusing." Jesper sounds like he's enjoying himself. "I believe there is only one way that gum arabic from North Africa could have made its way to northern England at or around 50 B.C.E. And that is through Camulodunon."

Agnes has a sense of expansion, she is dizzy. The basement anteroom where she is to put on her street clothes feels large all of a sudden, the air thin.

"What's Camulodunon?" she asks.

"The first Roman settlement in Britain. It was on the site of what is now Colchester, in Essex. It's a very well-preserved and well-researched site, but it would have been many days' ride away from Ludlow. We weren't aware of any trade or even contact between the Celts in the north and the Romans of this time period, until now."

"What does that mean?" she asks Jesper. "The woman, the body, was she Roman?"

"We don't know," Jesper says. "But at a minimum, it's likely that she traveled between Ludlow and Camulodunon, which would have been unusual for the time. And this is my speculation, but if she was in fact buried with both the lambskin and the pen—and given the dates on both it is likely that she was—then the objects were probably closely associated in some way. Perhaps she was merely transporting the lambskin from Camulodunon to Ludlow, but I think—especially given the presence of the pen, which still contained ink at the time it was submerged in the moss—I think that whatever the lambskin was meant to be or represent, she was its creator."

"How do we find out what it was?" Agnes asks.

"There are a number of possibilities—" Jesper says, and he begins to enumerate, but Agnes's phone is beeping, now, finally, Sunita is returning her call.

Time of discovery

A colony of moss does not notice or care about objects placed within it. But if such a colony were to speak on the items buried in its depths over the millennia, it might say this: Send more fruit. We especially enjoy apples, pears, and raspberries. Peaches are okay. Fruits provide us with nitrogen, which we need for turning sunlight into fuel. Also, they taste good.

Despite these fine qualities, humans have persisted in sending metal objects to us. We have received gold, silver, copper alloys, and, of course, iron; small rounds with complicated surfaces, long sharp spikes, and, just once, a thin tube full of a carbon-rich liquid. We never asked for any of these items (we never ask), but we do not complain (we cannot complain). In truth, we have found a use for some of the lengths of metal we've been given, though it has taken many lifetimes to come to fruition.

May 2018

"Did they have cholera in Camulodunon?" Ruby asks. "What about rats?"

She sits upright in the hospital bed, sipping apple juice through a straw. Above her head a machine boops and beeps. On her forehead are five fresh stitches. Despite her injury she looks unbowed, self-possessed, lightly indignant—this body she has always known to be unreliable has finally proved her right. Sunita sits in a vinyl-covered reclining chair next to the bed, looking watery and attenuated, her skin gray.

"I don't know about cholera," Agnes says. "I would guess they had rats. Why?"

"I'm just thinking, if she was Roman, or she'd been to the Roman city, there are so many more things that could have killed her."

Agnes sighs, she's had this thought too. She could sample the bone tissue for lead, perhaps, for signs of plague. But without a better idea of what she's looking for, Agnes risks abusing the body, taking and taking from it without giving anything in return. She thinks of what Danielle said, that someone else will discover what they cannot.

"It's true," Agnes says. "People will be working on her for a long time."

"What about you?" Ruby asks. "Don't you want to find out what happened?"

"I do," she says, "but my job here is ending soon. I might have to go back to the States."

"That's crazy," Ruby says. "Aren't you, like, famous now? Can't you get a job at the university?"

"It doesn't really work that way," Agnes says.

"Don't worry about Agnes, sweetie," Sunita says. "She came here to see you."

Agnes nods. She places on the tray beside the bed a frozen coffee drink, sweating in its plastic cup, that she now feels guilty for buying Ruby.

"How are you feeling?" she asks. "Your mum says you took a pretty bad fall."

Ruby shrugs. "I went to the bathroom in art class," she says. "And I saw this spot on my face and I started staring at it, like maybe if I looked at it from the right angle I could tell if it was skin cancer or not. Then my vision started to turn gray, like I was looking through smoke or something, and then I heard ringing in my ears and then I kind of couldn't stand up anymore."

"She had a panic attack," Sunita cuts in. "And she hit her head on the sink."

"I'm so sorry," Agnes says. "How are you feeling now?"

"My head hurts," she says. "And I'm bored. Did they have syphilis in Camulodunon, do you think?"

"Ruby—" Sunita begins, shaking her head.

The doctor comes in then, a tall man with a pleasant, compact face. "Ruby, good afternoon," he says, solicitous. "Evening, almost. How are you doing?"

"Better," Ruby says. "Can I go now?"

The doctor laughs and looks at Sunita, who acknowledges him only with a wan smile. "I think you can." He turns to Agnes. "But I'll have to ask your visitor to step out now so we can discuss some medical information."

Ruby looks annoyed. "Can't she stay? We're talking."

"You'll see Agnes soon," Sunita says, and then to Agnes, "We have a little party at the end of the year. I'll text you."

"I'll be there," Agnes says. "Ruby, I hope you feel better."

As she leaves, she hears Ruby talking to her mother.

"I'm not," she says. "I'm working on something."

○

"Will you stay for the trial?" Agnes asks.

Dorotea narrows her eyes; she still does not fully trust Agnes. And yet there is familiarity there, in the corner of the records room, with the faded pink walls, the nearly subsonic buzzing of the fluorescent light. The painting, Agnes realizes, is not abstract after all, but an ocean scene, the stripes indicating sand, sea, clouds, and sky.

"My husband is not well," Dorotea says. "He has Parkinson's. There is a nurse who comes, but—" She pauses and waves her hand dismissively in front of her face, as though she feels she has said too much. "I will be leaving Sunday."

She slides the toxicology report back into its folder and puts the folder in her purse. The lab has found no evidence of opiates or any other drugs in Isabela's bone tissue; her remains will be released to her niece for burial.

"I'm sorry," Agnes says.

Again Dorotea narrows her eyes. "For what?"

"For the delay," Agnes says. "And for . . . I'm sorry if we haven't answered your questions about your aunt. If I haven't."

Dorotea gazes at Agnes with a great stillness. "You were blaming her, and now, because the tests are negative, you are not."

"I never blamed her," Agnes says, affronted. "It's not about blaming. These are tests that you agreed to."

The two look at each other for a long moment, metal on metal.

"My grandmother, my mother's mother," Dorotea says finally, resignation in her tone and something else too, Agnes cannot identify it, "she was a very unhappy woman. My grandfather—they had a bad marriage. He hit her. She hit the children. My mother had a scar on the back of her leg where my grandmother burned her with a hot poker. My mother hugged and kissed us every day, she surrounded us with love, she never wanted us to feel what she felt. That fear."

"I'm sorry," Agnes says, her body, her nervous system standing down.

"My aunt, though," Dorotea goes on. "She—became violent. Once she cut my mother with a kitchen knife. Another time, a girl in their school, Isabela came up behind her and choked her with a hair ribbon. My mother only told us these stories when we were older, when she thought we could understand."

"Understand what?" Agnes asks.

Dorotea leans forward in her chair. "In your professional opinion," she asks, "did my aunt attack that man? Did she hit first?"

Agnes recognizes the second mood in Dorotea's voice and manner, the tension in the throat that makes her voice range higher. It is need.

"That's not a question I can answer based on the skeletal remains," Agnes says, stalling.

"What *can* you answer, then?"

Agnes takes a breath. To bear witness, she thinks—not only to hold knowledge but to carry it somewhere, to someone.

She opens her laptop, brings up her initial inventory of Isabela's remains.

"Your aunt," she begins, "she broke her ulna as a young child. Probably six or seven."

"She broke it?" Dorotea asks.

"She broke it," Agnes repeats, "or someone else did."

Dorotea nods slowly.

"You can tell this from her . . . from her bones?"

"That's right," Agnes says. "I'll send this to you. I'll write it all up in plain language, but I'll send you my numbers too. You can have everything I have."

Dorotea stands, she extends a ringed hand.

"It was a pleasure to meet you, Agnes," she says, and Agnes cannot tell if she is sincere, but she thinks their meeting has, at least, acquired some weight and import, they will remember each other, they have exchanged something that will endure.

"And you," Agnes says. "I hope the report is . . ." She struggles for the right words. "I hope it brings you some peace."

Dorotea smiles. "I do not expect peace," she says. "But I have done what I came here to do."

○

Agnes wants to buy a bottle of wine for the party, but all the bottles she can afford have ugly graphics of flowers or fish on them, and so at the last minute she instead buys something ridiculous: a giant bag of navel oranges.

Sunita's younger daughter, Maya, answers the door. She is seven or eight, with a straight back, a frank gaze, and the calm gravity of some young children. "Nice to meet you," she says. "The grown-ups are this way."

Tianna is in the kitchen surrounded by people. She looks like Maya, tall and cool, with short hair and big glasses and steady hands passing beer and wine around. An expression of confusion flashes briefly across her face when she sees Agnes's gift. Then Sunita darts out from behind the open refrigerator door, her body buzzing with energy and anxiety.

"Agnes!" she nearly shouts. "Thank goodness you're here! Ruby's looking for you."

"Where is she?" Agnes puts the oranges down on the kitchen island, where they are clearly in the way, then moves them to the counter, where they are also in the way.

Before Sunita can answer, Tianna calls to her from across the island, "You've got the asparagus?"

Sunita looks down at the foil-covered dish in her hands as though surprised to find it there.

"Sorry, yes, sorry," she says, handing it over. "What else was I getting here? The butter?"

She rummages in the refrigerator, knocking out a plastic container that opens and sends blackberries rolling over the tile.

"Oh, Jesus fucking Christ, Jesus Christ," she mutters, squatting, grabbing at the berries ineffectually with both hands. As Agnes kneels to help, a boy and a girl, four or five, run into the kitchen, their bodies tense with outrage. The girl shouts down into Sunita's face.

"Maya said I could play with her Spider-Man but he's not letting me play with her Spider-Man!"

"She's lying!" The boy's voice is ragged. He is near tears. "Maya said *I* could play with Spider-Man, not her."

Agnes is nervous on Sunita's behalf, she seems in no state to defuse such a conflict, but Sunita looks at the children with an expression of great seriousness, then reaches into a high cupboard and pulls out two bright plastic packages.

"Listen," she says. "I need your help with something. I have these parachute guys, and they really need to be thrown off the upstairs landing. But I'm really busy here in the kitchen. Do you think you could help me with that?"

The children laugh, they know it is a ruse but they love it, they grab for the packages. Sunita holds them back for a split second.

"I don't know," she says. "Do you have experience throwing guys off a landing? Do you think I should ask your daddy instead?"

A gray-haired man dressing a salad in a glass bowl raises his eyebrows at her. The children shout, "No!" They jump up and down, transfixed with glee. Sunita hands them the packages and they run away cackling at one another.

"Sorry," Sunita says. "Every year I say I'm not going to host another huge thing, and every year somehow I do."

But the encounter has calmed her; she looks taller, less pulled in on herself, even her breathing is slower.

Agnes remembers one terrible Christmas spent with her father's family; she must have been five or six, not much older than the little boy and girl. They flew to Denver, where there was snow on the ground, and instead of being excited Agnes felt she had stepped into an alien world; in the car on the way to her grandmother's house she got a nosebleed. For Christmas dinner she wore a plaid dress her grandmother had given her that morning, with long sleeves and tight elastic cuffs. She hated it but intuited somehow—surely her father had not told her, probably she had understood from the way he exclaimed over it when she opened the package wrapped in red and gold—that it was mandatory.

There were other children, her cousins, who all seemed to know each other, and adults who asked her questions she didn't understand; there was one woman in particular who made a special effort to speak to her, she had long pink-painted nails and Agnes's father was nervous and boyish around her in a way that made Agnes uneasy. But the person Agnes remembers most, who dominated her consciousness that day and for several weeks after, is her grandmother, a short woman, soft of hands and body, who hugged Agnes for too long and then looked at her with eyes both sad and appraising, like someone assessing damage, and all day and night kept talking about things they were going to do together, they were going to get her hair cut (Agnes's hair was long then, although her father sometimes let her cut small sections of it with safety scissors and measure them with a ruler), they were going to take her to a restaurant where she would learn how delicious hamburgers were (at that time Agnes refused almost all forms of protein), they were going to go ice-skating with all her cousins, they were going to teach her to tie her shoes, they were going to help her pick a sport, maybe soccer, so that she could spend more time with other kids.

All the while Agnes's grandmother was also fussing over her father—picking lint off his sweater, cleaning his glasses for him, offering him special dark meat she had saved out of the turkey when she carved it. The worst of it was the way her father seemed to relax into his mother's attention; Agnes could tell even then that it was comfortable for him, that he enjoyed being cared for in this way. When it was time to open presents Agnes hid in a spare room full of her father's old science fair ribbons and collections of rocks and minerals, and only emerged when it became clear that her father was disappointed and embarrassed by her behavior, and that the situation could only be salvaged by sitting on her grandmother's lap and accepting the brightly wrapped gifts that turned out to be dolls, a set of a barrettes with rhinestones, a pair of pink ice skates.

On the flight home Agnes's father asked her if she would like to be able to visit her grandmother more often, maybe even live a little closer, and Agnes burst into tears. She spent a week on high alert, a month nervous, a year periodically wondering when the announcement of a move would come, but—the relief seeped into her slowly, after the year was out—it was never mentioned again.

"Sorry," Sunita says again. "Where was I? Right, Ruby. And also you need a drink, and then I want to hear how the thing went, with Isabela—"

Tianna pours Agnes a glass of white wine, and then a man and a woman come in from the spring evening, calling Sunita's name, folding her in their arms. Agnes feels extraneous.

"It's okay," Agnes says. "We can talk later."

"Just one second—" Sunita says from inside the hug, but Agnes is already walking down the hallway, looking for Ruby while also trying to make herself invisible in the house.

The wine is sweet, and Agnes has never liked drinking, but she holds it to have something to do with her hands. In the living room are more kids playing and fighting, and three women arguing over the construction of a model shark clearly abandoned by a child.

Agnes is haunting a hallway lined with photos of Maya and Ruby—the two girls building a sandcastle together on an orange-lit beach; wearing soccer gear and expressions of winded elation; Ruby holding Maya as a newborn, swaddled and tiny, her little birth-crushed face nestled into Ruby's shoulder—when Ruby herself rollicks in from behind her with an older friend or cousin, a short laughing girl wearing big shoes that clomp on the floor.

"Your mum said you were looking for me?" Agnes says.

The other girl gives Ruby a look of confusion. She has braces on her teeth and wears makeup, dark-red lipstick and black liner swooping out from her eyes. A shadow passes over Ruby's face.

"What? No I'm not." She softens slightly, aware she sounds rude. "I mean, thanks for coming though. It's good to see you and everything."

She is turning away already, the older girl looks bored and impatient, Agnes is embarrassed in front of these children, but still she feels a tug, something is passing between her and Ruby.

"How are you?" Agnes asks Ruby. "You're okay?"

"I'm fine, I'm great," Ruby says. She starts to follow the older girl down the hall.

And then, a commotion in the kitchen: something shatters; Agnes hears crying and laughing and the sound of adults soothing tears. Ruby turns back, rolling her eyes.

"Come on," she says, "we'd better go see what that was."

In the kitchen Tianna and the gray-haired man are cleaning up oily lettuce leaves and spikes of broken glass. The little boy clutches a Band-Aided finger close to his chest, looking proud and aggrieved. Standing outside the fray, watchful but calm, is Danielle Muller, holding her baby.

"Agnes, good to see you," Danielle says. "This is Sabine."

Danielle wears a loose green dress and seems stronger, her back straighter, her gaze no longer backed by pain. Her baby has red-gold hair and can already control its neck and head; it is perhaps five months old.

"She's cute," Agnes remembers to say.

"Yes," Danielle says calmly. "She looks like me, I think."

And Agnes sees it, not only Danielle's angular beauty, reemerging from her weariness as though from behind clouds, but also her face reflected in the child's, the high forehead and wide, serious eyes. She has the urge to look at herself in the mirror, she wonders who she would see there.

"So what will you do now?" Danielle asks, bouncing the child.

"I don't know," Agnes says. "Now that we're finished, I kind of don't know what to do with myself."

Danielle looks mystified. She shifts the baby to her other hip.

"There are many things for you to do," she says.

Sunita calls the room to attention with the authoritative tone of her voice.

"Everyone get a plate," she calls. "We're not doing salad but we've got everything else."

Along the kitchen counters are laid platters of carved lamb, asparagus, roasted red potatoes cut in wedges, some kind of green sauce Agnes does not recognize, a basket of rolls. Someone has put Agnes's oranges in a blue bowl.

Ruby and the other girl grab rolls from the basket and leave. Agnes scoops food onto her own plate and then, seeing Danielle struggle with the baby and the serving spoons, realizes she should offer to make a plate for Danielle too.

"Thank you, yes," Danielle says. "A lot of lamb, please. All the time I was pregnant, and still now, all I want is meat."

The baby gnaws on her mother's shoulder with a look of determination.

"In a minute, Sabine," Danielle says. "You know I need to eat too."

The other guests sit in the living room, the plates balanced on their laps. Danielle looks around with consternation; she tries to lay the baby next to her on the couch, but the child's face cracks open in rage, she howls.

"I can . . ." Agnes begins, unsure what she's offering. "Do you want me to—"

"Yes please," Danielle says. "If you could walk her for just five minutes. Maybe take her to see the garden."

Agnes holds the baby in her arms. The child quiets, shocked by her new position. Small as she is, she has a firm, assertive presence. Her back is taut, she stares at Agnes with blue, lupine eyes. She opens her mouth and utters a single syllable: "O."

"She likes you," Danielle says. "You are friends now."

Agnes can feel the baby straining toward the doorway with her body, so she begins to walk. The child leads her as a rider leads a horse. They pass through rooms of people talking and through a sliding glass door into the backyard. The sun is setting, all the air is pink and violet. In the small garden tulips are blooming, their flowers orange globes of light. Almost immediately the baby begins to cry again. Agnes tries to bounce her the way she saw Danielle and Sunita do, but the movement is awkward and the baby cries harder. Agnes crosses the garden in a rising panic, making for the glass door, when she feels the baby lurch leftward, insistent. She turns to look and something flits rufous across her field of vision: a robin. It lights with delicate feet on the branch of a lemon tree, and then flits again to its destination, a feeder full of seed.

Agnes points the baby at the feeder and her crying stops, her body absolutely still with focus. They stand together in the dimming light as the bird hops from post to post, extracting seeds with its precise beak, its eyes black and glossy. Each time the bird moves the baby twitches, and Agnes adjusts her body to keep the child steady, until finally the bird eats its fill and flies over the fence and out of the garden. When Agnes rejoins the party and hands the child back to her mother, she resists for a moment, holding on to Agnes's arms.

The kitchen is empty when Agnes returns to it, except for Ruby, who is sitting on the kitchen island, trying to peel one of the oranges. In the light from the window, Agnes can see the tiny drops of oil spraying from the rind.

"I really was looking for you earlier," Ruby says. "I don't know why I said I wasn't."

Her body language has changed since Agnes saw her last, she looks smaller and more tentative. She glances over her shoulder, reaches behind her head to grasp and release a handful of braids.

"How are you really?" Agnes asks.

"I got some medicine," she says, "and they moved me up the waiting list for therapy. I start next week."

"That's good, right?" Agnes asks.

Ruby shrugs. She stabs at the orange with her thumbnail, scraping off small hard flecks of rind. Then she looks at Agnes with a tremulous expression.

"The medication helps a little," Ruby says. "But I'm still scared a lot of the time."

Agnes lifts herself up onto the island next to Ruby.

"I'm sorry," she says. "It'll get better, I think."

"What if it doesn't?" Ruby says. "What do I do then?"

Agnes turns to look at her. Her overbite, her high wide cheekbones, the chain of stitches still healing the skin of her forehead. Agnes wonders at herself. How small, she thinks, has been the circle of her attention, how narrow have been the limits of her care.

"Here," she says.

She holds her hand out for the orange. She slides a nail into one of the wounds Ruby made, the white pith slick on the pad of her finger. She begins to peel in a spiral, a muscle memory nearly as old as she is. When she is finished she bounces it, once, before Ruby's eyes and hands the peeled fruit back. Ruby splits it into two halves. They share.

"This is horrible," Agnes says, chewing the watery pulp. "I'm sorry."

Ruby laughs.

"Who brought this?"

"Me," Agnes says. "I brought this! You have two dozen now."

They both laugh then, eating the bad orange. Night falls outside, the windows blacken and reflect the warm interior light. A clock somewhere in the room is ticking minutes.

"Look," Agnes says. "I can't promise it's going to get better. But it's not going to be this way forever. It's going to be different."

Ruby nods. Agnes cannot tell if what she says is helpful, but she thinks Ruby is taking it in. Ruby pops the last orange slice into her mouth and pushes herself off the island.

"That's not actually what I wanted to talk to you about," she says. "Did you do a tox screen on the body?"

"What? On Isabela? Yeah, did your mom tell you?"

"No, I mean on the other body. The old one."

"I don't think a tox screen is really indicated in that case," Agnes says. "With Isabela we were looking for evidence of drug abuse. That's not really something we'd expect to see in the Iron Age."

"I wasn't thinking about drugs," Ruby says. Her face is different now—Agnes sees it again, that pinpoint concentration, the power of the mind behind it. Or perhaps it is not so different after all—the trembling Ruby and the one who vibrates with mental energy are two sides of the same coin. "I was thinking: The Romans were kind of famous for poisoning people."

Waxing Gibbous, Third Cycle

The day of the solstice festival was overcast. I spent the morning in purification: I fasted, consuming only hot water steeped with dandelion, and I worked on a special, sacred map, one I intended only for myself and for the druids who came after me, whoever they might be. When I finished I helped my mother prepare the mixture for the midday ceremony. I had seen her perform the same ceremony countless times before, and had also witnessed it performed by several visiting mystics, who danced in the clearing and sang of beautiful visions that even my mother could not access, but it would be my first time serving as the druid and taking the mixture myself. I was afraid—not of the draught, which was only mead mixed with dried mushroom, nothing to fear if prepared and consumed correctly—but of what might happen when I drank it down.

Every time I had tried to hear the speech of the gods I had failed, and had to rely on my own human wits, such as they were.

Today all the village would be watching, waiting for the vision that would set their path for the year ahead. They would be waiting too, to see how I performed; if I did not produce a satisfactory message from the gods, I knew my neighbors' fragile allegiance to me would crumble, and they would drift back over to Sego's side. As I poured the mead into the mixing jar, I imagined myself blinking emptily at the moss, my mind gray and dull, with only the buzzing of the summer flies in my ears.

My mother reassured me, telling me the gods had never failed to speak at a solstice festival, but her great hands shivered as she stirred the draught, and I could tell she was frightened too.

"Has Aesu been by?" I asked her as I changed into my solstice dress. It was very beautiful, dyed purple with blackberries and painted by the village children with flowers and wheat sheaves and, in one spot, a man with the head of a fish rising from a lake. I told myself that after the festivities were over, I would find out which child had added this detail, because whoever it was might benefit from druidic training.

"He hasn't," my mother said.

I had not spoken with my brother since our wager, so I was not sure how he had taken his loss—though he must have known of it, since the sons of several families I had visited were part of his watch. I felt sure that if Aesu was by my side at midday, then I could face whatever the gods showed me. If he did not come, however, I would be like a house built too shallow in the earth, and the slightest storm might sweep me away.

My mother rose after I had dressed to work my hair into its braids. She was more tender than usual—she'd always said a little pain was necessary to make sure they stayed in place—and as she twisted the locks one over the other, she spoke to me in a quiet voice.

"Sometimes I think I shouldn't have retired so soon," she said. "I'm still strong. I could have practiced another year, maybe two or three."

"Are you saying I'm not ready?" I asked, growing uneasy.

"No, of course not," she said, pulling my hair a little harder. "It's only that we are entering a time of change and danger, something I never saw in my divinations. I wish I could've been the one to bear the risk instead of you."

"I'm strong," I said. "You've made me strong."

But in truth her words made me more afraid.

◯

As always, we held the midday ceremony on the rise above the moss. The children soon to come of age were waiting at my mother's doorway to conduct us, with arms full of elder boughs and flowers in their hair. For the first time I walked at the end of the procession, as druid, with my mother before me to clear the way.

On the rise the fires were already burning, and the offerings were piled high: broadswords and daggers, wheat and flax, jars of milk and mead and salted fish. The young men and women were waiting in pairs and packs for the dancing to begin. The older ones were waiting for me. I scanned the faces of the crowd but Aesu's was nowhere among them.

I stood in the appointed spot, at the center of the rise, directly beneath the path the sun would travel as it made its way across the sky. From there, I could look over my right shoulder at the beeches that line the river, over my left shoulder at the houses of our village, and before me at the pines and oaks at the edge of the forest. When I turned, I could see the moss, its greens roiling bright and deep and pale, a heron hunting frogs at its margin and clouds of insects sizzling over every pool. With my eyes I followed the track to the offering place; when the festival was over I would go there alone with iron for the year ahead. It amused me to think how afraid I had once been of that simple journey, and this amusement gave me confidence; in only a few weeks I had grown stronger in my druidry, I told myself, and I would grow stronger still.

I began the festival by welcoming my neighbors, with special mention made of the babies born since the harvest season began, and of the oldest among us. Comux leaned on the arm of one of his daughters, giving me a cool stare that made me stumble over my words.

"We've had a rich harvest," I continued, "but I know it's been a difficult season. I know we face trouble from without and divisions within."

I heard a murmur in the crowd then, and saw Crab's face break out into a smile. Aesu had clapped him on the shoulder, and now approached the spot where I stood—Aesu, my little brother, seeming taller now than even the tallest men of our village, all of the meager light of the cloudy day accruing to his presence. If he was here, no harm could come to us, I felt it in the deepest part of my spirit, Aesu, my brother, my truest friend.

He carried something with him, dark but glinting: the goblet he'd been given by the king.

"I brought this for the mixture," he said. "To symbolize our new alliance."

I nearly wept with relief. I turned to my mother, who carried the mixture in its humble jar, ready for me to drink. For a moment she stood still, and I thought perhaps she wanted to remember us as we were that day, the first of many ceremonies we would perform together. Then she gave a single nod and handed Aesu the jar.

Our friends and neighbors watched silently as he poured a draught from the jar into the goblet, but as he handed it to me, a few began to clap and cheer. I heard Oconea shout. Even Comux, I saw, was smiling slightly.

I lifted the goblet above my head.

"We have been divided," I repeated. "But today we are here together, in all our strength, and we are ready to receive the wisdom of the gods."

I drank the mixture down. It was sweet from the honey mead but I could taste the mushroom, dark and earthy in the back of my throat, like the smell of the forest on a warm day. I began to speak the sacred words.

For a long time I felt no deviation from my ordinary state, and I feared that the gods had truly abandoned me. But then I began to notice that the faces gazing up at me were no longer those of my friends and neighbors: They were new faces, so unknown to me they seemed to have come from another world. When I turned to face the moss I almost wept, for I saw a land laid waste, all black and bare as though consumed by a terrible fire. Ah, but then: Then I saw, just at the corner of my vision, a single star. As I watched, this star seemed to split in two, then four, then hundreds, and then so many that they filled my sight, and I laughed and laughed, because I understood, finally, what the gods had been trying to tell me all this time.

May 2018

In graduate school, Agnes was given the opportunity, as part of one of her classes, to watch a mortician prepare a body at a funeral home. The man was quiet, short-faced and round-bodied, and moved with extraordinary grace. It was calming to watch him work. He cleaned the body, a very old, small woman, with alcohol pads. He combed her hair; he lifted each of her hands with his gloved hands and cleaned under her fingernails with a pin. As he inserted the tubes and started the embalming machine, he explained every step in his soft voice.

Agnes thinks of this man, the skillful reverence of his movements, as she and Danielle take samples from the body for the toxicology screen. Danielle cleans a two-inch square of the body's abdomen, on the right side, and prepares a wide-gauge biopsy needle. She looks at Agnes, as though for permission, before inserting it into the liver. Meanwhile Agnes uses a plastic rasp to scrape away the thin layer of preserved flesh at the truncated end of the left leg, revealing the surface of the tibia.

The bone tissue is straw-colored, with a waxy sheen and soft, spongy texture that makes Agnes think of honeycomb. It gives way easily under the blade of the scalpel; Agnes places a slice inside a specimen jar, then covers the raw end of the bone with plastic to protect it. She remembers the way the mortician laid a cloth across the body's hips to preserve her modesty, the way he referred to her, always, as Mrs. S.

Agnes pauses before she zips the body back into its container. When the embalming was finished, the mortician dressed the body. Then he made up her face using pink rouge and pale foundation. Finally, he produced a delicate tiny pot and painted the smallest amount of coral pigment on her lips. "I think of this step," he told the class, "as a little goodbye."

Agnes looks down now at the face of the body before her. She examines the expression: The forehead is furrowed, she now sees, not by a downward clench but by upward pressure, as though both eyebrows are being raised. Perhaps what she took at first for rage is shock, is even wonder.

○

Agnes receives the toxicology report in an email. She is sitting in her flat, in a chair she bought from the previous tenant. Its cushion is made of cheap upholstery foam covered in polyester; it is uncomfortable, she sits there for a long time as though she cannot move. Then she gets up and walks outside.

It is afternoon, the day is bright and open. A light breeze out of the west. She sits on the concrete steps of her building and looks out at the street, deserted except for a man with a slender, nervous dog. She feels a great emptiness inside her, a scooped-out sensation, an exhaustion, as though she has been crying a long time and must now rest her head on her crossed arms, spent. She will wonder, later, if this is what people mean when they talk about grief.

◯

Nicholas greets Agnes with a garland of yellow flowers. He looks gallant and rueful, sardonic and resigned, he lays the blooms about her shoulders, he holds her by the upper arms.

"Are you ready?" he asks.

Agnes has given a prepared speech only a handful of times—once as an undergraduate, when she was required to present a research project to a group of alumni donors, and once at a conference in her last year of graduate school. She barely remembers either; both times she experienced the audience as a blinding bright light, her own voice as a kind of clanging in her skull, and afterward she had to be told she had done well, had appeared knowledgeable, even witty. It was as though another person had briefly inhabited her body, leaving just in time for her to stumble through the lunchtime reception, awkwardly accepting congratulations and failing to field follow-up questions, an unfamiliar exhaustion heavying her limbs.

This time, however, Agnes feels a responsibility to keep her consciousness focused on the occasion. It is morning on the moss and clouds gather at the horizon; the air has an ozone smell. In the woods, the birds rejoice or panic as though anticipating something.

All along the rise the tents are strung with yellow flowers. A crowd of nearly a hundred has gathered, protesters and pagans, people Agnes does not recognize, some are flowered, some carry boughs of hawthorn or bunches of violets, they wear white and green and purple, Agnes can see sorrow and excitement in the tilt of their chins, the way their bodies cleave together and then part to let her pass.

Agnes stands in the center of the rise. She has written out what she means to say in her notebook. Ruby calls it a eulogy, Nicholas a testimony, but neither is exactly right—perhaps, she thinks, as she moves to address the crowd, what she is about to recite is best described as a record, something entered into evidence so that anyone who needs it in the future can refer back to it. The purpose of a record is not always clear to the recorder, it is not always obvious why or even if the information set down will be needed in the future, and this calms Agnes, she is doing her part in a process stretching indefinitely forward in time, she does not have to predict what the next part will look like, indeed she cannot predict it.

"On April 3, 2018, the body of a woman was discovered in the moss," Agnes reads. "After eight weeks of investigation, this is what we can say with confidence about her life: She was born here, in or near what is now Ludlow, in approximately the year 50 B.C.E. She ate a diet high in stone-ground grain, which led to tooth erosion. However, she was well-nourished, with no evidence of deficiency or severe illness. She would have been about one point five meters tall."

As she speaks, Agnes begins to spot familiar people in the crowd. Danielle has come for the ceremony, her tall healing body, her farsighted gaze.

"We believe that at some point in her life, she undertook a journey to the city of Camulodunon in southeast England. We also believe she acquired a pen there, a portion of which was found near her body. This artifact is the oldest such writing implement ever discovered in the region, and raises the question of whether written language arrived in northern England earlier than previously believed. Further research is needed."

Sunita is nodding, her wide keen eyes, her worrying hands, her long hair is loose in the wind.

"Shortly before she died, she sustained minor trauma to her skull. She was also badly wounded in the abdomen. Forensic analysis of both injuries revealed evidence of antemortem healing, suggesting that neither was the cause of death."

And now Agnes spots Ruby, next to her mother. She stands in an adolescent posture, arms crossed, shoulders rounded, but her face is upturned, defiant and proud. This child, her mind, Agnes imagines how she might stride, effortlessly, into her life: break, heal, break, heal, break, and heal again.

"A combined toxicological screening of both hard and soft tissues, however, reveals evidence of opiate poisoning. We have no record of opium use in northern England during the time period, but we know the drug was used throughout the Roman Empire both as an anesthetic and as a poison; thus, it is likely that the deceased acquired it during her journey to Camulodunon. Once ingested, a fatal dose would likely have produced hallucinations, followed by neurological and respiratory collapse. Death would have occurred within hours. The deceased was buried here, in the moss, in what may have been a special custom or ritual for her people."

Agnes closes her notebook.

"I want to acknowledge the work of Sunita Patel, Danielle Muller, Jesper Claasen, Kieran Davies, and Ruby Patel. It's only because of their efforts that I'm able to tell you these facts about the woman who lay here, and that her life and death will endure in human memory."

She steps away from the center and Nicholas steps forward. As their paths cross they meet each others' eyes.

"Thank you, Dr. Linstrom," he says, and it makes her stand taller, the way he speaks to her public self. "Thank you, everyone, for coming. Thank you, especially, to the druidic Order of the Oak, who have been teaching us some ways of thinking about and venerating this land. We've been learning from them about the holidays of the Celtic calendar, including Beltane, which traditionally falls on the first of May."

As he speaks the morning light begins to break apart in shafts and patches, a beam illuminates the flowers in his hair, then travels on across the faces of the crowd behind, their wrinkles and eyelashes, the veins at their temples, before giving way to the blue-gray shadow of a cloud.

"I know we don't necessarily feel like celebrating today. A lot of us are mourning what we're about to lose here. A lot of us are angry."

He gestures to the west at the yellow machines, which hulk inanimate on the living soil beneath.

"But the ovates of the order have been teaching me about the druidic attitude toward death and loss. For the druids—and I apologize if I'm muddling this—a funeral was an occasion of celebration and rejoicing, kind of like a wake. And maybe we can think of this as a wake, both for the person who was buried here and for the landscape that was her home."

Somewhere on the moss, the song of insects swells and goes silent.

"I've also learned that at Beltane—and I know I'm sort of mixing my druidic traditions here, I hope you'll all forgive me—it's traditional to walk the perimeter of one's home or fields, to ensure fruitfulness and confer protection for the year to come. And when I heard that, I thought, 'There's the ritual we need for today.' So now I'd like us all to just walk the footpath around the moss. For some of us it will be a way to say thank you for all that this land has given humanity over thousands of years, for others it will be a way to say goodbye. And if it offers a little protection against what's coming, well, we'll take what we can get at this point."

Nicholas leads the crowd down off the rise, and as the first of the protesters take their steps onto the path, thunder rumbles in the west and the rain, finally, begins.

The drops slap Agnes's skin; the water slicks and pools in the furrows. The moss greens triumphant in the gray air. A frog chimes; a commotion of thrushes disturbs the margins of the forest. Ruby, next to Agnes, pulls her hood up over her hair, and Sunita folds the girl into her jacket as though under a wing.

The smell of the peat in rain is new, is deep and vegetable, a smell of growing things. Agnes takes it in her lungs as she walks, into her blood, she feels herself existing in the matrix of this place, when she dies, her counterparts in the future will find its traces in her bones. She is looking too, with a new quality of attention now. She grants the shy grasses, the water strider in a puddle, the valiant integral moss, the care and curiosity she now sees that she owes them. And when she brings her mind and heart to bear in this way, she sees what she has not before: how she has lived for the last two months within a pattern of swirls and whorls, bounded by a curved rise, a river, a forest, and a town.

○

In the driving rain Ruby and her mothers gather over Agnes's phone, bending as though before a sacred object. She traces with her finger the square that forms the border of the lambskin.

"North." She points. "South, west, east."

And then the center, where the lines waver and swim. "It's a map of the moss."

Ruby is smiling, rain dripping from her nose.

"So what's this?" she asks, pointing to the symbol in the map's corner. "Is that where she was buried?"

"I don't think so," Agnes says. "That was in the north, close to the rise. This is in the southeast."

"Maybe it's nothing," Sunita says. "It could be a mistake, or a stain."

"It could be," Agnes says. "There's only one way to find out."

○

The rain lasts all day and into the night. Nicholas and Leah and some of the druids try to remove the rocks from drainage pipes, but they are stuck tight already with thick mud; instead they bail the water from furrow to furrow with plastic buckets in the failing light, trying to clear the land for digging. They soak to the skin, the blossoms from their crowns and garlands fall and disappear into the earth. The water sticks Agnes's sweatshirt to her back. As the night deepens their muscles tire, with every bucketful of water another bucket falls, with every shovelful of mud another shovelful slides in to take its place. The water comes in over the tops of Agnes's shoes. The beams of their flashlights are swallowed by the peat. One by one they give in to the weather and the impossibility of the task. The water pours over Agnes's eyebrows and into her eyes. When she rubs them, Nicholas is standing in front of her with his shovel in his hand. They are the only ones left.

In the tent, in the dark, they take off their wet clothes. They struggle with her sodden jeans, in the solemn heady sorrow of the night they are laughing; their teeth clack; they are quick and clumsy but she feels no fear or awkwardness; he puts his knee between her legs; that feeling of a fist tightening inside her; he holds her in both arms and breathes into her neck; the soles of her feet are hot; she tastes herself on his fingers, rust and salt, and then the taste of him at the back of her throat, sweat and seawater. She wipes her mouth, they are laughing still. Like teenagers, she will think later, except nothing was ever so easy when she really was a teenager, like setting aside all that was burdensome and finding her body a light and carefree thing.

Agnes is not sure when or if she sleeps, she has a sense of rushing around her, like she is floating in a river, or she is the river. When she feels the current shift, she opens her eyes. Nicholas lies asleep beside her. She opens the tent flap and something takes off from an elm tree, a blunt-headed bird. Agnes walks out into the very earliest part of morning.

The moss is empty. The rain is over. The air has the cool hard quality of a stone.

Agnes has no thought in her mind as she begins to work. The digging is easier now; the moss has drunk up some of the water, leaving space for her trowel. Agnes does not hope to find something, and she does not despair.

Later she will wonder what it was that guided her. Some change in the quality of the earth, its color or feel. A glimpse of red in the darkness. Below the level of her consciousness, the smell of iron.

Whatever it is, she begins to feel an intention in her forearms and fingers as she scoops the dirt and brushes it away. She moves not evenly in a layer, as she's been taught, but on the bias, slanting down, along some track she cannot see. And she is glad, but not surprised, when she breaks open a hardened carapace of peat to reveal something dense and weighty, with a dark shine locked inside its muddy mantle: the time-burnished pommel of a sword.

First New Moon, Fourth Cycle

My daughter, my daughter. Once when she was just of age, and beginning to learn divination and other skills, I told her my biggest fear: that I and all I had done in my life would be wiped away by the passage of time, that even the gods would forget me. And my daughter—she was not more than thirteen summers then—put her hand on my shoulder and said, "Mother, you never have to be afraid. I will take all your work and increase it. They will remember us for a thousand generations."

She was so arrogant, and no wonder—she was always my favorite, the one I raised most carefully while letting the others go their own way.

After she died, my fear came true, in a certain way. Aesu sought an alliance with Sego, who returned and placed the village under his influence and protection. Soon his men patrolled the river bend and the forest road and all the other borderlands where we were vulnerable. My neighbors were uncertain at first but soon welcomed them, forgetting all the promises my daughter had made once she was no longer there to fulfill them. At first I feared the king would send a force from Camulodunon to avenge my daughter's death and to bring Sego to heel, but no force came, and I heard through Comux's son who does business in the south that the king's attention had turned elsewhere, that he was preoccupied with war in the east and had no time to defend his interests here. Then I was angry that my daughter should matter so little to him that he would behave as though their alliance never existed.

I had a lot of time to nurture my anger because, although I had volunteered to assume the role of druid again after my daughter's death, it was decided that Bodeni, the dull and dutiful second son of my cousin, would take on the job instead. I mean that Sego decided it, and Aesu, who was daily gaining more influence in the village, did not oppose him. After this I truly felt I had lost Aesu, who had been so close with my daughter they were like twins; I felt I was losing my last link to my daughter, and I was despondent.

And yet, over the next season I began to notice changes in the village. First one, then two, then four young people left to seek their fortune in the south. Oconea's weak-chinned eldest son even sent word that he had found a wife there. Then too I heard that traders from the south had crossed the Small Willow River for the first time; our farmers came back from the markets with new fruits, dark-fleshed and seedy, and finespun cloth in bright colors like the petals of unfamiliar flowers. Morirex the miller brought back to the village a Roman coin, the first I had ever seen: a golden disk the size of a chestnut, with the face of a man stamped into its surface. I wondered if the man was the king at Camulodunon; if so he looked young, barely older than my daughter herself. It made me freshly angry, to think of this boy on the throne in the south causing so much trouble. And at the same time I thought this must be part of why my daughter agreed to follow him, that he was young, his gaze pointed at the future.

In time, our neighbors began to copy my daughter's maps, using them to travel beyond the neighboring towns to the larger markets in the south and west, coming back with sour drinks and ugly, sweet-fleshed birds. Then, stranger still, traders from far away began showing up in our little village, eager to try our herbs and divinations, which apparently had become famous. One of them even came to my door one foul-weather morning, seeking a Belgic spell for determining paternity. He spoke like a child with food in his mouth, the edges of the words all swallowed, but when we came to understand each other I asked him how on earth he had known to come to this place. He reached into his satchel and drew out a map that was just like one my daughter had made, except that some of the details were wrong and the lambskin was dotted here and there with strange symbols, like the herbs at the bottom of a cup when the water has been poured away.

With the increase in trade, our village began to grow: A man from the west met Comux's youngest daughter at the wool market, and married her, and they built a house on the rise by the moss and had twin boys, and soon they had convinced the western man's brother and cousin to move there as well, so that in no time what had been unoccupied land bustled with children playing, men felling trees, and women digging gardens.

I welcomed the changes: Our village became more prosperous, with a store of salt meat for the winter where once we had survived on withered turnips and fennel tea. And too it was a joy to me to learn the ways of the newcomers who had their own gods and forms of divination and their own healing practices that involved drawing fluid from the body.

Still it was strange to visit the moss once it became a place of daily living and commerce. I went there more frequently after we buried my daughter, making small offerings: the last of the season's blackberries, a leg of good goat meat wrapped in fat. At first I could feel the presence of the gods there, the closeness of the eternal world. But when the families came, with their children's shouts and the smells of their cooking, they seemed to pull the moss more firmly into this world, so that the gods seemed farther away, and I began to forget what it even felt like to sense them in a place, began to doubt whether I had ever sensed them at all. I wondered, not for the first time, if they had turned against me, perhaps as punishment for choosing my daughter as druid when, though I never told her this, the auguries suggested I choose Aesu instead. I wondered, in my darker moments, if I had ever enjoyed their favor, or if my entire service as druid had been a sham.

One day I was entertaining such black thoughts when Comux came upon me after visiting his daughter. I had just finished making an offering of cakes and honey, and I was sitting at the edge of the moss repeating an incantation in my native language, one I hoped might still have some power. The season was just turning from harvest-time to winter, a time of quiet and consolidation during which, in years past, you could almost hear the waters doing their work. But today some of the children were training a dog, and the sounds of barks and shouts drowned out anything else, so much so that Comux startled me when he arrived, even walking with a stick as he had for the last six or seven winters.

"Am I interrupting?" he asked, but I waved for him to sit down.

"It's just that everyone is so young these days," he said. "Sometimes I get exhausted."

I smiled. "I know what you mean."

"Please," he said, "you're young yourself. A blushing bride."

I laughed, shaking my head.

"I can't begrudge them," I said then. "After all I came here as a young person from far away, and made changes."

"And we're the better for it," Comux said.

"Are we? I wonder. Now sometimes I think, 'What if I never left Aremorio?'"

"Then we would be treating fever with pitch and settling disputes with blows," he said. "And your children would never have been born."

I looked out at the moss. The spot I had chosen for my daughter was on the north side, near a stand of pine—an auspicious site befitting her station. Sego had allowed me to perform her interment, even though I was no longer technically the druid. I think he knew how it would look to begrudge me this simple concession. And I think too that he felt guilty.

I do not know how my daughter died. Afterward there was much talk, loudest among Sego's closest allies, about the draught I had prepared for her, how the herbs and mushrooms in it might have been too much for her small body, already weakened by a recent wound. I knew this was ridiculous. The old druid, my predecessor, used to take the draught even when wasting sickness had shrunk him down to nearly nothing; indeed, it was in his last days that he had his most beautiful visions. There was nothing in the mixture that could harm a human being, as long as it was delivered as intended, without contamination.

Aesu stayed away from my house in the days after his sister's death; when he began visiting again, he did not meet my eye. What I think about this, along with his actions on the day of the festival—I do not let myself put it into words. But when I call on the gods on behalf of my children, I no longer ask for his success in all his endeavors. I only ask that they keep him safe.

He was not present on the rainy morning when I lowered his sister into the water of the moss. His older brothers helped me carry her, but I dismissed them when I reached the appointed spot. I did not want them to see me rage and cry, it's true, but more than that I did not want them to see me speak with uncertainty.

There are different schools of thought on what the gods do with human beings entrusted to them. Some believe that a person interred in a sacred place can attain the power of the gods themselves, essentially becoming one of them. Others say that the gods will protect the friends and punish the enemies of those entrusted to their care. I do not pretend to know which of these, if either, is true. I only wanted the gods to take notice of my daughter's death, and of her life. Though it was more usual to entrust a body to the waters with valuable or handy objects for use in the world beyond, I instead chose the objects I believed would help the gods know my daughter: her map and pen, along with herbs from our village and from my home. By putting her body in the gods' house, I wanted to force them to pay attention, and to remember her.

"I worry," I told Comux.

He smiled. "Only natural in these uncertain times."

"I worry that the noise will drive the gods from this place."

"You must think the gods are very weak," he said.

"It's just . . ." I began, searching for my words. "It's because of her that so many people have come here, and that the village thrives the way it does. It would be a shame if that thriving led her to be abandoned and forgotten."

"Is it the worst thing to be forgotten?" Comux asked.

"My father would say so. He always said the measure of a man is how many songs are sung about him after his death."

Comux shrugged. "No one will sing about me. What I make, fire will burn or time will wear away. When I'm gone, no praise or blame will attach to my story. To me, that's peace. I've lived lightly on the earth."

I put my hand on his arm. "I'll praise you, Comux," I said.

Though it was cold, we sat together for a time. A kite wheeled overhead and I did not bother trying to divine its meaning; I was past caring about auguries and signs. Instead I allowed my mind to fill with thoughts of my daughter, whose journey, I told myself, was not over, but stretched ever forward toward a destination it was beyond all my powers to see.

Time of beginning and ending

A colony of moss does not experience relief, joy, or gratitude. But if such a colony could express its condition, at a particular point in geologic time that is both consequential and entirely fleeting, it might say this: We are restored. The large machines roll away and do not return. In their place are small scratchings, a mild disturbance we tolerate and, at times, even enjoy. We wonder what the humans think they are doing, there above the earth. It amuses us to think of the meaning they attach to what they remove, occasionally, with great fanfare—the same iron hunks their ancestors put in.

We do not know how long they will persist, or how long this particular age of human activity will last, with its beeping, the smell of ashes, the hard slap of their rubber shoes as they walk quickly across our body. We do know there is more within us, holding fast, waiting for the day when it will be needed.

We know too that our current flourishing is not forever. The air is changing; the nights grow warm; in winter the earth no longer freezes as it once did. We are not, however, afraid of what is coming. One, a colony of moss does not experience fear. Two, we have always been able to make the world we need. Though we may pass through thirsty seasons, some extending across many human lifetimes, eventually, we triumph. We create the conditions of our thriving.

ACKNOWLEDGMENTS

Thank you to Julie Barer, my agent, for her indispensable guidance and wisdom. Thank you to Brooke Nagler for their help in matters large and small. Thank you to Callie Garnett for so thoughtfully shaping this book, and to Jillian Ramirez in the U.S. and Lettice Franklin and Alice Graham in the UK (special thanks to Alice for catching my Americanisms). Thank you to Barbara Darko and the copy team for fixing both my Latin and my English. Thank you to Rosie Mahorter, Marie Coolman, Lauren Moseley, Olivia Treynor, and everyone at Bloomsbury for their unflagging support and enthusiasm. Thank you to Jaya Miceli for a beautiful cover. Thank you to my writing group: Anthony Ha, Alice Sola Kim, Tony Tulathimutte, Annie Julia Wyman, James Yeh, and Jenny Zhang. Thank you to Marisa Macias, Allysha Winburn, and Sherry Nakhaeizadeh for their expertise. Any errors of fact or lapses in plausibility are mine. Enormous thanks to Transition Wilmslow for their hospitality and help, which were absolutely foundational to this book. Thank you to Greg Wayne for coming with me to the bog. Thank you to Seth Pomerantz for the air-jet loom. Thank you to my family, especially to my mom for answering my plant questions. Thank you to T., O., and F. always.

A NOTE ON THE AUTHOR

ANNA NORTH is a graduate of the Iowa Writers' Workshop and the author of three previous novels, *America Pacifica*, *The Life and Death of Sophie Stark*, and *Outlawed*, which was a *New York Times* bestseller and Reese's Book Club pick. She has been a writer and editor at *Jezebel*, *BuzzFeed*, *Salon*, and the *New York Times*, and she is now a senior correspondent at *Vox*. She grew up in Los Angeles and lives in Brooklyn.

QUESTIONS FOR DISCUSSION

Please note: Some of these questions contain spoilers.

1. *Bog Queen* begins with a voice that is not human. How did you understand this voice? And how did it combine with the discovery of a body in the next scene—a trope of the murder mystery or police procedural—to set up your expectations about what was to follow?
2. By trying to shield young Agnes from the truth about death, her father arguably made her more afraid. How did his intentions backfire? How did watching the house finch decompose transform Agnes's fear into fascination and even reverence? Why did this moment become so pivotal in her life?
3. What events led Agnes to take the posting in Manchester? Do you think this was a good choice for her life or a bad one? Why?
4. Consider point of view in the novel. Why do you think North wrote the druid's chapters in the first-person singular, the moss's sections in the first-person plural, and Agnes's chapters in the third person? How did these shifts affect your reading?
5. Throughout the novel, Agnes reflects on her social awkwardness, kicking herself for, say, bringing a big bag of navel oranges to a party. Do you think the other characters also see her as socially awkward? Why or why not?
6. Do you feel that Fiona, one of the self-professed "bad guys," was sincere in her offer to help Agnes? Why or why not?

7. Do we know for certain whether the druid's brother betrayed her? In the penultimate chapter we learn that the druid's mother had suspicions about her son, Aesu. If he did betray his sister, what drove him to make that choice?
8. How does the young druid's character grow throughout the novel? How does Agnes's character change? How are their individual stories similar, and how are they different?
9. What do you think the druid is experiencing at the end of her life when she has the thought, "Because I understood, finally, what the gods had been trying to tell me all this time"?
10. Do you think Agnes and Nick were attracted to each other the first time they met? Why do you think they ended up in the tent together after everyone had left? What do you think brought them together at that moment?
11. Self-belief or lack of confidence is a recurring theme throughout the novel. From your perspective, who are the most confident characters? Where does their confidence come from? Who are the more self-doubting characters? Did you notice your answers shifting and changing throughout the story? How so? Has your own self-confidence ebbed and flowed throughout your life?
12. Do you agree with Comux, who says of death and the prospect of being forgotten: "No one will sing about me. What I make, fire will burn or time will wear away. When I'm gone, no praise or blame will attach to my story. To me, that's peace. I've lived lightly on the earth"?
13. How do you understand Agnes's relationship with Ruby? How do they help each other throughout the novel? What do you think Agnes does after the novel ends? What about Ruby?